THE IMBROGLIO AT THE VILLA POZZI

An Angela Marchmont Mystery Book 6

CLARA BENSON

MOUNT
STREET
PRESS

The Imbroglio at the Villa Pozzi

While holidaying in Italy, Angela Marchmont is persuaded to postpone her trip to Venice and go to Stresa instead, to investigate a pair of spiritualists who are suspected of defrauding some of the town's English residents out of their money. But what starts out as a minor matter swiftly becomes more serious when one of the residents in question is found dead in the beautiful gardens of his home, having apparently committed suicide.

Seduced by the heady sights and scents of the Italian Lakes, and distracted by an unexpected encounter with an old adversary who seems bent on provoking her, Angela sets out to find out the truth of the affair and resume her journey to Venice before she forgets herself and loses her head—and her heart.

Chapter One

IT WAS UNSEASONABLY hot for early May, and the sun had been beating down uncomfortably all week on the tour party as they tramped up and down the cobbled streets of Florence, dutifully admiring every bronze bas-relief and cunning *trompe l'oeil* that was pointed out to them by their zealous and energetic guide. They had started on Monday, when their enthusiasm had been at its height, with the Cathedral of Santa Maria del Fiore, the bell-tower and the baptistery, and all had agreed they had never seen anything so awe-inspiring. Tuesday saw them gazing, tired but still impressed, at the Palazzo Vecchio and the imposing mass of the Church of Santa Croce, while Wednesday was dedicated to a lengthy tour of the Uffizi Gallery, in which they were treated to a detailed history of every Titian, Mantegna, Bellini, Botticelli and da Vinci contained therein, and given very little time for lunch. By Wednesday dinner-time, back at the hotel, some members of the group had begun to mutter together in corners, in that half-humorous English way which indicates a polite inclination not to give offence combined with a secret determination to follow one's own path. The results of these mutterings were soon seen: on Thursday, it was a much-depleted party (consisting of those who had paid their money and were bent on wringing every last included item out of it) that set off to visit the Palazzo Pitti and the Boboli Garden, while those less hardened to the demands of the organized tour disappeared in twos and threes on business of their own.

Angela Marchmont was one of this second group. She had initially been as impressed as anyone by the beauties of the city, and just as keen to learn about its art, architecture, religion and notable past residents, but after three days her very bones were aching and she was suffering from a surfeit of narrow, crowded streets, looming edifices and stifling heat, and she wanted nothing more than to find a café with outdoor tables and parasols and sit there all day, sipping cool drinks and thinking about nothing at all. She swiftly discovered that another member of the group, with whom she had become friendly, shared her feelings, and accordingly on Thursday she and Mrs. Peters slipped out of the hotel and escaped before they could be subjected to the occasionally misplaced enthusiasm of the tour guide, who could not understand why anyone might not want to sacrifice themselves on the altar of his beautiful home city, and who was likely to force them to come with him if he saw them.

Once out in the street and free they giggled together like schoolgirls at their own daring until they were well out of sight of the hotel, then stopped to consult, with the help of a rather dog-eared Baedeker's. It was soon agreed between them that they should escape the city altogether and make for higher ground, and an hour or so later Angela's wish was granted as she found herself sitting at a café table in Piazzale Michelangelo, admiring the panoramic views of Florence that it afforded and enjoying a refreshing breeze.

'Where do you go next?' said her companion Elsa Peters, a good-humoured widow in her forties.

'Venice,' said Angela.

'Oh, I do hope you like it,' said Elsa. 'I have been several times. Venice is even more beautiful than Florence, if possible.'

'So I understand,' said Angela. 'I confess I am rather looking forward to it. I've always wanted to see the place, ever since I read of it as quite a young girl, but somehow I've never had the opportunity.'

'Well, you must send me a postcard when you get there,' said Elsa. 'I want to know whether it lives up to your expectations. I shall be going to Stresa, on Lake Maggiore. Do you know it? It will be nice to have some peace and rest after the bustle of Florence.'

'I've never been, but I've heard a lot about it,' said Angela. 'An old friend of mine is married to the chaplain of the English church there. She invited me to visit her while I was in Italy, but I put her off until another time, as I didn't want to miss Venice.'

'I can't say I blame you,' said Elsa.

They sat in companionable silence for a few minutes, watching as the steam tram arrived and disgorged its passengers into the *piazza*. Among them were two figures they recognized, who were carrying knapsacks and portable easels.

'Look,' said Mrs. Peters. 'Isn't that those two students from our group?'

The two young men had evidently spotted Angela and Elsa too, for they waved and approached the women.

'Hallo there,' said the taller of the two, a light-haired youth who fairly brimmed with nervous energy. 'I see you had the same idea as us.'

'We thought we'd get away today,' said the other, who was shorter with dark hair. 'We've enjoyed the tour but we haven't had much of a chance to do any painting.'

'That's hardly surprising, is it?' said Mrs. Peters. 'They like to keep one busy on these tours—that's what we've paid for, after all.'

'Well, we've decided to have a day off,' said the first student.

'So have we,' said Angela, and they all laughed.

The young men sat down and introduced themselves as Christopher Tate and Francis Butler. They had come to Italy, they said, with the intention of staying a while and perhaps enrolling in one of the art schools in Florence.

'But I had some rather good news this morning from my parents,' said Christopher, the tall one, who also tended to do most of the talking. 'A neighbour of ours in England is a good friend of Jack Lomax, the painter—perhaps you've heard of him? He's rather well thought-of back at home, and people were going wild for his lake scenes a few years ago. He does oils and water-colours.'

'I think I know the name,' said Angela.

'Oh, you'd certainly recognize his work if you saw it,' Christopher assured her. 'Anyway, our neighbour wrote to Lomax and he has agreed to take us on as paying pupils, just for a couple of weeks. Isn't it tremendous?'

Mrs. Marchmont and Mrs. Peters duly offered their congratulations.

'He lives far to the North, by the lakes, so we're leaving Florence tomorrow and going to join him there,' went on Christopher. 'It's quite the most marvellous opportunity for us.'

Francis Butler merely nodded in agreement, being less inclined than his friend as a rule to transform his every thought into words.

'Where on the lakes?' said Elsa. 'I am going up to that region myself on Saturday.'

'Oh, it's on Lake—what's it called, Francis?'

'Lake Maggiore,' said Francis. 'The town is called Stresa.'

'What a coincidence,' said Elsa pleasantly. 'That is where I am going too. I look forward to seeing the results of your studies.'

'Oh, you shall,' said Christopher. The young men saluted the two women and went off to set up their easels by the stone balustrade.

'I must say, much as I love Florence, I am very much looking forward to seeing Stresa again,' said Elsa Peters. 'The views there are quite spectacular, and it is such a pleasure to take a trip out on the lake. Some of the islands are really worth visiting.'

'I am almost sorry not to be going, since you praise it so much,' said Angela. 'However, one thing I have learned this week is that one could quite easily spend years in Italy without seeing even half of what there is to see.'

'That's true enough,' agreed Elsa with a laugh. 'However, as you are to miss it this time, at least you will have a good excuse to return one day.'

They remained in Piazzale Michelangelo for some while, and then walked at a leisurely pace back down the hill, stopping now and again to admire a view or purchase a souvenir, then returned to Florence for an early dinner in a little *osteria* by the river which, they were pleased to find, was not quite as extortionate as they had feared. When Angela returned to the hotel, feeling quite refreshed after the little intermission, she found that a telegram had arrived for her in her absence. As she read it, her face assumed a slightly vexed expression.

'Not bad news, I hope,' said Elsa.

'Not exactly,' said Angela. 'It's from Mrs. Ainsley, my friend in Stresa. She is most insistent that I come and visit her as soon as possible.'

'But surely she knows you are going to Venice?'

'Yes, but apparently she needs my help,' said Angela.

'Oh? With what?'

'I can't imagine, but she says "they" are desperate. I assume she means herself and her husband.'

'Goodness!' said Mrs. Peters.

'Quite,' said Angela.

'Shall you go, then?'

Angela thought for a moment. Mary Ainsley had always been one for having her own way immediately without worrying too much about whether she was inconveniencing others. Mary's husband, too, was a little over-anxious and tiresome at times. However, they had not seen each other for several years and Angela had to admit that she *was* rather tempted by the thought of Stresa.

'Perhaps I could,' she replied. 'After all, it will only be for a day or two, and I can always go on to Venice afterwards.'

'Oh good,' said Elsa, pleased. 'Then we shall see each other again.'

'I suppose that's settled, then,' said Angela. 'I had better let Mary know I am coming.'

'Splendid. I promise you you'll like the place,' said Elsa.

Angela went off to send her telegram. She was a little disappointed not to be seeing Venice immediately, but consoled herself that there would be plenty of time afterwards. She was expected back in England in two weeks or so, for she had promised to visit her brother and his family —a thought she did not especially relish—but in the meantime she was determined to enjoy her Italian holiday as much as possible.

Chapter Two

MRS. MARCHMONT STOOD in the little square before the station and gazed out over the red rooftops of Stresa, which were bleached pink by the glare of the midday sunlight. The mountains loomed behind and around her, and through the trees ahead she could just catch a glimpse of Lake Maggiore in the distance. As Mrs. Peters had promised, the place did indeed look very attractive. The air was much fresher than in Florence and the vegetation more luxuriant, and people strolled by unhurriedly in twos and threes as though they had never heard of haste. A young man cast an admiring glance at Angela as he passed by, which lifted her spirits more than she cared to admit, and she began to think that perhaps there was something in the place after all.

By means of a slow exchange in halting Italian on her side, and equally halting English on the other, accompanied by many gestures, Angela had managed to procure a taxi, and she was now waiting for the driver to finish an animated conversation he had struck up with the porter, against whom he seemed to have a mortal grudge. The two men bellowed at each other in a heated manner for several minutes, and Angela was almost afraid that violence would ensue. Almost as soon as she had had this thought, however, the men's faces broke into beams and they clapped each other on the shoulder and saluted each other with the greatest good humour. The porter then disappeared back into the station and the driver opened the door for Angela then got in himself.

'*Andiamo*,' he said, and they set off.

The Ainsleys lived in an apartment in the centre of the town, and Mrs. Marchmont was very shortly set down with her luggage in front of it. The street was narrow and cobbled, and Angela was disappointed to see that there did not seem to be a view of the lake from here. The entrance to the apartment was through an arch that led into a little courtyard, in the centre of which was a fountain that hardly deserved the name, consisting as it did of a mere trickle of water.

'Angela, darling!' came a voice from above, and she looked up to see a woman's head looking over a balcony at her. 'Come in! The door is open.'

The head disappeared and Angela went to investigate. Just through the arch was the open door to the apartment building, and there she met her friend, who had run down to greet her. Mary embraced her with great affection.

'We'll have to carry your luggage upstairs ourselves, I'm afraid,' said Mary. 'Jonathan is at the church and won't be back until later.'

She picked up a bag and headed back up the stairs. Angela followed suit, and soon found herself in a dark, stuffy hall with a red-tiled floor. Mary led her into a little sitting-room, which was much brighter, having French windows that opened out onto the very balcony from which she had called just now. Angela was irresistibly drawn to it, but was again disappointed to find that there was no view.

'I don't suppose it's what you're used to,' said Mary, 'but it's comfortable enough.' She now took a proper look at her friend. 'Goodness, Angela, you *are* looking well,' she said. 'You hardly look a day older than when I last saw you.'

Angela returned the compliment, although privately she thought that Mary was looking rather worn and tired. Mary Ainsley had been brought up to wealth, but had disappointed her family by marrying a lowly clergyman, and it did not suit her. Jonathan Ainsley was devoted to his calling—to an excessive degree, Angela had often thought —and he was much given to seeing mountains where only molehills existed. Following her marriage, Mrs. Ainsley had discovered that her main task in life from now on would be to smooth the way forward for her husband, easing his worries and ensuring that any little obstacles that did arise were swiftly swept out of his way before they had the chance to distress him. Angela wondered what minor annoyance had thrown him into consternation this time—since she was sure it was a concern of Jonathan's that had caused Mary to summon her friend from Florence.

'How are you enjoying Italy?' said Angela, as Mary made some tea.

'It's nice enough, I suppose,' replied Mrs. Ainsley. 'Beautiful, of course—it would be absurd of me to suggest otherwise—but the Italians can be *so* trying at times, and not at all sensible. That's not to say they haven't welcomed us, and I will admit they are very friendly, but I confess I do miss England sometimes, and I don't get to return as often as I'd like, since of course we don't have a great deal of money. That's why we live in this apartment. I should have preferred a little villa in the hills with a view of the lake, but we simply couldn't afford it.'

She glanced at Angela's smart frock and then down at her own shabbier one, and a little sigh escaped her. Angela felt a pang of sympathy mixed with guilt, but suppressed it firmly, for she knew that Mary was inclined to take advantage of any such weakness in order to get what she wanted.

'Tell me about Stresa,' she said.

'I think you will like it,' said Mary. 'It's very pretty and the pace of life is much slower than it is elsewhere. We spent a few months in Milan when we first came to Italy, you know, but I didn't like it at all—far too dirty and busy. Stresa is very relaxing and the perfect place for a nice, restful holiday. Now, come and see your room. It's the smallest one in the house but I thought you'd like it as it has a partial view of the lake.'

The room was tiny and, as Mary had promised, did afford just a glimpse of the lake—if one stood on tiptoe, craned one's neck uncomfortably and ignored the lines full of washing that blocked most of the view. Angela sighed inwardly as she thought of the large, well-appointed hotel room overlooking the Grand Canal in which she had expected to stay that night. Had she kept to her original plan she would just be arriving in Venice now. Still, she was determined not to delay her trip by any more than was strictly necessary and decided to bring Mary to the point as soon as possible so as to waste no time.

'I read your telegram,' she said once Mrs. Ainsley had served the tea, 'and it sounded awfully mysterious. What is it you need my help with?'

Mary put down her cup with a clatter and regarded her friend ruefully.

'It's Jonathan,' she said. 'But of course you'd guessed that already.'

Angela smiled and admitted as much.

'He has a bee in his bonnet,' said Mary. 'I know what you're going to say: he always has a bee in his bonnet—and it's true, he does. But this one is bothering him much more than usual.'

Since Jonathan Ainsley's bees tended to take the form of edicts from the Bishop of Gibraltar, against whom he had a whole list of grievances, Angela wondered what she was expected to do. Perhaps the bishop was about to visit and she had been summoned to swell Jonathan's congregation, which could only be a small one.

'I'm afraid we're having a problem with spiritualists,' went on Mary unexpectedly.

'Spiritualists?' said Angela in surprise. 'Do you mean fortune-tellers?'

'That's what Jonathan calls them,' said Mary, 'but there's more to it than that, of course. Mrs. Quinn is a medium—or so she says.'

'Oh, a medium. I see. Yes, I know the sort of thing you mean. They claim to speak to the dead for five shillings. I've seen their advertisements in the paper.'

'Yes, that's it,' said Mary. 'Mrs. Quinn and her daughter conduct séances—you know, with automatic writing and suchlike. They also claim to be clairvoyant. They came to Stresa a few months ago and they have been living here ever since. It's all nonsense, of course, but Mrs. Quinn is very plausible and seems to have won over some of Jonathan's congregation, since he has noticed lately that some of his—shall we say less fervent—worshippers have stopped attending church quite so frequently.'

'Oh dear,' said Angela.

'Quite,' said Mary. 'Of course, he's terrified that we'll end up with no congregation at all and the church will have to close, and he'll be reduced to conducting services at the big hotels in the summer months.'

'Do you think it will come to that?'

'Well, we don't have a terribly large number of worshippers to start with,' said Mary, 'although we do get more at this time of year, naturally, when all the tourists arrive. Unfortunately, Mrs. Quinn has begun placing advertisements in the English newspaper and leaving bills in all the hotels, and Jonathan is convinced that she is winning his flock away from him. She's a rather charming woman—very pleasant, as a matter of fact—and to tell the truth I think that is partly what annoys Jonathan so much.'

'I can imagine it would,' said Angela, who could easily see why Jonathan's somewhat dour, intense manner might put off potential worshippers. 'Is there nothing he can do to win them back?'

'Naturally he's doing everything he can,' said Mary, 'but the fact is that people come abroad to have fun and forget about being virtuous for a while, and here in the sunshine plain old religion simply can't compete with the latest thing. Spiritualism is all the rage, and Mrs. Quinn offers it at a very reasonable price. The tourists can get their fill of the immaterial and then go away and enjoy the rest of their holiday without being reminded of their sins.'

'I expect you're right,' said Angela. 'But Mary, why do you need *my* help?'

Mary was about to reply when the front door to the apartment opened and in came her husband. Jonathan Ainsley was a slightly-built man with a permanently troubled air about him. His sparse hair and beard were limp and untidy, and he had a nervous habit of rubbing his head frequently. A few years ago he had been a pleasant-looking man, but time and constant worry had not been kind to him, and his face was now lined and sunken. He greeted Angela cheerfully enough, and remarked on how well she looked, but immediately afterwards his frown reappeared and he turned to his wife.

'That woman is doing it again, my dear,' he said. 'I've been talking to Mrs. Smithson. They are going home next week, you remember, and I just said in passing—pleasantly, of course—that I hoped we should see them in church tomorrow. Well, you simply can't imagine how she prevaricated. She hummed and hawed and simpered, and said she wasn't quite sure, but she *believed* they were booked onto a trip to Milan. Naturally, I didn't believe a word of it, but didn't say anything, but then just at that moment Mrs. Quinn walked past and quite brazenly—really, that is the only word for it, brazen—waved and called to Mrs. Smithson that she would see her for their appointment tomorrow morning as agreed.'

'Oh dear,' said Mary. 'What did you say to Mrs. Smithson?'

'I confess I was caught so much by surprise that I didn't say anything at all,' replied Jonathan. 'However, I did manage to muster a *very* disappointed look, and at least she had the grace to look embarrassed. Then she hurried off before I could collect my thoughts enough to give her a kindly lecture.'

'I don't suppose we'll see them again, then,' said Mary regretfully. 'They go on Wednesday.'

Jonathan now turned to Angela.

'I dare say Mary has been telling you all about our woes,' he said, then as Angela assented, went on, 'This Mrs. Quinn is shameless, absolutely shameless. She is peddling the most egregious and dangerous nonsense to people who really ought to know better than to listen to it —although, of course, many visitors do find the attractions of Italy so seductive that they lose their heads for the duration of their trip, and so they are particularly susceptible to this kind of foolishness.'

'I suppose that's true,' said Angela, who was still no clearer in her mind as to what the Ainsleys expected her to do about the problem.

'It most certainly is true,' said Jonathan. 'I have been here for several years now, and am ashamed to say that in that time I have seen normally decent English people behaving in the most disgraceful manner, and getting up to things they would not dream of doing at home.'

'Oh yes?' said Angela, intrigued. She waited with interest for further details, but Jonathan pursed his lips and went on:

'And now Mrs. Quinn is taking advantage of this temporary loss of sense to induce people to embrace the dark arts—yes, for that is what I *will* call them, dear,' he said to his wife, who had been about to speak. 'They are neither more nor less than dark arts. And of course, as I said, it is all nonsense—why it's simply absurd to think that one can really summon the spirits of the dead by rapping on a table. The Quinns are committing fraud, and that is the truth of it.'

'I don't believe in spiritualism myself,' said Angela, 'but if they are doing it fraudulently, as you say, then "dark arts" hardly seems to be the most appropriate description for it, since they are not actually calling upon any supernatural forces.'

'They are meddling with things that ought not to be meddled with,' said Jonathan, who was becoming rather agitated. Mary hastened to intervene.

'Well, dear, Angela is here now, and she's promised to help,' she said.

Angela had done no such thing, but saw that she was

about to be driven into a corner and prepared to resign herself to the inevitable.

'What exactly do you want me to do?' she said.

'Why, expose her, of course,' said Mary, as though it were obvious.

'But, pardon me, is she actually doing anything illegal?' said Angela. 'I am not clear on the law as it relates to mediums and spiritualists—especially here in Italy—but I can only imagine that many of Mrs. Quinn's clients part willingly with their money in return for the chance to participate in a séance. I don't suppose half of them really believe that they are about to speak to their dead Uncle Henry or whomever it may be. I have always assumed that most people who pay for the services of a medium treat it as one might a fortune-teller in a fairground—a harmless diversion for an hour or so, but nothing to be taken too seriously.'

'I cannot take the thing as lightly as you do, Angela,' said Jonathan, 'but if it were only that I should be less disturbed. However, I firmly believe that Mrs. Quinn is actively defrauding some of her more gullible clients out of their money.'

'Oh?' said Angela.

'Yes,' said Jonathan. 'I have heard indirectly of several instances recently in which people have handed over large amounts of money to the Quinns, or have promised to remember them in a will. I believe Miss Frome, for example, pays Mrs. Quinn regular sums in the form of a retainer for her services, which is simply absurd in my view —but then of course she is terribly rich and has always been rather eccentric in her views on established religion. Then there is Mrs. Rowe, who is quite bedridden. Mrs. Quinn visited her frequently all last winter and, I am sure, made every effort to insinuate herself into the old woman's confidence. I know of this because Mrs. Rowe's son came out to visit her a month or so ago, and was most dismayed to find out what had been happening. He came to see me about it and said that his mother was planning to leave Mrs. Quinn a significant amount of money in her will and was there anything he could do about it?'

'If he had cared enough about her to visit her more often himself, then perhaps she wouldn't have done it in the first place,' said Mary reasonably.

'True enough,' said Jonathan, 'but he is her only son, and surely deserves to have some say in the matter. And then of course there is Raymond Sheridan, who really ought to know better, given that he is not a weak-minded old woman but rather a perfectly sensible man in all other respects.'

'Who is Raymond Sheridan?' said Angela.

'He lives here in Stresa with his wife,' said Jonathan. 'They are a very pleasant couple—he in particular is very friendly and a valuable part of the little English community we have here. They frequently hold large parties and gatherings at their home, and we have benefited from their hospitality many times.'

'Oh, yes,' agreed Mary.

'Unfortunately,' went on Jonathan, 'he, too, appears to have fallen for the wiles of Mrs. Quinn recently. She has saved him from financial ruin more than once—or that is what he believes, at any rate. On two occasions he happened to mention in passing an investment he was considering, and she warned him against it. Apparently each time she was right, and the company in question went to the bad. He therefore considers himself in her debt.'

'Now *that* is a useful talent to have, if she really does have it,' said Angela, 'although I shouldn't say it necessarily required any clairvoyant ability. One can often predict these things merely by reading the newspapers with a close eye.'

'A *man* might, but I doubt a woman could understand complicated financial matters of that sort,' said Jonathan dismissively.

As it happened, Mrs. Marchmont lived a very comfortable life thanks to her understanding of complicated financial matters of that sort, but she merely raised her eyebrows a little and did not reply. Instead, she said:

'Then you think all these people have been induced by dishonest means to give Mrs. Quinn money?'

'I've no doubt of it,' said Jonathan. 'She is a cunning and insinuating woman who has succeeded in charming her way into the confidences of some of the weaker members of our community, and I want her stopped.'

Angela was becoming a little impatient at Jonathan's intransigent attitude to what seemed to her a fairly harmless activity. She shook her head and was about to speak but before she could do so she was forestalled by Mary, who saw that her friend was not entirely sympathetic to Jonathan's cause, and was determined to rescue the situation.

'I know it sounds a little absurd,' she said in her most persuasive voice, taking Angela's hand, 'but we'd—I'd be most grateful if you'd agree to help, Angela. You won't have to do very much, you know—just make an appointment to sit for Mrs. Quinn and then tell us your impressions afterwards. I'd do it myself, but of course it's impossible in my position, and you were always *so* clever at seeing through people. If she's up to no good then I just *know* you'll be able to tell straightaway.'

'But what if there's nothing to discover?' said Angela. 'I dare say she employs various tricks and artifices to create effects during her séances, but that's hardly proof that she is committing the more serious crimes of which you suspect her, is it? To discover evidence of outright fraud would take more than a half-an-hour appointment, surely? Why, it would require a proper police investigation, and I can't help you with that.'

'If you don't discover anything then we'll consider the matter settled and say no more about it,' said Mary.

It was an empty promise, as Angela knew full well, since Jonathan was not one to abandon a perfectly good *idée fixe* once it had taken hold. She was about to demur again but the sight of Mrs. Ainsley's careworn face and hopeful expression caused her to hesitate. Mary's life could not be an easy one, and they *had* been good friends at one time. And a day or two would not make much difference to her holiday, she supposed. Venice could wait. There was one thing on which she was determined to stand firm, however.

'I had better not stay here with you,' she said, 'or everyone will surely suspect what I am about. Is there a decent hotel in Stresa?'

Mary saw that the game was won.

'I was just thinking the very same thing,' she replied. 'Of course you must go to the Hotel del Lago. It's quite the best one in the place, and all the English people go there, including the Quinns. Mr. Morandi is the owner and he's the most incorrigible gossip. You'll easily be able to learn all kinds of things you couldn't possibly find out if you stayed with us. It's still early in the season so there are bound to be rooms available.'

'I had better go there, then,' said Angela. 'It sounds the very place.'

'Then you'll do it,' said Mary, clapping her hands together with pleasure. 'Thank you, Angela, I'm so glad. You can go to the hotel tomorrow, but you must stay with us tonight. It's the least we can do after spoiling your holiday.'

'You haven't spoilt it at all,' said Angela, and it was not entirely a lie, for although she did not see eye to eye with Jonathan in the case, she had never sat for a medium before, and was in truth rather intrigued by the idea. Besides, she liked the look of Stresa and was keen to see more of it. A day or two of fresh air would be delightful; a much-needed pause for rest and refreshment before she ventured into the close and heady atmosphere of the city once again.

And so Angela resigned herself to her fate.

Chapter Three

As its name suggested, the Hotel del Lago was situated down by the water, and commanded spectacular views of Lake Maggiore itself, as well as of the mountains and villages on the opposite shore at the point where the lake forked, its right-hand branch stretching miles into the distance up to and beyond the Swiss border. The hotel itself was a stately edifice, although not more than about fifty years old, and flaunted its gay grandeur shamelessly, its white-painted façade and flower-bedecked balconies seeming to betoken a state of permanent spring-time. It was pleasant to sit on the hotel terrace in the shade of a striped canopy, idly watching the little boats and the steamers cross to and fro as they ferried their passengers to their various destinations. Thus was Angela occupied, in company with her friend Elsa Peters, the very afternoon after her arrival in Stresa. She had left the Ainsleys' cramped apartment without much regret that morning, and had secured herself a large, well-appointed room at the hotel. It had a four-posted bed, a lake view and a balcony, all of which pleased her very much, and caused her to reflect that in such comfortable surroundings perhaps a little light detective-work would not be so unpleasant after all. Moreover, she had soon discovered that Mrs. Peters was staying at the same hotel, and the two ladies were now sipping cool drinks and making plans to visit various places in the vicinity, while Angela studiously forgot the fact that she was only meant to be staying for a day or two.

'You can't go without first seeing the Borromean Islands,' Elsa was saying. 'The Isola Bella has the most magnificent terraced gardens. I never come to Stresa without taking a trip out on the lake. Let's go together, shall we? What about tomorrow? I always love to see people's faces when they see it for the first time.'

Angela laughed at Elsa's enthusiasm and agreed to the proposal.

'Ah, Mrs. Peters, I see you are instructing your friend in the beauties of our *lago*,' said a voice just then, and the ladies looked up to see a jovial-looking man of middle age and luxuriant moustache standing by their table. He beamed at Elsa and gave a little bow to Angela. '*Buongiorno signora*, I am Morandi, the owner of this hotel, and you are Mrs. Marchmont, yes?' Angela assented, and he went on, 'You see, it is my business to know the names of all of my guests—especially the beautiful ladies. The English women are all *elegantissime*.'

He said it so sentimentally and was so patently sincere that Angela had to suppress a smile.

'Mr. Morandi knows absolutely everything, and is extremely helpful to us poor, ignorant English tourists,' said Elsa. 'He has been most kind to me, too—especially when I came here shortly after my husband died a few years ago. I believe you gave me the best room, although I hadn't paid for it, didn't you? Come now, admit it.'

Mr. Morandi looked about him in exaggerated fashion and put his finger over his lips.

'Quiet!' he said, 'Or everyone will think I am not a hard business-man and you will ruin me.' He beamed again and invited himself to sit down. He and Elsa were evidently old friends, and Angela listened in silence as they gossiped about mutual acquaintances and exchanged news of their families. Mr. Morandi was a widower too, with a son who worked in the hotel restaurant and gave him nothing but worry, being a lazy *fannullone*. The ladies duly expressed their sympathy and their hopes that young Vittorio would shortly come to his senses and become a useful member of society. Mr. Morandi shrugged expressively and glanced up at the heavens as though to say that the matter was out of his hands.

'Isn't that Mr. Sheridan?' said Elsa, who had just spotted someone. Angela looked and saw a well-built, smartly-dressed man of forty-five or so emerging from the hotel onto the terrace. He sat down at a table in the corner and summoned a waiter, then caught sight of Mr. Morandi and held up his hand in salutation.

'I think I've heard his name,' said Angela. 'Doesn't he live here?'

'Yes,' said Mr. Morandi, acknowledging the gesture. 'He and his wife live at the Villa Pozzi, not far from here. Perhaps you have seen it? It is the yellow house with the very beautiful gardens, set a little back from the lake.'

'No, I haven't seen it,' said Angela.

'I dare say you will,' said Elsa. 'Mr. Sheridan is very sociable and likes nothing better than to invite everyone he meets to come and see his exotic plants. I met him and his wife when I came here last year and we had a very pleasant picnic at the villa one afternoon.'

'I am afraid you will not see Mrs. Sheridan this time,'

said Mr. Morandi. 'She is in England, visiting her family.' He glanced up and started, for another man had just then appeared silently at his shoulder. 'Ah! It is D'Onofrio. I did not see you there. Mrs. Peters, Mrs. Marchmont, this is Mr. D'Onofrio, our *capo di polizia*. It is his job to protect us all from thieves and assassins.'

'Goodness,' said Elsa. 'Do you have a lot of that sort of thing here?'

'Very little,' said Mr. Morandi slyly, 'thanks to D'Onofrio.'

Mr. D'Onofrio nodded impassively. He had the wary, observant expression of many policemen and an air about him which suggested that nothing could ever surprise him. He was duly invited to sit down and did so.

'Morandi is right,' he said. 'It is very quiet here. There is not the violence and the criminality of Milano, for example.' An expression of disgust passed briefly across his face at the mention of the undisciplined city. 'In Stresa there are one or two people who like to steal things from the foreigners, but we know who they are and we catch them quickly. And sometimes a man shoots his wife when she looks at another man,' he went on almost as an afterthought. 'But that is a problem only for her. The tourists know nothing of it.'

He fell silent as two men in military uniform passed by and nodded politely at him. He returned the nod and watched them with narrowed eyes as they continued on their way. Once they were out of earshot Mr. Morandi said something in a low voice in Italian and D'Onofrio replied shortly in the same language. The ladies knew better than to ask questions, and in any case Angela had just spotted something else that interested her, for two women had come out onto the terrace and were making their way to Mr. Sheridan's table. The older woman was short, middle-aged and plump, with a cheerful expression and an evident addiction to quantities of rouge, while the younger one, a girl of eighteen or so, was taller and strongly-built, with a dark and unsmiling aspect. Both of them were dressed in far too many layers of clothing for the warm weather. Angela watched as the older one approached Mr. Sheridan and engaged him in conversation, while the girl hung back. They were too far away to be audible, but Sheridan appeared delighted to see them both and indicated the empty chairs next to him. The older woman shook her head and by her gestures seemed to say that they were in a hurry. Mr. Sheridan said something to the young girl and she replied but did not smile, although the other woman gave a cheery laugh. After a minute or two they saluted each other and the women moved away. They were about to descend the terrace steps into the garden when the older one spotted the little group at Angela and Elsa's table, and made towards it, the girl tagging behind.

'Hallo, hallo!' the woman said brightly. 'Isn't it a fine day?'

'Indeed it is, Mrs. Quinn,' said Mr. Morandi. 'And good afternoon to you, Miss Quinn. I hope you are both well.'

'Oh, pretty fair, thank you,' said Mrs. Quinn. 'Just a touch of the arthritis in my left knee as usual, but the weather's warming up now and that usually helps. I always say there's nothing better than the Italian climate to do wonders for one's health.'

'I quite agree,' said Elsa Peters with a smile. 'Hallo, Mrs. Quinn. We met yesterday, didn't we?'

'Indeed we did. Hallo, Mrs. Peters,' said Mrs. Quinn. She glanced at Angela and held out her hand. 'Adela Quinn,' she said.

'Angela Marchmont,' said Angela, shaking the proffered hand.

'Mrs. Quinn is a medium and clairvoyant,' said Elsa. 'I understand she is recommended by many people here.'

'That's kind of you to say so,' said Mrs. Quinn. 'One doesn't like to boast, but I will say that my clients do tend to return more than once.'

'Indeed?' said Angela. 'I've never consulted a spiritualist before. It sounds most interesting. What services do you offer?'

'Oh, the usual,' said Mrs. Quinn. 'Table-turning, automatic writing, full séances, card-reading—anything you like. I'd love to tell you all about it now, but I'm afraid I'm already rather late for an appointment. However, I do have something—'

She patted her many pockets and eventually unearthed a slightly battered card, which she handed to Angela.

'We're here most days, so I dare say I'll see you again,' she said. 'I do a special rate for new clients, in case that sways it for you.'

'I shall give it some thought,' promised Angela.

Mrs. Quinn smiled pleasantly, satisfied at the thought of a new customer, then she and her companion went off.

'Is Miss Quinn her daughter?' said Angela, when they had gone.

'Yes,' replied Elsa. 'Her name is Asphodel, I believe. Rather a mouthful, don't you think?'

'It is certainly unusual,' said Angela. 'They don't look a bit alike, do they?'

Mr. Morandi was shaking his head.

'Don't you like spiritualists?' said Angela with a smile. 'They are not to everybody's taste, I understand.'

Mr. Morandi was too polite to give his true feelings on the matter, but his expression said much.

'What about you, Mr. D'Onofrio?' said Elsa. 'I don't suppose they're doing anything illegal, are they?'

The policeman shrugged.

'As long as they do not cause trouble then there is no problem,' he said.

He stood up and took his leave. Angela watched him go and wondered whether Jonathan Ainsley had ever tried to report the Quinns to the police. D'Onofrio was clearly not a man who liked to make work for himself, and was perhaps unlikely to be receptive to a complaint unaccompanied by supporting evidence. On first acquaintance, Mrs. Quinn seemed genuine enough—as far as that went, of course. Angela did not believe herself, but she supposed that spiritualism must bring comfort to some people. At any rate, her task was proving very easy so far, since she had already met Mrs. Quinn. The next thing would be to make an appointment to sit for her.

Mr. Morandi excused himself a few minutes later, and Elsa said:

'I didn't think you were the type to fall for all that spiritualist nonsense, Angela.'

'I'm not,' said Angela, and debated whether to tell her friend her real purpose in coming to Stresa. Elsa might be persuaded to sit for Mrs. Quinn too. Mrs. Peters was a sensible woman and unlikely to be fooled by an act, and her opinion would be valuable. Angela reached a decision.

'How would you like to help me in a little detective-work?' she said.

Elsa was surprised, but all ears, and Angela explained the situation.

'Well!' exclaimed Elsa. 'That certainly sounds intriguing, and I should love to help if I can. What do we do? Make an appointment to see her, I suppose?'

'That will be the first thing, certainly,' agreed Angela.

'After that, I'm not quite sure. I don't see how we can discover whether or not she is defrauding people of their money without speaking to the people in question, and they're not likely to admit anything.'

'You mentioned Mr. Sheridan as being one of her regular clients. We can certainly speak to him about it, at any rate. A séance, though: now, that is exciting. I've never done anything of the kind before.'

'Nor have I,' said Angela. 'I think I shall have to invent a dead husband or two.'

'You can have mine if you like,' said Elsa. 'If he turns up then I'll *know* it's all rot, as Tom had no patience at all with that kind of thing and would never have dreamed of returning to haunt his poor family.'

'He died a few years ago, I think you said,' said Angela.

'Yes,' said Elsa. 'The silly ass crashed his aeroplane when he was messing about and showing off. He always was a reckless idiot, and he paid for it in the end.' Despite the epithet, she spoke fondly. 'And now the children are all grown up and I can please myself, so I spend my time travelling the world and meeting new people.'

'That sounds delightful,' said Angela.

'It is,' said Elsa, 'although I do miss him terribly. We were both very sociable types, you know, and it's difficult when there's just the one of you. I confess I do get lonely at times. Still,' she said, brightening up, 'we have the trip on the lake to look forward to tomorrow.'

'So we do,' said Angela. 'And after that you can help me find out about this Mrs. Quinn.'

'I shall look forward to it,' said Elsa.

Chapter Four

THE NEXT DAY was fine and sunny, and by ten o'clock Mrs. Marchmont and Mrs. Peters were down by the landing-stage where Elsa, whose Italian was better than Angela's, was briskly negotiating terms with a boatman for a visit to the islands. As Angela stood by feeling rather useless, she heard a voice calling her name and turned to see the two young students they had met in Florence approaching.

'I say, how splendid to see you here,' said Christopher Tate. 'I didn't realize you were coming too.'

'I wasn't originally, but I changed my plans,' said Angela. 'I take it you're going to paint, today,' she went on, for the young men were again weighed down with various items of artistic paraphernalia.

'Yes,' said Christopher. 'We're just waiting for Lomax and then we'll begin. I simply can't tell you how pleased I am that we came here, Mrs. Marchmont. Why, under Lomax's tutelage we've both come along more in two days than we should have in a month in Florence—I'm quite convinced of it. Don't you agree, Francis?'

The more taciturn Francis Butler nodded, and Christopher went on:

'You absolutely *must* meet him, Mrs. Marchmont. His brush-work is *quite* the best I've ever seen—and his sense of perspective and colour! Why, the man's a genius. Those blues! I've never seen such blues!'

'Well, I suppose if one's fond of blue then a lake in sunny weather is an excellent place to indulge one's taste,' said Angela, amused at the young man's raptures. Since his arrival in Stresa he seemed to have rapidly developed a severe case of hero-worship. Francis let out a short laugh; he had evidently noticed it too.

They were then joined by Elsa, who had concluded arrangements to her own satisfaction, and after a few more minutes spent exchanging pleasantries the two young men went off and the ladies allowed themselves to be handed into the boat. As it drew away from the quay, Angela saw a figure approaching the two students, who waved a greeting to him. She pointed the newcomer out to Elsa.

'That must be Jack Lomax, I suppose,' she said. 'Have you met him?'

'I believe so, briefly,' said Elsa. 'Rather a strong, silent type. He's a great friend of Mr. Sheridan's, I gather. I dare say he'll turn up at the hotel sooner or later. Everybody does.'

They now turned their attention to the scenery, and Elsa pointed out the nearest of the islands, Isola Bella, which was to be their main port of call. The next few hours were spent very pleasantly indeed, exploring the delightful *palazzo* and its gardens. As she ascended slowly from terrace to terrace and admired the splendid cedars, magnolias and orange-trees, Angela conceded that her friend had not exaggerated in her description of the place, and was forced to admit that she was very glad she had come.

At about five o'clock they arrived back at the hotel where they parted, since Elsa wanted to go to the post-office. Angela pondered the possibility of a glass of iced lemonade on the terrace, but before she could act on her idea she was spotted and joined by Mr. Morandi, who wanted to hear all about her day and insisted on strolling through the garden with her until he was quite satisfied that she had enjoyed herself as much as was required. He then began to instruct her in the history of the islands, and was in the middle of a lengthy discourse on the various exploits of the noble Borromeo family when he happened to catch his son idling under a tree smoking, and stopped to upbraid him in vehement Italian. Angela walked on tactfully, but her attention was still on the little family scene behind her and she was not looking where she was going, so she did not see the man who just then emerged from another path at a brisk pace and they cannoned full into each other with some force. They both exclaimed in surprise and began to apologize, then stopped.

'*Oh!*' they said together.

Mr. Morandi came hurrying up.

'*Accidenti!*' he said gaily. 'I hope nobody was hurt in the collision. Ah, I see it is you, Mr. Smart. So you are back again from your travels. This is Mrs. Marchmont, one of our English guests. Mrs. Marchmont, Mr. Smart.'

Angela had quickly recovered her self-possession, and held out a hand.

'How do you do, Mr. Smart,' she said. 'I am Angela Marchmont.'

He took her hand and muttered something that might have meant anything, and then passed on hurriedly without another word.

'Mr. Smart is one of our occasional English residents,' said Mr. Morandi as they walked in the direction of the terrace. 'I believe he has a house outside Stresa. He was not very friendly today, which is quite unusual—but perhaps he is tired from his journey.'

Angela was only half-listening, for her mind was busy. As they ascended the steps she glanced back and saw that Mr. Smart had stopped and was gazing intently after her, eyes narrowed. When she looked again he was gone.

'Will you take a drink?' said Mr. Morandi.

Angela brought her thoughts back to the present with some difficulty.

'As a matter of fact, I think I should like to lie down for a little while,' she said. 'The fresh air has quite tired me out, I believe.'

'A very good idea,' said Morandi. 'Tonight we have a most excellent orchestra, and you must be refreshed for that.'

He beamed a goodbye then went off to the kitchen to make sure his son had returned to his duties, and Angela went up to her room to reflect on the events of the day.

As Mr. Morandi had promised, there was music after dinner, and the hotel bustled with more than the usual activity that evening. Angela and Elsa sat together and were soon joined by Mr. Morandi and Mr. D'Onofrio, who felt it incumbent upon himself to join in the revels for the sake of the protection of the public, as he assured them. After one or two drinks he unbent slightly and decided that it was time to teach Angela some Italian. They were laughing together at her attempts to pronounce *quaran-taquattro* when Angela suddenly had the strangest feeling that someone was watching her. She glanced up and around and saw the man called Smart leaning against the hotel bar, smoking. He was not looking in her direction but she had no doubt that his were the eyes she had felt upon her. She in turn watched surreptitiously from under her lashes as he stubbed out his cigarette and came over to her table, where he entered into conversation with Mr. Morandi, although the music was very loud and she could not hear what they were saying.

The number came to an end and the introduction to a gentler one was struck up, and as soon as he could make himself heard Mr. Smart asked Angela to dance. She was momentarily surprised but agreed, and joined him on the floor in a state of some apprehension. Once the music had fairly begun he glanced to his left and right as though to be sure they could not be overheard, then said:

'Hallo, Angela.'

'Hallo, Mr. Valencourt,' she returned with the utmost politeness.

'Rather a surprise to see you here,' he said.

'I might say the same,' she replied, and indeed the sudden appearance on the scene of a notorious jewel-thief and former adversary was a factor with which she had not reckoned. She went on, 'I suppose you've come to Italy to enjoy the health-giving benefits of the fresh mountain air.'

His mouth curled up in amusement.

'Naturally,' he said. 'I sit in my easy chair all day long with the windows open and a blanket tucked about my knees, sipping weak tea. I find it does me no end of good. You look quite stunning, by the way.'

'Thank you,' she said warily.

'Why *are* you here, as a matter of interest?'

'For a holiday, of course,' she said. 'In actual fact, I was supposed to go to Venice, but I changed my plans at the last minute.'

'And I can tell you're regretting it now,' he said. She did not reply, and he laughed. 'You ought to be more careful of that face of yours, Angela,' he said. 'It gives away more than you know—to me, at any rate. I can read it as easily as a book.'

'Can you, indeed?' she said coolly. 'How very dull for you.'

'On the contrary, I find it fascinating,' he said.

'Very well, then, Mr. Valencourt,' said Angela with a sigh. 'Let us agree that my face is the equivalent of the Bible and the entire *oeuvre* of Dickens combined and have done with it. But that's quite beside the point. What exactly do you want?'

'Well, to start with I'd like you to stop calling me Mr. Valencourt. Can't you call me Edgar? Everyone else does.'

'Oh, I see. You're afraid I'll give away your real name in front of everyone,' she said. 'Don't worry—I won't.'

He was about to speak but then stopped and looked at her searchingly.

'You're still angry with me about what happened in Cornwall, aren't you?' he said in surprise.

'Not in the least,' said Angela.

'Oh, but you are, I can tell. Look how rigidly you're holding yourself, and the distance you're keeping. Why, there must be six inches between us, at least. We must do something about that.'

Before she could reply he whirled her round suddenly and at the same time pulled her tightly against him. Angela's eyes flashed.

'I should rather like to breathe, if it's all the same to you,' she said.

He gave a short laugh and released his hold just a fraction.

'If anyone ought to be angry, it is I,' he said, 'but I don't hold grudges. Life's too short for that sort of thing.'

Angela said nothing. For some reason he seemed determined to provoke her, and she would not be provoked, although she was feeling prickly and hot and the music suddenly seemed discordant and too loud in her ears.

'And now you won't speak to me,' he said. 'Have I offended you that much?'

She made an effort.

'I don't see that we have anything to say to one another,' she said. 'And quite frankly I have no idea why you sought me out this evening, since if you'd had any sense at all you'd have run a mile as soon as you saw me this afternoon. Don't think I don't know what you've been up to lately. I do read the newspapers, you know. The police have been searching high and low for you after your latest escapade. They didn't mention your name but I knew immediately it was you.'

'Ah, yes, that little adventure in Vienna,' he said. 'I shouldn't normally have given it a second thought, but the thing was so easy it would have been foolish of me not to.'

'Well, naturally,' said Angela.

He laughed again.

'You don't approve of me, do you?' he said.

'Not much. Tell me, why do you do it?' she could not resist asking curiously. 'You're an intelligent man; surely you don't need the money.'

'Of course I don't do it for the money,' he said. 'I do it because I get the most tremendous kick out of it. And what about you? What do you do for fun, Angela?'

'I teach at Sunday school and knit clothes for the poor,' she said tartly.

'That sounds delightful. Could you teach me to be a good man, do you think?'

'Don't ask *me* to do it,' she said. 'I won't take the responsibility. Your immortal soul is your own affair.'

'So it is, and I'm afraid I've neglected it shockingly over

the years. I've lied and stolen and cheated, and worst of all I'm quite foul-tempered first thing in the morning before I've had my coffee. In fact, most people would say I'm a thoroughly bad lot. Do you like that, Angela?'

Angela was by now becoming very irritated, which was most unlike her.

'You're being ridiculous,' she said. 'And you still haven't told me what it is you want.'

He did not reply directly but held her gaze for a moment with a glint of mischief in his eye, then turned his head until his mouth was close to her ear and murmured something. It was in French, but Angela understood it perfectly. She drew in her breath sharply and pulled away from him, her face reddening.

'If your intention was to make me blush, then you've succeeded,' she said angrily.

'My word, I have, haven't I?' he said, entertained. 'You ought to blush more often—it rather suits you.'

But Angela was not in the least amused.

'I think I should like to sit down now,' she said, and would have broken away from him there and then, but he would have none of it and insisted on escorting her back to her seat.

'Are you quite all right, Angela?' said Elsa. 'You look a little unwell.'

'Yes, thank you,' she replied. 'I just got rather hot, that's all, and wanted a rest.'

She took out a cigarette and pointedly turned away her head so that Valencourt could not light it for her. He shrugged easily and took his leave of them all, then headed for the door, stopping to talk to someone at another table as he did so. Angela was unable to prevent herself from glancing after him, and as she did, she noticed a woman she had not seen before, who was standing alone and regarding Valencourt narrowly, although he did not seem to have noticed her. The woman was dark, and clearly a foreigner, although something about her suggested that she was not Italian. Her clothes were expensive but slightly gaudy, and she was decked out in festoons of gold jewellery. Valencourt left the room and shortly afterwards the woman did the same, leaving Angela with nothing to do but compose her ruffled feelings as best she could.

Chapter Five

WHILE ANGELA WAS DANCING with Edgar Valencourt, Mr. Sheridan had come to join their table and they were now introduced. His manner was friendly and pleasant, and in conversing with him Angela gradually recovered at least some semblance of her usual equanimity and cheerfulness. Raymond Sheridan was very neatly and tidily dressed for such a bear of a man, and clearly took some care with his appearance. He seemed to live only for his garden at the Villa Pozzi, and soon enough he was telling Angela all about it and enumerating with enthusiasm the rare plants he had collected therein over the years.

'Of course, I don't do it all myself,' he said. 'It's far too big for that, but I oversee as much of the work as I can, and the men do quite a splendid job. I'm afraid my wife often complains that I am neglecting her.'

Angela told him about her trip to the Isola Bella that day and how much she had liked the gardens there. He knew them well, and nodded.

'Yes, they are magnificent, are they not? The gardens at the villa are not terraced, naturally, and they are a little less formal, but I flatter myself that they are a worthy rival to those on the island. I was thinking of organizing a little picnic at home in a day or two. I do it quite often at this time of year. You will come, won't you? Mrs. Peters has already agreed, and I dare say there will be a few other people. Do you know the Ainsleys? They usually come along.'

'Yes, I know them very well,' said Angela.

'Then you absolutely must come. My wife is away at present and I should be glad of the company.'

Angela said she would be delighted. Their number had now swelled considerably, for they had been joined by Christopher Tate, Francis Butler and Jack Lomax, whom Angela now saw close to for the first time. As Elsa had said, he was a man of few words, although he did not seem unfriendly. He had the slightly untidy aspect frequently seen in artists, but it sat well on him, and Angela thought he was rather attractive. Christopher was hanging about him and agreeing with everything he said, and Angela wondered how Lomax could stand it. He did not seem to notice it, however, and on the contrary treated his two students with perfect courtesy.

'He knows which side his bread is buttered on,' said a voice in her ear. It was Elsa, who had noticed her friend studying the trio.

'Do you mean Jack Lomax?' said Angela.

'Yes,' replied Elsa. 'He may be quite well known but I gather he's penniless, and needs the business. That's why he puts up with that sort of thing.'

'Christopher is certainly enthusiastic,' said Angela. 'I wonder Francis can get a word in at all.'

Mr. Sheridan was nearby and had raised his eyebrows in polite interest, and Elsa explained to him that they were talking about the two students.

'Your friend Mr. Lomax seems to have found himself two very apt pupils,' she said.

'Oh, yes,' he said. 'Jack is a most able teacher, although I can't help thinking that it's rather a shame that he is not able to make his living just by his painting. He had an exhibition in London a few years ago, you know,' he went on confidentially. 'It was very well received and great things were expected of him, but as so often happens, it all ended in nothing. I told him he needed to do more to sell his work, but I'm afraid he is somewhat shy and modest and lacks the ability to talk about himself, and so things rather came to naught. Still, it must be a comfort to him to have such keen students.'

'So it must,' said Elsa. She glanced over at the little group musingly. 'I was just thinking that Francis reminds me a little of my youngest son. They are not unlike physically.'

'What does he do?' said Angela.

'He is going to be a doctor,' said Elsa, 'and he'll be a jolly good one. He's awfully clever, even if I do say so myself.'

'I'm sure you are very proud of him,' said Mr. Sheridan. 'My wife and I have not been fortunate enough to have children, which will always be a source of regret to me. What a blessing they must be!'

'A mixed blessing, perhaps,' said Elsa dryly, and they all laughed.

Angela now remembered her purpose in being there, and so began:

'I was wondering, Mr. Sheridan—I was introduced to Mrs. Quinn yesterday, and was thinking of consulting her. I gather you think very highly of her. Should you advise me to do it?'

Mr. Sheridan beamed enthusiastically.

'Indeed I should,' he said. 'I have known Mrs. Quinn for several months now and have found her powers to be quite remarkable. I must confess that I was unconvinced at first—I'd always been one of those people who looked down on spiritualism as the worst kind of nonsense, you know—but then something happened that caused me to change my views.'

'Oh yes?' said Angela.

'Yes,' he went on. 'Of course, in the beginning I should never have dreamed of paying for a sitting, but as it happened I didn't need to, since it was she who came to me. I was sitting in a café in the *piazza* reading my news-paper and looking at the stocks, since I'd been turned on to what was supposed to be rather a good thing by a friend of mine, and I was just making some notes about it when Mrs. Quinn happened to walk past my table. She stopped and said—quite politely—that she hoped I'd excuse her interference, but she could not help noticing that I was taking an interest in B— stock. She knew it was none of her business but she felt she ought to warn me against it, since she was getting vibrations which told her that no good could come of it. Naturally, I thought she was talking nonsense but I thanked her politely and prepared to ignore her advice and go ahead with the investment, since my friend was absolutely certain that the price was about to go up sharply and I did not want to be too late. As luck would have it, however, I wrote out a cheque for quite a large sum of money but forgot to post it for nearly a month, and by the time I remembered it the stock had plummeted to less than a fifth of its value. Had I posted the cheque I should have ended up in no little financial difficulty.'

'Goodness me!' said Angela, who privately thought that anyone who had even considered investing in B— stock must have been quite mad, and applauded Mrs. Quinn if not for her vibrations, then at least for her good sense.

'The same thing happened again a little time later,' continued Mr. Sheridan. 'The second time I was talking to Mrs. Quinn and just mentioned in passing that she had been right in what she had said about B—, and what did she think about F— Holdings? I was joking of course, but she immediately shook her head and said she thought the company was very unstable. This time I did not write a cheque but merely watched to see what would happen, and sure enough, a week later the scandal blew up, which you may remember. After that I was convinced, and I have consulted her regularly on a professional footing ever since. I am happy to say that she has never disappointed me.'

'Then you will vouch for her as being genuine?' said Angela.

'Oh, absolutely.'

'I *had* heard that some people suspect her of trying to defraud her clients of large sums of money,' went on Angela cautiously.

'Why, that's simply nonsense,' said Mr. Sheridan. 'I suppose Jonathan Ainsley has been getting agitated again. He's a good fellow but I'm afraid he is quite blind where Mrs. Quinn is concerned, and is convinced she is some kind of criminal just because one or two of her clients have taken it upon themselves to acknowledge their gratitude for her services in the form of hard cash. In fact, I shouldn't be surprised if he suspects her of dabbling in witchcraft and human sacrifice to boot.'

Angela thought he was probably right, and resolved never to mention the word 'witchcraft' to Jonathan in connection with the Quinns, for fear of giving him ideas.

'Is it just Mrs. Quinn who does the sittings?' she said. 'Or does her daughter take part too?'

Mr. Sheridan hesitated.

'Miss Quinn's gifts are a little different from her mother's,' he said. 'Mrs. Quinn is well-versed in all the standard spiritualist methods—table-turning, séances and all the rest—but her daughter's methods are less formal.'

'In what way?'

'She has the gift of the second sight,' he said, 'but has not yet learned to harness it usefully. She has visions, but is unable to summon them at will or control their frequency or timing, and can only act on them when they come to her.'

'I see,' said Angela. 'And are her visions accurate?'

He shifted uncomfortably.

'I don't know,' he said. 'As a matter of fact, she has told me several times recently that I am in danger of something, although she can't say what it is exactly.'

'That's not very helpful, is it?' said Elsa in some amusement. 'How are you supposed to protect yourself from the danger if you don't know what it is?'

He seemed about to say something but then changed his mind. Instead he gave a smile.

'I dare say she thinks I ought to wear a hat in the midday sun, or something of that sort,' he said.

'Well, then,' said Angela, 'from what you have told me I think I certainly ought to make an appointment with Mrs. Quinn. It all sounds most interesting.'

'Do,' he said. 'I assure you you won't be disappointed.'

It was getting late, and shortly afterwards the party broke up and Angela thankfully headed to bed. Her mind was still in turmoil following her bad-tempered encounter with Edgar Valencourt and she felt the need for a few minutes' quiet reflection. When they had collided in the garden he had evidently been as astounded to see her as she was to see him, but why had he insisted on returning to the hotel that evening, instead of disappearing as quickly as he could? After all, he was a wanted man and he knew full well that she could identify him to the police. It was foolhardy of him in the extreme to remain in Stresa while she was here. And why had he taunted her so? As she gazed at herself in the little glass over the wash-basin she flushed again as she remembered his insolence, and bent to splash some cool water onto her hot cheeks. At any rate, she thought as she slid into bed, she should not have to suffer anything of the sort again. Presumably he had got his fit of pique—or whatever it was—out of his system and would now slip away quietly, leaving only a bad memory behind him. It was small comfort, though, and she lay awake far into the night, staring into the darkness.

Chapter Six

ANGELA AWOKE LATE the next day with a nagging headache, and so decided to indulge in the luxury of breakfast in bed. By mid-morning she was feeling much better, and she emerged from her room with the intention of speaking to Mrs. Quinn and arranging a sitting with her. Her task proved to be an easy one, for as she emerged from the lift she saw the medium and her daughter standing in the hall talking to a small group of hotel guests. Angela made for the little rack of brochures offering day-trips which stood outside the Cook's office, intending to leaf through them as she waited for the Quinns to finish speaking, but she had reckoned without Mrs. Quinn's sharp eye for a new client.

'Good morning, Mrs. Marchmont,' she said as soon as the other people had moved away. She and her daughter came and joined Angela by the stand. 'Thinking of booking a trip to Milan?' she said, looking at the pamphlet in Angela's hand. 'It's not far by train, although I've never been myself.'

'Yes, I was considering it,' replied Angela. 'The cathedral is meant to be rather magnificent, I understand. I'm only in Stresa for a few days, unfortunately, and there is so much to do that I'm finding it difficult to fit everything in.'

Mrs. Quinn laughed.

'That's not the first time I've heard that from a visitor,' she said. 'In fact, I can name two or three people who've said that to me and next thing I know they're moving here for good!'

'I don't suppose I'll go that far, tempting though it is,' said Angela with a smile. 'But I must confess that I've been surprised to discover just how many English people do live here. I wonder whether the Italians feel as though they are being pushed out.'

'I doubt it,' said Mrs. Quinn. 'The English bring too much money with them. I know what you mean, though. A good half of my clients live here permanently.'

Angela saw an opening.

'Such as Mr. Sheridan, for example?' she said. 'I was speaking to him last night and he was singing your praises most highly.'

'Oh, Mr. Sheridan. We know Mr. Sheridan very well indeed, don't we, Saph?' said Mrs. Quinn to her daughter. 'He's a very pleasant gentleman and one of our best clients.'

Miss Quinn nodded in agreement.

'Mr. Sheridan has been very kind to us,' she said, in an unexpectedly deep voice.

As always, she was standing a little back, and Angela now got her first good look at the girl. Asphodel Quinn was no beauty, it was true, but she had an arresting presence and an air of immense and barely-suppressed energy. Angela wondered whether she had been instructed by her mother to keep her distance in order to prevent people from being frightened away by the expression of intensity in her large, dark eyes.

'Indeed?' said Angela. 'And does Mrs. Sheridan sit for you too?'

'She came once,' said Asphodel darkly, 'but I foresaw trouble for her and she never came back again. I foresaw trouble for both of them, as a matter of fact—him too—but he took it badly when I warned him about it.'

'You oughtn't to send letters about personal matters to people you hardly know, then,' said Mrs. Quinn. 'I've told you before you'll never do well in this business unless you learn how best to approach people. Part of the job is knowing how to get them on their right side, and sending threatening letters to people who've never asked your advice is the worst way to do it.'

'It wasn't a threatening letter,' said Miss Quinn. 'I meant to be kind and save them both from a dreadful mistake. There was no need for him to send me that rude note.'

'You put his back up,' said her mother. 'You ought to have spoken to him personally, or asked me to do it. Now he'll never listen to you.'

Angela had been following this exchange with great curiosity, but forbore to ask impertinent questions, although she was burning to know what it all meant.

Mrs. Quinn saw her interest and said, 'Saph has the Gift much more than I do, don't you Saph? It's a fine, strong one she's got, but she hasn't learned how best to use it yet. One day she will, but in the meantime I take care of the social etiquette side of things.'

She laughed, and Angela glanced over at Miss Quinn to see how she took the dig, but the girl did not seem to be offended, or even appear to be listening with great attention. Instead, she was staring at Christopher Tate and Francis Butler, who were just then walking across the hall in the direction of the terrace. After a moment she glanced away and directed her eyes at the floor.

'Mr. Sheridan told me you had saved him from making one or two bad financial decisions,' said Angela.

Mrs. Quinn laughed again.

'Oh, yes, I did that all right.' She lowered her voice. 'To be perfectly truthful, Mrs. Marchmont, it was nothing that anyone with good sense wouldn't have been able to do, but people do like to attribute things like that to my Gift. Not that my Gift is nonsense, of course—no, I can tell you *that's* real enough—but it would be useless without a healthy dose of common sense. That's partly what people pay for, you see. They come to me with a problem and they think that if I summon their dead father or whoever you like then the problem will be magically resolved, but of course it's not like that at all. Nine times out of ten the dead father would have had no idea how to solve the problem even if he were alive, and so I have to offer a little advice myself and push them gently in the right direction.'

Angela was disarmed by Mrs. Quinn's forthrightness and apparent honesty.

'Then if I consult you about my husband it won't do me any good to speak to him in person—is that what you mean?' she said with interest.

'That all depends on your husband,' said Mrs. Quinn. 'We don't have to speak to him, and sometimes it's simpler not to if he was a ne'er-do-well in life—no reflection meant, my dear, but so many of them were. But I always tell clients that I can often get the same result by sitting quietly with my hands to my head as I can with a planchette, and so we don't have to summon anyone if they don't want to. Of course, they usually *do* want to.'

'I should very much like to try it,' said Angela. 'As a matter of fact there *is* something—' she tailed off delicately, as though embarrassed.

'Oh, no need to tell me about it now,' said Mrs. Quinn briskly. 'We can discuss it better in private. We have a room at home that we use for sittings—it's quite separate and very comfortable. Or perhaps in your room here at the hotel? I'm busy all day today but I might be able to come here tomorrow morning if Mrs. Hargreaves goes to Lugano tomorrow, and I'm pretty certain she will. I can send a note later to confirm it, if you're in agreement.'

Angela assented, and Mrs. Quinn beamed.

'Then that's settled,' she said. 'Saph and I will see you here tomorrow at ten, Mrs. Hargreaves permitting.'

'Might I bring a friend?' said Angela, suddenly remembering Elsa, who would hate to be left out.

'Why, certainly,' said Mrs. Quinn as she prepared to move off. 'The more the merrier. Bring anyone you like.'

Angela watched them depart, and thought back to their conversation. It had certainly been most interesting. Mrs. Quinn had been cheerful and charming, but it was the daughter, Asphodel Quinn, whom Angela found most intriguing. What exactly had she seen that had induced her to write to Mr. Sheridan? She thought back to their conversation the night before. Sheridan had admitted to receiving a warning from Miss Quinn, but had claimed that the girl could not say what the danger was. Had he been lying? And why did Asphodel say that he had been angry about it? When Angela had seen them together, Mr. Sheridan had been perfectly courteous and friendly to both the Quinns—and in fact had said nothing at all to suggest that he was angry with anyone. It was all most mysterious. At any rate, now that Angela had made the appointment, she could at least say that she was doing something useful in the way of investigation, and she looked forward with interest to the next day.

Chapter Seven

THAT AFTERNOON, Angela went into Stresa in search of Mary Ainsley, as she wished to report on her progress. As she expected, she found her friend in the town's tiny English church, which was tucked away in a gloomy side-street that got no sun before five o'clock. Mary was standing at a little table, polishing a small collection of sad-looking brass articles. There was no sign of Jonathan.

'There you are,' said Mary brightly. 'I was just wondering whether to come and look for you at the hotel. How are you getting on? I hope you like your room.'

Angela assured her that she did, and explained somewhat sheepishly that she had not got very far yet as she had unaccountably been side-tracked into taking a trip out on the lake the day before. However, she had now made the acquaintance of the Quinns and expected to have her first sitting the next day.

'Oh, good,' said Mary. 'What do you think of them so far?'

'I should say that Mrs. Quinn is very charming and

undoubtedly knows what she is about,' said Angela. 'She is disarmingly honest, it seems to me.'

'Yes, she is, isn't she?' agreed Mary. 'I rather like her myself.'

'As to whether she is defrauding anyone,' went on Angela, 'of course I can't say, but I did put the question as tactfully as possible to Mr. Sheridan last night and he rejected the notion completely—at least as regards himself. I don't suppose he can speak for other people.'

'No,' said Mary.

'I'll do what I can, of course,' said Angela, 'but I'm afraid Jonathan is almost certainly going to be disappointed.'

'I think you're probably right,' said Mary. 'I didn't really expect much to come of it, you know, but at least Jonathan can't accuse me of not trying to help if I've had you investigate it and give your honest opinion.'

It was on the tip of Angela's tongue to say that Mary might as well have saved her efforts and let Angela go to Venice in peace for all the effect the investigation was likely to have on Jonathan's unshakeable conviction, but she kept quiet.

'Good luck with the sitting, anyway,' went on Mary, 'and do let me know straightaway what you thought. You can send a note if you like.'

'Won't I see you at the Villa Pozzi tomorrow?' said Angela. 'Mr. Sheridan said you were coming to the picnic. We can speak then.'

'What's tomorrow? Oh, Wednesday, of course. So we can,' said Mary. 'I must say, you seem to be filling in your time here quite nicely. I should have thought you would have wanted to get straight off to Venice tomorrow afternoon, once you've seen Mrs. Quinn.'

'Perhaps I'll go on Thursday instead,' said Angela,

forgetting for the moment that she had half-agreed to go to Milan with Elsa on Thursday.

'Careful, Angela,' said Mary with a smile, 'or you'll turn into one of those people who comes to Stresa and never leaves.'

'Oh, I don't think so,' said Angela.

She took leave of her friend and went out. The shops were just now beginning to open after their long lunch-time *pausa*, and since Angela had one or two things she wanted to buy she remained in town and entertained herself by looking at the various gaudy souvenirs on display and buying several postcards, which she sat down to write on a bench under a shady tree. After making her purchases and visiting the post-office she was about to turn her steps back to the hotel when to her surprise and discomfiture she saw a familiar figure coming towards her up the street. It was Edgar Valencourt, whom she had imagined as being miles away by now. She was still furious with him, and was preparing to cut him magnificently and pass on when he stopped in front of her and said formally:

'Mrs. Marchmont, I should like to apologize for my appalling behaviour last night. It was quite inexcusable.'

Angela glared at him.

'It most certainly was,' she said severely. 'What on earth did you mean by it?'

'I don't know,' he said. 'I have no idea what got into me —the devil, I suppose. I had the most awful shock when I saw you in the garden yesterday afternoon, and I'd had rather more to drink than was good for me last night, but to insult you like that was completely uncalled for. I'm terribly ashamed of myself and I apologize unreservedly.'

'Do you behave like that to everyone you bump into unexpectedly?' said Angela.

'No,' he said, looking uncomfortable. 'Just you, it

seems. I'm sorry, Angela, truly I am. If it makes you feel any better I was awake half the night kicking myself for being such an unmitigated ass. Please say you'll forgive me. I'll do anything to make it up to you. Just say the word. What shall I do first? Shoot myself?' he said with a half-smile, in something more like his old manner.

'Oh, no need for that when I can do it for you and save you the trouble,' said Angela sweetly.

'Shouldn't you like to call me some names before you do it?' he said. 'I can think of a few choice words you might want to apply to me.'

'Don't worry, I've thought of plenty of my own,' she said. 'Luckily for you, however, I was very nicely brought up and should never dream of saying them out loud.'

'Well, at least you're speaking to me,' he said. 'That's something, at any rate.'

'It doesn't mean we're friends, though,' said Angela.

'Oh no,' he said. 'Naturally I shouldn't dream of aspiring to that until I've served at least ten years' penance. For the moment I shall be quite content to get through this afternoon without being beaten soundly about the head with a parasol. By next year perhaps you'll even smile at me again.'

'Oh, very well,' said Angela, who could see that he had no intention of leaving her alone until he had won her round. 'Let's forget it, shall we? It's too hot to argue and I don't like being cross.'

'Thank you,' he said. 'I always suspected you of having a generous heart and now you've proved me right. Come and have tea with me and I'll show you that most of the time at least I'm perfectly capable of behaving myself in the company of women.'

But Angela was having none of it.

'No, Mr. Valencourt, I'd much rather not,' she said. 'As a matter of fact, I think you ought to go away now.'

'Go away?' he said. 'Ah, yes, I thought it might come to that.'

'Of course it's come to that. By staying here you put me in a very difficult position. I promised once not to give you away to the police, but it's not fair of you to expect me to hold to that promise forever.'

'No, I suppose not,' he said.

'By rights I ought to have reported you to Mr. D'Onofrio as soon as I saw you,' she said. 'I didn't, of course, but my conscience is uneasy and it's telling me that it's my duty to do it. I don't like being in this position. It makes me very uncomfortable and if you were any sort of gentleman you'd disappear now and let me continue my holiday in peace. Can't you see I'm a danger to you?'

'You're perfectly right,' he said, 'although if you want to save yourself some trouble I'd advise you not to bother talking to D'Onofrio about me. He and I have a little—arrangement, let us say.'

'Oh?' said Angela. 'I'm surprised. He doesn't seem like the type to give himself unnecessary work, but I should have thought he'd want to stamp out your sort of—er—activity. Besides, there must be some credit to be had for arresting you.'

'I'd be most offended if there weren't,' he said. 'Listen, D'Onofrio is a good fellow, but he's mostly concerned with catching cheating hoteliers and petty thieves, and making sure the foreigners keep on coming back every year. I take good care not to cause any trouble while I'm here and in return he leaves me well alone. However, you're right—if you wanted to turn me in you'd find a way to do it. Very well, I promise I'll leave as soon as I can.'

'Thank you,' she said. 'And now I must go as I'm in rather a hurry, I'm afraid. Goodbye.'

She was not in a hurry at all, but she wanted to get away from him, and so she smiled politely and walked off as quickly as possible. Unfortunately, in her haste she did not notice that she had dropped one of her parcels. He picked it up and ran after her.

'If you're in a hurry then at least let me help you carry your things back,' he said. She hesitated but did not object as he took her parcels and walked alongside her. They had now reached the lake-front and the first thing Angela saw there was Jack Lomax and his two pupils sitting under an awning with all their art equipment piled about them, while the owner of the café looked daggers at them for blocking the way to several of his tables. A strong smell of turpentine hung about the party.

'We're practising painting light today,' said Christopher, once the greetings had been got over with. 'Look, this is my attempt at capturing the lake at midday.' He picked up his portable easel and showed Angela what he had been doing. 'In a little while we're going to have a go at the sunset.'

Angela duly admired his work, which as far as she could tell showed some signs of competence. Christopher's painting style was careless and exuberant, and he favoured the use of dramatic splashes of colour, which gave his work a certain appeal. Francis's work was much more precise and calming in tone.

'I see Mr. Lomax has been working wonders with you both,' said Angela. Lomax disclaimed the compliment but did not seem displeased.

'Oh, yes,' said Christopher. 'I think my art tutor at home will be very happy with how I've come on. Francis, too. We're both learning how to put more of ourselves into our paintings.'

'Do you paint, Mrs. Marchmont?' said Francis Butler.

Angela laughed.

'Not at all,' she said. 'I fear the artistic muse was looking the other way on the day I was born. I distinctly remember as a child sketching what to my mind was a beautiful portrait of my mother, but when I showed it to her she kissed me and said, "Why, you've drawn a pig, darling, how delightful." I rather gave it up after that, but I do admire those who can do it.'

While they had been talking Jack Lomax had been busy with his pencil, drawing something on a scrap of paper. Valencourt craned his neck to see what it was. Lomax signed it with a flourish then handed the paper to him. Valencourt looked at it then passed it to Angela with a smile. She glanced at it in turn and then exclaimed in surprise, for it was a sketch of her, quite neatly done in only a few lines.

'Goodness!' she exclaimed. 'How clever you are, Mr. Lomax! I shouldn't have thought it possible to capture someone as well as that in only a minute or two, but you've done it.'

She handed it to Christopher and Francis, who bent their heads to look at it and comment. The café owner was now showing signs of agitation at the number of non-paying visitors taking up the seats in his establishment, so Angela and Valencourt took their leave and walked on towards the Hotel del Lago. As they entered they came upon the Quinns, who were on their way out.

'Oh, Mrs. Marchmont,' said Mrs. Quinn, 'I've just left a note for you. Mrs. Hargreaves is certainly going to Lugano, so we can do tomorrow as we planned. Ten o'clock, wasn't it? We'll see if we can't get that husband of yours to speak to us.'

With the utmost effort Angela managed not to blush, although she determinedly kept her face turned away from Valencourt, who was staring at her in astonishment.

'Thank you, that will be perfect,' she said.

The Quinns moved on. There was a short silence.

'You're not really going to see the Quinns, are you?' said Valencourt at last. 'Why, Angela, I shouldn't have thought you were the type to fall for that kind of nonsense.'

'Why not?' said Angela, who had no intention of telling him why she was really doing it. 'I'm not presumptuous enough to suppose that we know everything there is to know about the world. Perhaps there are forces at work of which we are totally unaware.'

He was not fooled for an instant.

'You're up to something, I can tell,' he said. 'Speak to that husband of yours, indeed. Is he really dead?'

'I have no idea,' said Angela frostily.

Her manner prevented him from inquiring further, but he was about to pursue the subject of the spiritualists when his attention was suddenly caught by someone who was just then passing through the hall. It was the woman Angela had seen last night following him out of the room. It seemed that Valencourt was seeing her for the first time, for a look of surprise passed briefly across his face.

'Good afternoon, Mr. *Smart*,' said the woman in meaningful tones, then glanced at Angela and walked on before he could reply.

'Who is that?' said Angela. 'She was here last night. She followed you when you went out.' She immediately bit her tongue, for now he would know she had been watching him, but he was distracted and did not seem to have noticed.

'I don't know,' he said. 'I—er—must have met her somewhere. Her face seems familiar.'

He then took leave and departed, somewhat to Angela's relief. She was standing deep in thought when Mr. Morandi came in through the front doors and greeted her with pleasure. She returned his salutation, and then said, 'Who was that woman who went out just now? The dark one wearing all the gold.'

'Ah, yes, I know her,' he said. 'She is La Duchessa di Alassio—or at least, that is what she calls herself.'

'Do you mean that's not her real name?'

Mr. Morandi shrugged.

'I do not know,' he said, 'but let us say I suspect it. The title is not familiar to me. She is not Italian, at any rate.'

'Where is she from, do you suppose?' said Angela.

'That I cannot tell you. I love all my guests, of course, but not all of them are as friendly as you and Mrs. Peters, Mrs. Marchmont. If they choose not to talk to me then that is their right.'

From the coolness of his tone, Angela surmised that Morandi's friendly approaches to La Duchessa had been rebuffed.

'Ah, *eccola*! Here *is* Mrs. Peters,' said Mr. Morandi in a more cheerful voice, as Elsa just then came in from the garden. 'Now *signore*, I insist you both come and have a drink with me. Have you tried Campari? It is a little drink we make here in Italy and I assure you it is quite delicious on a hot evening such as this.'

They went out onto the terrace. Dense, black clouds had begun to move across the sky in sharp contrast to the blazing sunshine of only an hour earlier, and the atmosphere was starting to feel close and stifling, even outside.

'I'm glad I got back when I did,' remarked Elsa. 'It

looks as though it's going to rain soon.' And indeed, as she spoke the first fat drops of a summer downpour began to land *spat* on the canopy above their heads. Their drinks arrived and they sat comfortably under the shelter and prepared to enjoy the sight of everyone else getting wet but themselves.

The shower soon eased off but the clouds did not dissipate and the weather looked set to be dull and overcast for the rest of the evening. Angela saw two people she recognized, and watched as Christopher and Francis trooped dejectedly along the lake-front, having presumably given up any attempt to paint the sunset for that day.

'Do you think it will be like this tomorrow?' said Elsa. 'It won't be much of a picnic if it is.'

'Who knows?' said Mr. Morandi. 'The weather is very changeable at this time of year, but I hope it will be fine.'

He then got up and went off to harangue the waiting-staff, as dinner-time was approaching, and Angela said to Elsa:

'By the way, I've made us an appointment to sit for Mrs. Quinn tomorrow morning. I hope you're still keen.'

'Am I!' said Elsa. 'I wouldn't miss it for the world. What are you going to ask her?'

'I'm not sure,' said Angela. 'I haven't quite decided yet.'

'You said something about inventing a dead husband. Presumably that means your husband is still alive,' said Elsa.

'He was alive and well the last time I saw him, but that was quite a long time ago,' said Angela. 'We're separated, I'm afraid,' she explained as she saw her friend's curious look, 'but as a general rule I try not to bring it up in conversation, since people can be rather tiresome on the subject.'

'Oh, I'm sorry,' said Elsa sincerely. 'Well then, let's forget the live one and think up a really good dead one for you.'

Angela laughed and agreed, grateful for her friend's tact in not inquiring further.

'But we must come up with something convincing,' she said. 'I've the feeling that Mrs. Quinn isn't so easily taken in.'

'Yes, and that daughter of hers too,' said Elsa. 'She makes one quite uncomfortable with that way she has of making one feel as though she's staring into one's very soul. Do you suppose she really does have second sight?'

'We'll soon find out,' said Angela.

They put their heads together, and after rejecting several tales about buried treasure and missing heirs as being anything from somewhat unconvincing to plain absurd, they finally agreed to tell Mrs. Quinn that Angela's husband had died suddenly while she was away with friends, and that Angela had always felt guilty about her absence and wanted to be sure that he did not think too hardly of her.

'There, that will do nicely,' said Elsa. 'It has the ring of truth about it and won't require you to tell too many lies.'

'True enough. And what shall you say?' said Angela.

'Well, what I'd really like to do is give Tom a piece of my mind for being stupid enough to go up in that plane of his during a storm, but I shan't. Instead I shall put on my saddest widowly face and say merely that I want to be sure he is well and that the children send their love.'

She assumed a doleful expression, then giggled mischievously.

'I think this might turn out to be rather good fun,' she said.

Chapter Eight

THE NEXT MORNING Angela threw open the doors to her balcony and discovered that the weather was once again fine and sunny, although grey clouds hung over the mountains on the other side of the lake, away in the distance. Angela squinted at them and hoped they would dissipate soon rather than drifting across to spoil the picnic, which Mr. Sheridan had confirmed was to take place that afternoon. There was to be a little group of them, and Angela was rather looking forward to seeing the Villa Pozzi and its grounds, of which she had heard so much.

After breakfast, Angela and Mrs. Peters returned to Angela's room and waited with some trepidation for the arrival of the Quinns. Although they had been laughing about it the day before, both were feeling slightly nervous, and Angela in particular was worrying that they would spot her lies immediately and that she would be exposed as a fraud—which would be ironic in the circumstances, she thought with a wry smile.

At ten o'clock prompt, Mrs. and Miss Quinn knocked on Angela's bedroom door and were admitted.

'Here we are, as promised,' said Mrs. Quinn, as cheery as ever, while Asphodel Quinn stood by, a silent presence in a dark and heavy worsted frock. 'And good morning, Mrs. Peters. Are you joining our sitting today?'

'Yes, if you don't mind,' said Elsa.

'Oh, there's no problem at all,' said Mrs. Quinn. 'Four is a nice, convenient number.' She looked about her. 'Now, we'll need a table,' she said. 'A round one would be best.'

'What about this one here?' said Angela, indicating a little table which stood to one side of the window.

'It's a bit small,' said Mrs. Quinn, regarding it with her head on one side, 'but since there's nothing else it will have to do.'

She carefully put down the bag she had brought with her, pulled the table away from the window and into the middle of the room and then set out three chairs around it.

'There are no more chairs, so one of us will have to sit on the bed, I'm afraid,' she said.

'I'll do that,' said Asphodel.

Mrs. Quinn now busied herself about the room. First she closed the curtains and switched on the lamp, then she delved into her bag and brought out several candles, which she placed here and there and then lit. The room immediately seemed smaller and stuffier, and it began to feel rather warm.

'Does Mr. Ainsley know you're doing this, Mrs. Marchmont?' Mrs. Quinn said as she worked. 'I gather he and his wife are friends of yours.'

Angela started guiltily at her words, but luckily neither of the Quinns was looking in her direction.

'I haven't mentioned it,' she lied. 'Why do you ask?'

'No particular reason,' said Mrs. Quinn blandly, 'except that we're not exactly favourites of the reverend, are we, Saph?'

Miss Quinn gave a short laugh.

'You might say that,' she said.

'No,' went on Mrs. Quinn. 'He doesn't hold with the Art, and he's taken very much against us since we came, although it's not as though I've done anything to interfere with him. As a matter of fact I understand he's been spreading all sorts of rumours about us in the town— which I call uncharitable, as I've never said a bad word about him. I'm a good Christian woman, I am, and I do my best to love my neighbour, even if he doesn't think much of me.' She straightened up and looked about her with satisfaction. 'Now, then, that ought to do the trick,' she said. 'For my part I'd happily let the light and the fresh air in but the spirit guides don't like it, you see, and they're the ones in charge so we have to go along with it.'

'What is your spirit guide's name?' asked Elsa, who had been watching the proceedings with interest.

'Thutmose. He's an Ancient Egyptian,' replied Mrs. Quinn. She saw Mrs. Peters' sceptical look and said amiably, 'Yes, dear, they so often are, aren't they? It's a bit hackneyed, I know, but that's what he told me and I can't prove otherwise so I don't bother arguing with him. Now then, shall we sit? Mrs. Marchmont, it will be best if you and Mrs. Peters sit opposite each other.'

Angela and Elsa glanced at one another and sat gingerly in the chairs indicated, and Mrs. Quinn burrowed in her bag once again and brought out an object, at which they gazed curiously. It was a flat, wooden board, rather chipped and battered, with rounded corners, on which the alphabet was printed in large, black letters in two curved rows, with below it the numbers from one to ten. On the board the medium placed a smaller, heart-shaped piece of wood which was mounted on three little casters.

'Why, it's a talking board,' said Angela.

'That's right,' said Mrs. Quinn. 'You can buy these in the shops, but I had mine made especially to my own design. It's ash, which I always find is the most powerful wood for clearing a channel between this world and the next.'

'Oh,' said Angela, glancing at Elsa again.

'Are we ready to begin?' said Mrs. Quinn, sitting down. Miss Quinn followed suit and perched upon the end of the bed.

'What do we have to do?' asked Elsa.

'Oh, it's easy enough,' said Mrs. Quinn. 'First of all I'll summon Thutmose—always assuming he's in the mood to join in, of course. He can be a bit mischievous at times, I'm afraid, and sometimes he flatly refuses to help. There used to be another guide who came occasionally—a Roundhead from Norwich, he was, and much more sensible—but I haven't seen him recently. Anyway, I shall ask Thutmose if he knows of anyone who would like to give you a message, and then we'll see what happens after that. It's best to give the board its head, by the way,' she went on. 'I don't say you ladies would do it, naturally, but there *are* some people who think it's a good idea to try and direct the planchette to their own advantage, so I'm just giving you a friendly warning to advise you not to do that, as no good ever comes of it.'

The sitters promised solemnly that they would not attempt to influence the board in any way, and Mrs. Quinn nodded in satisfaction.

'Very well, then, let's start. Now, everyone place two fingers on the planchette, please, and let's see if Thutmose is nearby.'

Angela did as instructed and waited as Mrs. Quinn closed her eyes and began to sway gently. After a minute or two her eyes snapped open and she said, 'Nothing there yet. Let's try again.' She closed her eyes again and this time began to hum tunelessly under her breath.

Angela was so busy watching her that she was caught completely by surprise when the planchette jolted suddenly and began to zigzag wildly across the board—so much so, in fact, that her fingers lost contact with it altogether.

'Connection's lost,' said Mrs. Quinn briefly. 'Let's try again.'

Angela looked at Elsa and saw that she looked as startled as Angela felt. They all placed their fingers back on the planchette and Mrs. Quinn began again. This time, when it began to move Angela was more prepared and kept her fingers on it.

Mrs. Quinn said, 'Thutmose, is that you?'

After a short pause the planchette began to move across the talking board. It came to the letter Y and stopped.

'Are you able to speak to us today?' said Mrs. Quinn.

Again the planchette moved, and this time it spelt out a longer message: 'W-H-O A-R-E Y-O-U.'

Mrs. Quinn gave an impatient noise.

'You know very well who I am, Thutmose. It's Adela. Are you going to be a naughty boy today? You know how cross I get when you play tricks.'

There was a pause, then the board spelt out 'H-A H-A.'

'Oh dear,' said Mrs. Quinn. 'I have the feeling he isn't going to be very helpful,' and indeed the planchette was now jerking backwards and forwards repeatedly between the W and the Z.

'Wzwzwz,' said Elsa. 'Is that a word? Perhaps it's Ancient Egyptian.' Angela glanced up at her. Elsa's face was perfectly serious but there was a glint in her eye.

'I don't think so,' said Mrs. Quinn. 'Let's do it one last

time and if it's no good then we'll give it up. Thutmose,' she said more loudly, 'Mrs. Marchmont is here, and she would like to speak to her husband. Is anyone there with you?'

This time there was no reply.

'Well—' began Mrs. Quinn, but was unable to finish as the planchette suddenly sprang to life and began to spell something out rapidly. All eyes were upon it as it moved across the board and paused for a split second at each letter, then came to a halt. There was an embarrassed silence, then Elsa began to giggle uncontrollably.

'That was very rude of you, Thutmose,' said Mrs. Quinn. 'I've told you before not to use words like that in front of the ladies. I won't speak to you any more if you're going to be like that.' She picked up the planchette and set it firmly on its back. 'Well, that wasn't much help, was it?' she said. 'I'm sorry about that, but sometimes it does happen, I'm afraid.'

Angela was also having great difficulty in keeping a straight face.

'Not to worry,' she said. 'I didn't really have much hope, to be perfectly honest.'

Mrs. Quinn rubbed her chin.

'I don't like leaving a client with nothing to show for our efforts,' she said, 'but when Thutmose is in that kind of mood there's not much I can do with regards to speaking to the dear departed. I know it's not the same, but I could read your cards if you like. A lot of people look down on fortune-telling but it can be useful sometimes.'

'Very well, then,' said Angela, who thought she may as well experience all the services on offer while she was there.

Mrs. Quinn delved into her bag again and brought out a crumpled and greasy pack of playing-cards that looked as though they had seen better days. She handed them to Angela.

'Now, dear, give them a good shuffle if you please, and then cut them,' she said.

Angela did as she was instructed, and then Mrs. Quinn took the cards and laid them out in three rows of three. She turned over the first row and regarded the cards closely, muttering to herself.

'Now, this represents your past,' she said. 'Here, the cards tell us where you have come from and the events leading up to your present situation. Now you see there the Five of Diamonds. That means happiness and success, or it can refer to the birth of a child. You don't have children, I suppose?'

Angela shook her head.

'Well, then, you have had success in the past, perhaps in business. But here is the Two of Spades. Spades are bad luck, in general. This one's a bad card. It denotes deceit or separation. Someone in your past has deceived you.'

'That's true,' agreed Angela, and indeed it was true enough, although the same might be said of most people, she thought.

'Hmm. Hmm. Ten of Diamonds. Money. No surprise there,' said Mrs. Quinn almost to herself. 'Now, let's look at your present situation,' she went on, and turned over the second row of cards. 'Jack of Clubs. Have you an admirer, Mrs. Marchmont?'

'I don't think so,' said Angela, and exchanged glances with Elsa, who raised her eyebrows.

'Then it must refer to a friend,' said Mrs. Quinn, and went on, 'Three of Hearts. You must think twice before giving your heart.'

'Excellent advice at all times,' said Elsa.

'Eight of Diamonds,' continued Mrs. Quinn. 'That

means travel and a new love. Well, the travel part is right enough.'

'So it is,' said Angela. So far she was not especially impressed by the reading, which seemed to be very vague, and might apply to almost anybody.

'And it looks as though you're going to fall in love, too, Angela,' said Elsa slyly. 'Who shall it be? My money's on Mr. D'Onofrio.'

'He seems pleasant enough, certainly,' replied Angela, 'but I shall try and resist him if I possibly can, since I don't think his wife and seven children would be particularly happy about it.'

They all laughed and Mrs. Quinn began turning over the last three cards.

'Now, these represent your future. Dear me,' she said, as the last spread revealed a row of Spades. 'Dear me.'

Angela had no time to ask her what she meant when her attention was arrested by a sudden movement and a noise like a groan. They all looked up and saw that Asphodel Quinn had fallen backwards onto the bed and was lying there, rigid, staring at nothing and twitching slightly. Angela and Elsa jumped up, exclaiming in surprise and concern, but before anyone could do anything Mrs. Quinn said comfortably:

'Oh, there's no need to worry. Just leave her be. She's having one of her turns. She'll come out of it in a minute or two.'

'Oughtn't we to fetch a doctor?' said Angela. 'Does she often get these fits?'

'It's not a fit—at least, not as such,' said Mrs. Quinn. 'It's a vision, or a visitation, or whatever you care to call it. She'll come to soon enough.'

They all gazed at the girl, and sure enough, after a

short interval she stopped twitching, blinked once or twice and then sat up.

'Too late!' she cried in distress. 'Mother, it's too late! Something has happened, I know it, but what? It was there, just out of reach and I tried and tried to see it but I couldn't. Oh, why couldn't I help him?'

Her face crumpled up and she put her hands to her face and began to weep.

'Are you quite certain?' said Mrs. Quinn. Under the rouge her face had gone quite pale.

'As certain as I can be,' said Asphodel. 'And it's all my fault.'

'Hush, child, of course it's not your fault,' said Mrs. Quinn. 'You can only help those who choose to listen. The rest is out of our hands.'

'I must go,' said Asphodel. 'I can't stay here a moment longer.'

'Very well, dear,' said Mrs. Quinn. She turned to Angela. 'You won't mind, will you?' she said. 'Saph is unwell and I'd better take her home now.'

'Not at all,' said Angela. 'Is there anything I can do?'

'That's kind of you, dear, but no need,' said Mrs. Quinn. 'I'll put her to bed and she'll be as right as rain by tea-time.'

Together she and Angela helped Asphodel to her feet while Elsa busied herself extinguishing candles and collecting Mrs. Quinn's things together. Then the two of them left, the mother clucking anxiously around the daughter.

'Well!' exclaimed Angela when they had gone and the curtains had been opened again, allowing some light and air back into the room. 'That was quite an experience. Will Miss Quinn be all right, do you think? Do you suppose she really did see something, or was it all part of the act?'

'The latter, I expect,' said Elsa doubtfully. 'It was very convincing if it was, though. What did you think of them?'

'Pretty much the same as I thought before,' replied Angela. 'They seem harmless enough. The card-reading might have applied to anybody, and the automatic writing —well, that's easily done.'

'True, although I almost believed in it for a moment when the planchette started moving the first time.'

'So did I,' agreed Angela. 'Now, confess: was it you who wrote that message?'

'Of course not! As a matter of fact I rather thought it was you.'

'I'm afraid I don't have that kind of facility with language,' said Angela. 'As a matter of fact, I rather wonder whether Mrs. Quinn suspected us of being not entirely sincere and decided to play a little joke on us.'

'How very mischievous of her, if she did,' said Elsa. 'She's not at all stupid, is she?'

'No,' said Angela. 'I should say that she knows perfectly well what she is about. She is clever enough not to pretend to take it all *too* seriously, and she has admitted herself that much of her ability is down to common sense—and yet she and her daughter have enough of the other-worldly about them to leave open a tiny chink of uncertainty as to whether it might not all be true.'

'Then you don't think you can help Mr. Ainsley at all?' said Elsa.

'No, I don't,' said Angela. 'He hates everything Mrs. Quinn stands for and I believe that is affecting his views of her. There is nothing he can do to stop her practising as a medium, and so I think he desperately wants her to be guilty of defrauding people out of their savings so he has an excuse to drum her out of town.'

'And of that there is no evidence.'

'Not as far as I can see. Of course, the logical thing to do would be to go and talk to everyone who has ever sat for the Quinns, but I can hardly ask a lot of complete strangers about their financial arrangements, can I? What could I say? "Tell me, has anybody persuaded you into changing your will in their favour lately?" Why, it's unthinkable. No, I believe I shall have to retire from the investigation—such as it was, since I seem to have spent most of it in enjoying myself. If Jonathan wants to find some evidence of fraud then I don't think I can help him.'

'No,' agreed Elsa. 'If they really are guilty of something then it will be a job for the police.'

'I suppose I had better break the news to Jonathan this afternoon,' said Angela.

'I hope Miss Quinn will be all right,' said Elsa. 'She did look remarkably unwell. I wonder what she saw, and who needed help.'

'Well, whoever it was, it's too late, apparently,' said Angela.

Chapter Nine

THE HEAVY GREY clouds had been drifting slowly across from the other side of the lake all morning, and by early afternoon the sun had gone completely and the air was heavy and still, with the threat of rain. Raymond Sheridan had promised to send a message if he thought the weather was not good enough for the picnic, but they had heard nothing, and so Angela and Elsa duly presented themselves downstairs in good time to be conducted to the Villa Pozzi by Mr. Morandi in his motor-car, since it was far too hot to walk even the half a mile or so from the Hotel del Lago.

The villa stood on the outskirts of Stresa, and was set a little back from the lake, at the top of a long drive. Angela looked about her as they drove through the grounds, admiring the lush vegetation, tall trees and expansive grassy areas. The effect was formal without being too stiff, and it certainly looked as though plenty of hard work had gone into creating and maintaining it.

They passed a little octagonal summer-house, whose windows and doors were shut up tight as though for the depths of winter, and continued up the straight road, then drew up by a fountain which stood in front of the house. There they alighted and Angela now saw the Villa Pozzi properly for the first time.

'As you can see,' said Mr. Morandi, who could never resist an opportunity to show off his knowledge, 'the building is in the early Palladian style, but to a smaller scale. It does not have the adornment or grandeur of the later Palladian architecture—it has none of the columns and pediments that so characterized Palladio's later work, for example—and is in fact quite plain.'

Angela regarded the house with interest. It had a creamy yellow façade and a red roof, and was graceful in its symmetry. A long flight of steps at the front led up to the entrance, which was concealed under a loggia of three arches. It was larger and much more impressive than Angela had imagined, although she noticed that here and there the paint was peeling and some of the brick-work was crumbling. Perhaps Mr. Sheridan had invested most of his time and money in the garden rather than the building.

'Shall we go in?' said Mr. Morandi.

'Yes please,' said Elsa. 'I should like to have a few minutes inside and escape this horrid heat.'

Indeed, even in the past hour the air seemed to have become hotter and more humid, and the sky darker and heavier. It hardly seemed the right sort of weather for a picnic.

'Surely it must rain soon,' said Angela.

'Not before we have eaten,' said Mr. Morandi gaily. 'I shall not allow it.'

They climbed the steps and passed through the loggia into the villa's gloomy entrance-hall, where they found the Ainsleys waiting for them. It was just as hot in here as it was outside, and there seemed no escape from the oppressive heat. They all exchanged greetings.

'Where is Mr. Sheridan?' said Mr. Morandi.

'We don't know,' said Mary. 'Nobody has seen him today, although the women were given instructions yesterday to prepare the picnic, so we've got that at least.' She indicated two baskets that stood at her feet. 'We were just waiting for you and wondering what to do.'

'Perhaps he got called away on business,' said Elsa. 'Do you think we ought to wait? Or shall we start before the rain does?'

'I vote for the latter,' said Jonathan Ainsley. 'I oughtn't really to be deserting my duties, and the sooner we start the better, I think, so I can get back.'

'Oh, nonsense,' said Mary. 'You work hard enough. Even the bishop isn't going to begrudge you a little fun now and again.'

'Then that is settled,' said Mr. Morandi. 'Let us start immediately. Mr. Sheridan can join us when he will.'

They carried the baskets out through the loggia and down the steps. After a minute or two it was decided between them that they would lay out the picnic under the branches of a nearby chestnut tree which had particularly thick and luxuriant foliage, in case it began to rain while they were eating. The blanket was spread out and the food unwrapped and they set to as well as they could in the sweltering heat. Mr. Morandi, indeed, seemed to have suffered no diminution in appetite at all—but as he said, he had been born and brought up in the area and was perfectly accustomed to this type of weather, which did not bother him in the least. Angela ate very little and Elsa barely anything at all, much to her regret.

'It all looks so delicious that I feel terribly guilty,' she said, 'but this heat is so overwhelming that I fear I shall explode if I allow one of those enormous rolls to pass my lips.'

'I know what you mean,' said Mary. As everybody seemed to have finished she began wrapping the leftover food up and putting it back into the baskets. 'Perhaps Raymond can have what we've left for supper, since it doesn't look as though he's going to turn up today.'

'I wonder where he's got to,' said Jonathan. 'It's not like him to miss a picnic.'

'It's not, is it?' said Mary. 'Still, at least he was thoughtful enough to leave some food for us. It's just a shame we couldn't finish it.'

'At any rate, I'm glad they put in sandwiches instead of risotto and cold vegetables,' said her husband. 'The Italians may pride themselves on their food but they have no idea how to do a picnic, generally speaking.'

Mr. Morandi and Elsa were talking together, so Mary took the opportunity to say to Angela in an undertone, 'How did you get on with Mrs. Quinn this morning?'

Angela hesitated. Jonathan was listening, and she had no desire to upset him, so she merely said cautiously, 'It was very interesting.'

'But what did you think of her? Did you find anything out?'

Angela was about to reply when Elsa said, 'If we stay sitting here much longer in the heat I shall go mad. I must walk, and find a breath of air *somewhere*.'

Angela shook her head at Mary and indicated that she would speak to her later, and the party began to disperse. Jonathan was anxious to get back to his duties, and so he and Mary agreed that they would return the picnic-baskets to the house and see if Mr. Sheridan had come back. If he had not, then they would return to town. Meanwhile, the others would take a little walk in the gardens which, after all, were what they had come to see.

Accordingly, Angela, Elsa and Mr. Morandi set off at a

leisurely pace in the opposite direction from the villa, for Mr. Morandi assured them that there was a fine view of the house to be had from the top of a little rise a short distance away, where there were no trees to block the view.

'How steep is this rise, exactly?' said Elsa. 'I think I shall melt if I have to climb a proper hill.'

'It is very gentle,' Morandi assured her. 'You will have no trouble at all—and if you do, then I will carry you. You also, Mrs. Marchmont,' he added as an afterthought.

'Well, with that kind of threat hanging over us I suppose we'll have to climb it ourselves, Angela,' said Elsa, and they all laughed.

They were a little distance from the house when Elsa suddenly said, 'Why, Angela, where is your jacket?'

'Dear me,' said Angela, 'I must have left it in the car. It was so hot I simply couldn't bear to wear it, but if it rains I'll get drenched, won't I?'

'You certainly will, in that thin frock of yours,' said Elsa.

'I will fetch it for you,' said Mr. Morandi.

'No, no,' said Angela. 'Thank you, but I can get it myself. I'll catch you up in a few minutes.'

She set off briskly back the way they had come, but had not gone fifty yards before she felt a *spat* on her arm, and then another on her cheek. A second later there was a blinding flash of lightning, quickly followed by a thunderclap such as she had never heard before, and then the heavens opened and the downpour which had been threatening all afternoon was unleashed with all the force that gravity could provide and more.

Angela had only read of the Indian monsoon, but it seemed to her that she had now found herself in the middle of it. Within seconds she was soaked to the skin, and she began to run as fast as she could towards the nearest shelter, which happened to be the little summer-house they had seen on the way up to the villa. As she arrived she barely noticed that the door, which had been firmly shut before, was now open, and she ran inside thankfully, intending to wait until the worst of the rain had passed. The window shutters were all closed and it was dim, almost dark inside, and it took a second or two for Angela's eyes to get used to the light. As soon as they did she realized that someone had arrived before her, and she started as she recognized Edgar Valencourt, who was standing in the centre of the room looking up at something. When she entered he glanced towards her, but barely seemed to register her presence and immediately turned his eyes back up towards the thing he had been staring at before. Angela followed his gaze and immediately clapped a hand across her mouth for there, hanging from an overhead beam and quite beyond help, was Raymond Sheridan.

Chapter Ten

THE HEAT inside the summer-house was suffocating, almost overwhelming, and for a moment or two Angela was sensible of nothing but the sound of the rain drumming incessantly upon the roof and the beating of her own heart. Gradually, however, her senses returned and she noticed that the body was swaying gently, causing the rope to creak against the beam to which it was attached. She turned a questioning gaze to Valencourt.

'I knocked against him when I came in,' he said, as though reading her mind.

The air was dead and flat. Angela glanced up at the mortal remains of Mr. Sheridan, who had been talking to her so cheerfully about his garden only two days ago, and then back at Edgar Valencourt, who had now turned his attention away from the thing in the middle of the room and towards her. They stared at each other. Angela's mind was a rush of jumbled thoughts but for the moment she was unable to give voice to any of them. The sound of the rain seemed to be getting louder and louder in her ears, and she felt the pressure in her head growing.

'What happened?' she managed at last.

'I don't know,' said Valencourt, without taking his eyes off her. 'I'd only just got here when you arrived. I know as much as you do.'

'Is it suicide?'

'It looks like it, don't you think?'

'But why?'

He said nothing, but continued to stare at her. She turned away and back towards Mr. Sheridan. She could not bear to look at the contorted face of the hanging figure but her eyes took in his clothes, his hands, his feet. One of his shoes had come off and was balanced precariously on the leg of the overturned chair below him, and his jacket hung open, unbuttoned. Angela glanced back at Valencourt, who was still regarding her intently.

'What is it?' she said.

'You're wet through,' he said, and began to move towards her. She backed away slightly and looked down at her thin summer dress, which was quite ruined.

'Yes,' she said. The pressure in her head was mounting and her breath was starting to come rapidly. He continued to advance slowly, his eyes on her all the while, and she kept on backing away until she reached the door.

'I have to get out,' she whispered at last, as panic started to overcome her.

She turned and would have run blindly into the rain, but he said:

'You can't go out like that. You're soaking wet and shivering.' And indeed it was true: she was trembling, although it was not from cold. 'Look here,' he said, 'you'd better take my jacket.' Before she could protest he took it off and threw it around her shoulders. 'Now,' he went on, 'we'll have to run if we don't want to drown. Ready?'

Angela nodded, and he took her hand and together

they ducked out into the rain and ran as fast as they could up the drive and back to the house. The other two had evidently made it back before them, for as they ran up the steps Angela saw Elsa looking out from under the loggia.

'Well, I believe you're even wetter than we are, if that's possible,' said Elsa as they arrived, drenched and breathless. 'Hallo, Mr. Smart, where did you spring from? Why, Angela, what's the matter?' she said as she saw Angela's face. 'You look as though you'd seen a ghost.'

'You're not far wrong,' said Valencourt grimly.

'What do you mean?'

'We've just found Mr. Sheridan,' said Angela. 'He's in the summer-house. I'm afraid it looks very much as though he has killed himself.'

'Oh, *no!*' said Elsa, putting her hand to her mouth in dismay.

'*Dio mio!*' said Mr. Morandi at the same time, and crossed himself.

Now that Angela had escaped from the oppressive atmosphere of the summer-house she was starting to feel much more like herself. She explained briefly what had happened, and then said, 'Is there a telephone here? We must call a doctor, and the police too.'

She saw, or rather felt, Valencourt start a little at this, but she set her jaw and ignored it.

'Yes, yes, indeed,' said Mr. Morandi. 'There is a telephone. I will call the doctor and tell him to come as a matter of urgency.'

'Don't you think you ought to sit down?' said Valencourt to Angela, indicating a chair. 'You did get a bit of a shock.'

'I'm quite all right now, thank you,' she said. Nevertheless, she did as he suggested and sat.

They waited for the doctor to arrive, Morandi and Elsa

talking and exclaiming over the dreadful event, and Angela and Valencourt in silence. By the time the doctor came the rain had stopped, the clouds were beginning to disperse and it looked as though it would be a fine evening.

Mr. Morandi had insisted on taking charge, and so he entrusted his friend Mr. Smart with the task of conducting the ladies back to the Hotel del Lago with many instructions on the proper management of his motor-car, while he remained behind to escort the doctor to the summer-house and direct operations. Despite Morandi's fears, Valencourt successfully managed to convey them the half-mile to their destination without accidentally driving the car into the lake, and they all alighted and went up the steps onto the terrace. Elsa disappeared to change and Angela was about to do the same but Valencourt said, 'Wait.'

He pointed to a seat and ran off. Angela sat down and waited, surprised, but all was explained when he returned shortly with two glasses of brandy.

'You'd better have this,' he said. 'You look pretty done in. In fact you can have both of them if you think you need it.'

'One will be quite enough, thank you,' said Angela.

She took a sip and immediately felt the warmth flowing into her.

He swallowed his own drink in one mouthful and then said, regarding her closely, 'Are you sure you're all right?'

'Quite all right,' replied Angela, 'except that I feel rather an idiot for panicking like that. I don't know what got into me.'

'Don't feel like that,' he said. 'I felt a bit like panicking myself. One doesn't expect to bump into a dead body when one takes shelter from the rain.'

'Is that what you were doing?'

'Of course. It was coming down in buckets and I didn't

especially want to take a bath. Why, what did you think I was doing? Skulking about, waiting to entrap my next victim, having dispatched Sheridan by hanging him from the ceiling? What do you take me for? He'd be far too heavy for me to lift, for a start.'

'That's not what I meant,' said Angela, who was not entirely certain what she *had* meant by her question. 'I was just surprised to see you, that's all. I thought you'd gone.'

'I am going. But I was meant to be meeting Sheridan on Friday and I was going up to the house to tell him I shouldn't be able to come.'

'Were you friends?' said Angela. She had not supposed a man such as Edgar Valencourt would have friends.

He shrugged.

'Not close friends, but in the sense that all the English people here are friends with one another, yes, we were.' He saw her look and smiled wryly. 'I live a perfectly respectable life much of the time, you know. One can't always be running.'

'I suppose not,' she said, eyeing him over the rim of her glass. She wanted to know more but would not ask.

'And you'd better stop looking at me like that,' he said, 'or before I know it I shall find myself giving away all my secrets, and that would never do.'

She shook her head and looked away.

'I wonder why he did it,' she said after a pause. 'Killed himself, I mean. He seemed so cheerful and content when I was talking to him the other night.'

'What did you talk about?'

'I don't know. He talked about the gardens at the house, I do remember that. He was very enthusiastic and mentioned a delivery of rare plants that he was expecting soon, although I couldn't tell you what they were. And then we talked about Mrs. Quinn and he was telling me all about how she had saved him twice from financial ruin, and then—oh!' She paused.

'What is it?' asked Valencourt.

'I've just remembered something else he said,' said Angela. 'He told me that Miss Quinn had warned him several times that he was in danger.' She paused again as her mind darted back to the events of that morning. 'How very odd. I wonder if that's what she saw today.'

'What do you mean? What *who* saw today?'

'Miss Quinn,' said Angela. 'Elsa and I sat for them both this morning. We did automatic writing and Mrs. Quinn read my cards.'

'And did you manage to speak to your—er—husband?'

'Don't be silly, of course I didn't,' she replied. 'But something rather strange happened while we were there. Miss Quinn had a funny turn which Mrs. Quinn claimed was a vision, and when she came to she seemed to think something dreadful had happened. She kept saying, "Too late! Too late!" and asking why she hadn't been able to help him. I wonder whether she mightn't have meant Mr. Sheridan.'

He looked sceptical.

'You don't really believe in all that stuff, do you?' he said.

'Not really,' said Angela. 'But you must admit it's rather odd.'

'I expect she put it on just to impress you,' said Valencourt.

'Perhaps she did,' said Angela. 'The automatic writing didn't go terribly well, and perhaps they wanted to convince us they really are in communication with the spirit world.'

'Then I should advise them to try harder,' said Valencourt.

'What would it take to convince you?' said Angela curiously.

'Why, I don't think anything could,' he said. 'Unless—' he stopped, and did not finish the sentence. 'No,' he went on, 'I think it's fair to say that I am unassailable in my disbelief.'

Something had just occurred to Angela.

'Who is going to tell Mr. Sheridan's wife?' she said. 'I understand she is in England at present. Someone will have to let her know what has happened to her husband. I should hate to be the one to have to tell her, poor thing. I imagine it will come as an awful shock.'

'I dare say it will,' said Valencourt.

'Do you know her?' said Angela. 'What is she like?'

'She's a pleasant enough woman,' he replied. Something about the way he said it caught her attention, and she glanced up.

'You don't like her, do you?' she said.

'I have nothing against her at all,' he said. 'But no, Mrs. Marchmont, in answer to your impertinently direct question, I don't think much of her.'

'Why not?'

'Because she won't do a thing for herself,' he said. 'She's one of these wide-eyed, clingy types who can't seem to set foot out of doors without someone to help her —usually a man. And now you've got that much out of me, I shall say no more. I'm supposed to be behaving myself, and talking ill of dead men's wives is hardly charitable.'

'You're right,' said Angela, 'but I promise I won't hold you to account for it, since I'm the one who forced it out of you.' She looked down at her glass. 'Do you think the police will have to be told?' she said.

'I don't know,' he said.

'I think perhaps I ought to speak to Mr. D'Onofrio about it,' she said tentatively.

'Do whatever you think best,' he said. 'But I'm sure you'll excuse me if I keep well out of it.'

'I thought you said you had an arrangement with him.'

'I do,' he replied, 'but it requires me to keep away from him as much as possible and not cause him any more trouble than I can help. I'm not sure where mysterious suicides come into it, but I don't particularly want to spoil things by finding out.'

'No,' said Angela. 'Still, it oughtn't to be too much of a problem for you, since you were leaving anyway.'

'Yes,' he said, throwing her an odd look. 'Are you feeling better now? Then I should advise you to go and change out of that frock before you catch your death of cold.'

The evening sun was so warm that her dress was now quite dry, but she was hardly looking her best and so she went off to do as he suggested. Back in her room, as she combed her hair, she thought back to their encounter in the summer-house, and about the feeling of menace that had almost overwhelmed her, and shivered involuntarily. Where had the sensation come from? Had it simply been caused by the grisly discovery she had made, or was there something more to it than that? She tried to put out of her mind the thought that had shot immediately into her head when she first ran into the summer-house and discovered Valencourt there with Mr. Sheridan's body, but it was no good: there was no getting away from it. He had even joked about it afterwards. Angela stopped what she was doing and stared at herself in the glass, her thoughts anything but reassuring.

Chapter Eleven

Naturally, the news of Raymond Sheridan's sudden and tragic death spread around the Hotel del Lago like wildfire, and by dinner-time it seemed that there was not a person in the place who had not heard about it. Everyone knew, too, that Mrs. Marchmont had been the one to find him, and Angela was forced to fend off any number of attempts —both veiled and open—to get the story out of her. To all inquirers she merely said yes, she had been the one to find the body, but she preferred not to speak of it as it had been rather upsetting. Nobody seemed to be aware that someone else had got there before her, and Angela to her annoyance once more found herself in the position of having to keep silent on behalf of Valencourt, who unlike herself could presumably go about his business in peace without having to answer ghoulish questions about what a dead body looked like.

Fortunately for her, Mr. Morandi returned shortly after dinner and came to join her and Elsa at their table, and he was able to take over the disagreeable business of answering inquiries. Of course, Angela and Elsa were full of their own questions, and Mr. Morandi was more than happy to answer them. He said that between them, he and the doctor had managed to get Mr. Sheridan down, and that the doctor had now taken the body away for examination.

'What did the doctor say about it?' said Elsa. 'Presumably it *was* suicide?'

'Yes, I think there is no doubt that he died by his own hand,' said Mr. Morandi. 'There seems to be no other explanation.'

'But why?' said Angela. 'Was there a note?'

'Not one that we could find,' said Morandi. 'You did not find one yourself in the summer-house, I suppose?'

Angela shook her head.

'We looked in the principal rooms of the house,' he went on. 'His bedroom, for example, and the *salone*, and all the other places where one might expect to find one, but we found nothing.'

'Not all suicides leave a note,' observed Elsa. 'It might have been quite a spur of the moment thing.'

'When did he do it?' said Angela. 'Those women we saw at the house—when did they last see him?'

'He spoke to them yesterday afternoon, to give them instructions about the picnic,' said Mr. Morandi. 'They expected him to speak to them again today, but he did not, and so they merely carried on with what they had been told to do. Of course, I asked them whether they had noticed anything unusual about Mr. Sheridan's manner— was he angry or depressed, for example?—but they are not the most observant of women and they could tell me nothing.'

'And what about the other servants?' said Angela. 'Have you spoken to them?'

'The Sheridans do not keep a large number of servants

at the house,' said Mr. Morandi. 'Most of the people they employ live out and we have not seen them yet.'

'I see,' said Angela. 'Then we have no way of knowing anything about Mr. Sheridan's state of mind in the hours leading up to the event. That's a pity.'

'Has Mrs. Sheridan been informed?' asked Elsa.

'Yes,' said Mr. Morandi soberly. 'I telegraphed her myself and she will be here as soon as she can.'

'Poor woman,' said Elsa. 'What a thing to return to.'

Just then the Ainsleys turned up. The rumour had evidently arrived in town and they had hurried back to the hotel to ascertain its veracity or otherwise. When assured of the truth of the matter, they sat down, looking appalled.

'And to think that while we were waiting for him the poor thing was there all the time in the summer-house!' said Mary. 'If only we'd gone there sooner—he might have been still alive then and perhaps we could have prevented it in some way.'

'Do not distress yourself,' said Mr. Morandi. 'I think there is nothing any of us could have done. Once someone has resolved to do a dreadful thing such as this then they will always find a way of doing it.'

'I suppose so,' said Mary. 'But to die like that! Angela, you poor darling, it must have been such a shock. Are you quite all right?' Angela assured her that she was, and Mary went on, 'But someone said Mr. Smart was there too. What was he doing?'

'Taking shelter from the rain, apparently,' said Elsa. 'It was rather a deluge.'

'Yes,' said Jonathan. 'Unfortunately it got in through the window of my office and ruined the notes for this week's sermon. I shall have to begin again—or perhaps I shall rewrite it and take the opportunity to tell the story of the Flood instead.'

'I think something about turning to God in times of despair might be more appropriate, in view of what's happened,' said Mary soberly.

They left shortly afterwards, and Elsa and Angela decided to remove outside to the terrace since it had turned out to be a beautiful evening, while Mr. Morandi bustled off to see to business.

'Look, it's the Quinns,' said Elsa suddenly, as she caught sight of Mrs. and Miss Quinn sitting at a little table apart, conversing earnestly in low voices. 'Why, it was only this morning that we were holding that silly séance, but what a lot has happened since then! Do you think we ought to give it another try? We still haven't talked to the dead, and we invented such a beautiful husband for you it seems a shame to waste him.'

Angela looked across at the Quinns. Mrs. Quinn had a serious expression on her face which was quite unlike her, while Asphodel was looking as pale and gloomy as ever. As she watched, they stood up and walked down the terrace steps and into the garden, presumably on their way home.

'Wait here,' said Angela to Elsa, then jumped up and ran after them. She had remembered Miss Quinn's supposed vision of that morning and was curious to know more about it.

'Oh, Mrs. Marchmont,' said Mrs. Quinn in her usual manner as she saw Angela. 'Isn't it a pleasant evening after all that horrid rain?'

Angela did not reply, but said to Asphodel, 'Miss Quinn, what exactly did you see this morning in my room?'

Miss Quinn and her mother glanced at each other and hesitated, and Angela went on, 'I beg your pardon, I didn't mean to be quite so blunt, but you've no doubt heard about what happened this afternoon at the Villa Pozzi, and

I just wondered whether there was any connection between your vision and—what I found.'

It sounded ridiculous even to her own ears, but the Quinns did not seem at all surprised at her question.

'I knew something had happened,' said Miss Quinn, ignoring her mother's warning glance. 'I knew he was—' she stopped, unable to go on.

'You knew he was dead?' said Angela gently.

Asphodel looked down at the ground and gave the tiniest of nods.

'I couldn't see where, or how, but I knew it,' she said. 'And it was all my fault, too. I ought to have done more to try and save him. He might still be alive now had I known what to do.'

'You couldn't have done anything,' said Mrs. Quinn.

'It's all because of Mrs. Sheridan,' said Miss Quinn suddenly. 'I told you I foresaw trouble, didn't I? And I was right. I only wish I'd known how to put a stop to it before it happened.'

'Now, there's nothing you can do for those who are bent on self-destruction,' said Mrs. Quinn. 'I've told you before you can only show the way. If people choose to ignore you then that's their own affair.'

'But it is my fault,' said Miss Quinn miserably. 'I sent that letter, and you were right—it only irritated him. I ought to have spoken to him in person instead. Perhaps I might have shown him the danger that lay ahead.'

'Hush,' said Mrs. Quinn. 'It's too late now, and least said's soonest mended. You must try and forget that it ever happened. You can't live other people's lives for them. I'm only sorry it's come to this, but it's best you learn it sooner rather than later or you'll go through life in agony. Now, let's go home.'

They went off and Angela returned to her seat to muse

on this most interesting and cryptic conversation. Elsa was as mystified as she was, and they spent a few minutes speculating discreetly as to what Mrs. Sheridan might have done to cause her husband to take his own life, but soon gave it up, feeling a little guilty.

Shortly afterwards they were joined by Francis Butler who was alone for once, since his friend was not well and had gone back to their little *pensione* with the intention of having an early night.

'Nothing too serious, I hope?' said Angela.

'Oh, no, nothing that a little bed-rest won't cure,' he replied. 'I don't suppose Chris told you, but he came abroad to recover from what I suppose one might call a nervous illness.'

'Oh?' said Elsa in concern. 'I'm sorry to hear that.'

'Yes,' said Francis. 'We've been friends since childhood, you know, and he was always pretty highly strung even as a boy, but he had a complete nervous collapse a few months ago, poor fellow, and his parents sent him out here for some sunshine and warm weather, with me to look after him. He'd been doing very well, but he went out this morning and came back upset about something or other, and then the thunderstorm this afternoon set off one of his headaches, and after that we heard the news about Mr. Sheridan, which I don't suppose helped either. I dare say he'll be as right as rain tomorrow, though.'

'How did Mr. Lomax take the news?' said Angela. 'I understand he was a close friend of Mr. Sheridan's.'

'I don't know,' said Francis. 'Truth to tell I don't even know whether he's heard, as when the rain started we had to stop work, of course. He went off somewhere and I haven't seen him since. I expect he'll be pretty cut up about it when he finds out.'

'I should imagine that he more than anyone will know

about Mr. Sheridan's state of mind before he died,' said Elsa. 'It doesn't look as though there was a note, you see.'

'Is that so?' said Francis. 'Well, then, I think you're probably right. As a matter of fact, I do seem to remember his saying something about dropping in on Sheridan on his way home last night, after our attempts to paint the sunset were so rudely interrupted by the rain. Perhaps he noticed something then.'

Angela nodded but was only half-listening, for she had just spotted Edgar Valencourt standing in the garden in close conference with the woman who called herself La Duchessa. Out of the corner of her eye Angela watched as La Duchessa appeared to discourse at length, with many gesticulations. Valencourt glanced around and then replied. As far as Angela could tell, he seemed to be suggesting that he and the woman go somewhere less public to continue their conversation. La Duchessa smiled the smile of a woman who was very pleased with herself indeed, then took his arm and they walked away until they were quite out of sight.

After that little scene she might have wasted the rest of the evening in useless speculation, but fortunately for her Jack Lomax just then turned up. His jaw was set even more firmly than usual and he seemed even less likely than usual to talk unless forced to, but it was evident from the haunted look in his eye and the sympathetic clucks of Mr. Morandi, who was with him, that he had heard the news.

'I saw him yesterday evening,' he said at length, after some gentle pressing, 'and he was perfectly well then— physically, at least.'

He seemed inclined to sink back into his own thoughts, but Mr. Morandi said:

'But what of his mental state? Did he give you any idea that he was planning something of this kind?'

'No, none at all,' said Lomax, then swallowed and reddened. Angela had never seen such a poor attempt at a lie. Lomax evidently realized it himself, for he went on, 'Well, not suicide at any rate.'

'Do you mean he was depressed about something?' said Elsa.

Lomax hesitated.

'Don't like to talk about a man when he's not here to talk for himself,' he said.

'But you are the only person who can help him talk for himself,' said Angela, 'since you may have been the last person to see him alive.'

'Hadn't thought of it like that,' said Lomax. He looked remarkably uncomfortable. 'He was depressed,' he said at last after a pause. 'He and Virginia had a row—I don't know what about—and that's why she went home to England.'

'Oh, dear,' said Elsa. 'Do you mean she'd left him?'

'Don't know, exactly,' said Lomax. 'Perhaps. I thought she'd probably come back once things had cooled down, but he seemed to think she'd gone for good. We had a drink or two and he said life wasn't worth living without her, but I thought it was just one of those things one says on the spur of the moment.'

Everyone was silent. It seemed clear enough what had happened: Raymond Sheridan, having taken a few drinks and become maudlin over the departure—possibly permanent—of his wife, had decided to act on his mood and had taken himself off to the summer-house and hanged himself. Had it been true depression or merely a moment of temporary insanity? Perhaps they should never know.

That night, Angela lay awake for some time, unable to get the events of the day out of her head. Now that she was alone in the peace and quiet of her room, her thoughts had become clearer, and she considered the matter as dispassionately as she could, although she could not escape a feeling of sadness at what had happened. Poor Mr. Sheridan—he had seemed so cheerful when he had spoken to her, but now it appeared he had been nursing a secret sorrow that had driven him to take his own life. How long had he been there in the summer-house, she wondered? And, furthermore, how often was the summer-house used? Had he expected that he would be discovered so soon, or had he chosen that spot as a refuge, assuming that he would not be found for days?

One thing was certain: he had not been planning to kill himself two days earlier, or he would not have invited several people to join him on a picnic. No—the urge to do it must have come afterwards. Perhaps his mind had been disturbed by a sudden, overwhelming impulse that he had not been able to resist. Why, it looked as though he had been so caught up in his intention that he had not even thought to leave a note.

But there were one or two other things that Angela could not explain to herself. They seemed odd, but who could explain the workings of a suicide's mind? At any rate, she thought, she would speak to Mr. D'Onofrio the next day and tell him of her doubts, and then at least her conscience would be clear. One person, she knew, would not be especially happy if she approached the police, but she refused to let it bother her. She put all disturbing thoughts firmly out of her mind and went to sleep.

Chapter Twelve

ANGELA KNEW that Mr. D'Onofrio often stopped at the Hotel del Lago for his morning coffee and so she looked out for him carefully at his usual time the next day, intending to speak to him before she could change her mind. Sure enough, there he was, sipping his tiny cup of strong coffee and glancing around with his customary wary expression. She approached his table just as he was rising, and he greeted her politely.

'Good morning, Mr. D'Onofrio,' she said. 'May I speak to you?'

'Of course,' he said. He saw that she did not wish to do it in public, and went on, 'Perhaps the garden?'

'Yes, that's probably better,' said Angela, and he motioned to her to lead the way.

'You want to speak to me about the death of Mr. Sheridan, yes?' he said once they were safely out of range of all listening ears.

'I thought you might have guessed,' said Angela. 'Yes, I do.'

She could not find the words to continue, so he said helpfully,

'Do you have some evidence to explain why he did it? A note, perhaps?'

'Oh, no, nothing like that,' Angela said. 'And to be perfectly honest I've been in two minds as to whether or not to bother you with it, but there was something I noticed yesterday which didn't quite seem to fit in with what happened.'

'And what was that?' said Mr. D'Onofrio.

'His shoe-laces were undone,' she said. It sounded very little when spoken out loud. He continued to look at her politely, and she went on, 'One shoe was so loose it had actually fallen off. And his jacket was unbuttoned too.'

He was gazing at her so thoughtfully that for a second she wondered whether he thought her mad, but then he nodded.

'I understand,' he said. 'A man does not walk out of his house and hang himself in the garden without first fastening his jacket and tying his shoe-laces.'

'Yes, that's it exactly,' said Angela in some relief. 'I just thought it rather odd, that's all, and decided I'd better tell someone about it.'

'And now you have told me. What do you want me to do?'

'Why, I—' Angela began. Of course, she wanted him to investigate it, but did not feel able to demand it of him, since he appeared to be something of a law unto himself in the matter of policing.

'Were you alone, by the way, when you found Mr. Sheridan?' he asked suddenly. 'I thought I heard that someone was with you.'

Angela hesitated. They were now getting onto delicate ground.

'No, I wasn't alone,' she said after a moment. 'Mr. Smart was there too.'

'Did you arrive at the summer-house together?'

'No,' said Angela. 'He wasn't at the picnic with us, and I didn't know he was at the villa at all until I met him.'

'Then did you arrive at the scene first, or did he?'

'I don't remember,' said Angela, and immediately kicked herself for an idiot.

'You do not remember?' he said. His face was as impassive as ever but Angela knew he did not believe her.

'Well, I think he might have arrived a second or two before I did,' she said reluctantly.

'A second or two? Then you must have seen him go in,' said Mr. D'Onofrio.

She was fairly caught.

'No, I didn't,' she admitted.

'*Ecco*,' he said, almost to himself. He regarded her reflectively and then said, in the manner of one giving advice, 'Some people are not to be trusted, *signora*.'

'Oh?' said Angela politely.

'Yes,' he said. 'Be very careful.'

'I thank you for your concern,' she said, 'but I assure you it's quite unnecessary.'

Their eyes met and he nodded.

'Do not worry about Mr. Sheridan,' he said. 'At present there is every reason to believe he killed himself, but if any evidence to the contrary reveals itself then you can be sure I will act on it. You have my word.'

'Thank you,' said Angela.

'Morandi tells me you are a detective in England,' he said.

'Not a paid one,' she replied, 'but it's true that I have done a little investigating in the past.'

'Then I will rely on you to tell me if you discover anything else,' he said.

'Don't worry, I shall,' she said.

He took leave of her and went off, and Angela breathed a sigh of relief that the interview was over. It had been an uncomfortable few minutes, and she was annoyed at herself for feeling guilty about having brought Edgar Valencourt into it. Still, she reflected, at least she had done her duty. The police might do as they saw fit now, and Valencourt would have to take care of himself. After all, no-one could say she had not given him plenty of opportunity to leave the place.

She walked slowly up the terrace steps, deep in thought. Her mind had wandered back to the Quinns, and in particular Miss Quinn's insistence that she had foreseen trouble for Mr. and Mrs. Sheridan. Trouble had come for them both, right enough, but Angela could not help feeling that there was something she had not understood; something she had missed. Perhaps she would speak to Miss Quinn about it again when she next saw her.

She was brought out of her reverie by Elsa Peters, who wanted to know what she had been talking to Mr. D'Onofrio about. Angela was unwilling to share her suspicions, based as they were on such slight evidence, so she merely said vaguely that they had been discussing Raymond Sheridan's suicide.

'Oh, yes,' said Elsa. 'I hear that Virginia Sheridan is arriving tomorrow. I wonder how she will cope, the poor thing. She's rather delicate, you know—not the capable sort at all. I hope she won't find it too hard, although I imagine there will be plenty of people who are only too willing to help her. She's one of those women who tend to inspire protectiveness in others.'

Angela's thoughts were immediately driven back to

what Valencourt had said. Clearly he did not admire the type himself, but presumably many people did. Angela found herself growing very curious to meet Mrs. Sheridan.

'Now, then,' went on Elsa. 'Have you decided whether or not to come today? I only ask because there's a train in three-quarters of an hour and we can be in Milan by lunch-time if we set off soon.'

'Oh, I'd quite forgotten about it,' said Angela. 'It's not very far, is it?'

'Only about an hour,' said Mrs. Peters. 'Now, *do* say you'll come. I'll be dreadfully bored without someone to help me poke fun at people.'

'Well, if you put it like that, how can I say no?' said Angela. 'I suppose a day away from all the unpleasantness here in Stresa won't do us any harm, will it?'

'No indeed,' said Elsa. 'I should say quite the opposite, in fact. Now, go and get ready and we'll be off in no time.'

Angela did as was suggested, and shortly afterwards she and Elsa were sitting in a railway carriage with their heads bent over the trusty Baedeker's, trying to decide what to see first. The afternoon was spent ostensibly in admiring the stately buildings of Milan, and in gazing at the *Last Supper* and politely pretending it was not a disappointment, but the city was hot, dusty and uncomfortable and Angela found it a struggle to maintain the appearance of interest, being unable to tear her thoughts away from what had happened the day before at the Villa Pozzi. She felt some relief, therefore, when they arrived back at the Hotel del Lago in the late afternoon and she could seek the solitude of her own room. An hour or two's rest would be just the thing, she thought, to refresh her and restore her to her customary good humour. Before she could go up, however, she was informed that someone had left a message for her. Angela took the note. It was from Mary Ainsley, who wanted her to come and visit the next morning. The message hinted at some mysterious purpose, and Angela bit back an exclamation of impatience then put it out of her mind. No doubt all would be revealed tomorrow, she thought as she headed upstairs.

Chapter Thirteen

'BUT IT'S TRUE,' said Mary as they sat in the little sitting-room of the Ainsleys' apartment. 'We had it from Mrs. Bernini, who had it from Miss Frome, who heard it from the Quinns themselves. I believe they come into quite a large sum of money from Raymond Sheridan.'

'Are you quite certain?' said Angela. 'Do you mean the solicitor has already spoken to them? I've never seen the law act so quickly, if so. Why, it's been less than two days!'

'Well, Mrs. Bernini swore that's what Miss Frome told her,' said Mary.

Angela looked sceptical. It seemed highly unlikely to her that so soon after Mr. Sheridan's death his solicitors would rush forth into action and begin telling all his beneficiaries of their good fortune before the body was even cold. Why, the deceased's wife—presumably the main beneficiary—had not even returned from abroad yet to identify him. No, it was unthinkable, and Angela told Mary so.

'I see what you mean,' said Mary, considering, then blushed a little. 'Oh dear, I seem to have got rather carried away with the gossip, don't I? How dreadful of me, after all the efforts I make every day to prevent that kind of thing in our little community here. Of course, you're right. Nothing is likely to happen with the will for ages, I suppose.'

'And whatever one thinks of the Quinns, I can't quite picture them going around boasting about an inheritance gained under such tragic circumstances,' said Angela.

'True,' conceded Mary. 'I don't think even they would be so crass as that. Very well, I shall make every attempt to discourage all gossip about the will. But it won't be possible to put a stop to all of it, unfortunately,' she went on. 'Poor Raymond. I'm afraid this is the most exciting thing to have happened in Stresa in years. It will be the talk of the place for months at least.'

'I imagine it will,' said Angela.

Just then, Jonathan Ainsley came in.

'Hallo, Angela,' he said. 'I trust you're feeling better now after what happened on Wednesday. No ill-effects, I hope?'

'None at all, thank you,' said Angela.

'Angela has just been saying that we ought to put a stop to all this gossip about the Quinns,' said Mary.

'Gossip?' said Jonathan, pricking up his ears. 'What gossip?'

'About the Quinns having inherited some money from Raymond Sheridan, of course,' said Mary.

'I didn't know they had,' said Jonathan. 'Why didn't you tell me?'

'I thought I had, dear,' said Mary. 'I must have forgotten. But that's exactly the point—we're not supposed to talk about it, since it may not be true.'

But Jonathan's mind had immediately latched on to the idea of the inheritance and he was not interested in the rest.

'How much did he leave them? Was it a large sum?'

'We don't know that he left them anything,' explained Mary patiently. 'I was just saying that people have been talking and spreading rumours about it when they really oughtn't. News travels so fast here in Stresa, and people can't resist passing on a really good story.'

'But that's rather serious, if it's true,' said Jonathan.

'Is it?' said Mary. 'Why?'

'Why, because it gives the Quinns a strong motive for desiring his death, of course,' he said.

'Good gracious!' exclaimed Mary. 'Surely you can't be suggesting that they killed him? Why, Jonathan, what on earth has got into you? I'm beginning to think that your dislike of the Quinns amounts to an obsession.'

'Don't be ridiculous,' said Jonathan. 'Of course it isn't an obsession. I don't deny I dislike them, but I should never dream of making unfounded accusations against innocent people.'

'Well, that's what it sounds like to me,' said Mary.

'But if what you say is true about the inheritance then I'm not so sure they *are* innocent,' went on Jonathan obstinately.

'How on earth could they have killed him?' said Mary in exasperation. 'Raymond was a big man. They'd never have been able to lift him up—and even if they could, how does one murder a man by hanging him? Why, he'd never stay still! It's simply nonsense. Angela, tell him he's being absurd.'

'It might be possible to kill someone that way,' said Angela, who was unwilling to take Jonathan's side in this argument but was forced to admit that he might have a point.

'What?' said Mary in surprise.

'Well, they might have drugged him first,' said Angela.

'I'm talking in general terms, of course, but if one wanted to kill a man and make it look like suicide, it would in theory be possible to give him something to knock him out and then hang him when he was unconscious. I don't say that's what happened here—as you say, Mr. Sheridan was a well-built man and even two women would have found it very difficult to lift him—but it certainly might be done.'

'You see?' said Jonathan to his wife. 'But as a matter of fact, I wasn't talking about anything so obvious. Even I don't believe the Quinns would stoop to violence of that sort. No—I have something much more subtle in mind. We all know how charming Mrs. Quinn is, and how she and her daughter have managed to insinuate themselves into the lives of many of our residents. That must take no little ability on their part, and I have on occasion wondered whether they might not have some kind of hypnotic powers which enable them to influence others and bend them to their will.'

'That seems a little far-fetched,' said Mary.

'Oh, believe me, my dear, I have heard of such things being quite normal in spiritualist circles,' her husband assured her. 'Many so-called mediums have been caught attempting to hypnotize their subjects in order to convince them that what they see during a séance is real, rather than a tawdry trick on the part of the practitioner. It's quite common among that type of people, as I understand it.'

'Then you think they may have hypnotized him and convinced him to commit suicide?' said Angela, pondering this new idea.

'It would be easy enough for them, don't you think?' said Jonathan. 'They had his full confidence, and he was always more than happy to listen to what they had to say. What could be easier than for Mrs. Quinn to exercise her powers of suggestion upon him and convince him that his wife was not going to return and that, as a consequence, there was no reason for him to go on living? Why, they wouldn't need to touch him at all, or even go near him. All they would have to do would be to goad him enough to make him take his own life.'

'That's always assuming, of course, that they knew he was leaving them some money—if indeed he did,' said Angela. 'Otherwise I can't see what possible motive they could have.'

Jonathan was about to develop his theory further when the doorbell rang. Mary peeped out over the balcony.

'Oh!' she said. 'It's Virginia.'

She ran downstairs and shortly afterwards returned in company with a slight and delicate-looking woman with dark hair and large, expressive eyes. Virginia Sheridan was some years younger than her husband, and Angela was struck by the contrast between the two, since Raymond Sheridan had reminded her of nothing so much as a bear, whereas his wife was more like a tiny fawn, wide-eyed and frightened. She was carrying a handkerchief and had evidently been weeping, but was now quite composed, although white and ill-looking.

'Oh, Mary,' she said. 'How shall I bear it?'

'I don't know, dear,' said Mary, taking Mrs. Sheridan's hand in hers. 'It's horrid, I know, but you must do the best you can to remain strong. Jonathan and I will be here to help if there's anything at all you want us to do. I know Jonathan is quite willing to take care of all the dull, difficult stuff if you don't want to bother yourself with it—you know, death certificates and all the other formalities.'

'Naturally,' said Jonathan sincerely. 'I shall be more than happy to do anything you require, Virginia. We are always here, as you know, day or night. There is no need to trouble yourself with anything you don't want to.'

'Oh, how kind you are,' said Virginia Sheridan. 'I'm afraid I still haven't quite got over the shock of all this, and I simply don't know how I can cope with anything.'

'But you must look after yourself, dear,' said Mary. 'Why, you look positively ill—not well at all. There's no use in your making yourself sick with worry and grief, you know.'

Mrs. Sheridan held her hands to her face.

'Yes, I'm afraid I do feel rather sick,' she said. 'Travelling disturbs my health even at the best of times, but this whole thing has made me feel quite unwell.'

'Perhaps you ought to have something to eat,' suggested Mary. 'Why don't you stay to lunch, and then afterwards I shall come with you back to the house and help you unpack—or I can do it while you lie down.'

'Is—is Raymond still there?' asked Mrs. Sheridan fearfully.

'Of course not,' said Jonathan.

'Shall I have to identify him? I don't think I could bear to see him like that.'

'No, I don't suppose it will be at all necessary,' said Mary. 'I'm sure Jonathan can do it for you. You needn't trouble yourself at all.'

'You're both so kind,' said Mrs. Sheridan with a wan smile, then her face crumpled and she exclaimed, 'Oh, how dreadful it all is! I feel as though I'm in the middle of the most awful dream, and I expect to wake up at any moment, but it's not a dream at all, is it? And it's all my fault!'

'Of course it's not,' said Mary. 'How can it be your fault? You weren't even here.'

'But that's just it, isn't it?' said Mrs. Sheridan. 'I never ought to have left him. I knew at the time it was a mistake, but we'd had a silly row—I can't remember who started it

—and I was furious with him. I know one oughtn't to let the sun go down on one's anger, but I did just that, and I'd been promising to visit my sister for ages, so I packed my bags and went back to England without speaking to him again. As soon as I got there I regretted it and wanted to make it up, but it's difficult to do that from hundreds of miles away, and my sister wasn't well, and so I comforted myself with the thought that he'd have forgotten it by the time I got back. But he didn't, did he? He must have thought I'd left for good, and now I shall never be able to forgive myself.'

She put the handkerchief to her eyes and gave a sob.

'Did he ever give you the impression he was planning something of the sort?' said Angela gently.

'No—yes—I don't know,' replied Mrs. Sheridan. 'He was always a little prone to depression, but he always came out of it quickly and I swear I never dreamed he'd do something like this. Of course I should never have left him if I had. Poor, darling Raymond. He died alone and it was all my fault. Oh, it's too much! Mary, I'm going to be sick!'

Mary gave an exclamation of concern and ran to fetch a cold cloth, and after a minute or two's application of that to the face and wrists, followed by several sips of water and a dry biscuit, the sickness receded and Mrs. Sheridan declared she felt much better.

'I was just being silly, I'm afraid,' she said ruefully, 'but it won't do, will it? I must exert myself for Raymond's sake.'

Angela had been observing the scene with interest in view of what she had already heard about Raymond Sheridan's wife, and decided that she rather agreed with Edgar Valencourt's assessment, having seen how neatly Mrs. Sheridan had convinced the Ainsleys, within five minutes of her arrival, to volunteer to take over all the unpleasant tasks associated with her husband's death for her.

Mary brought some more biscuits for Mrs. Sheridan, and while she was doing so the bell rang and Jack Lomax arrived.

'Hallo, Virginia,' he said gruffly. 'Just came to say how terribly sorry I am about all this. Dreadful business, I say. Can't tell you how much I regret it.'

'Oh, how kind of you, Jack,' said Mrs. Sheridan. 'It wasn't you who found him, was it?'

'No. It was Mrs. Marchmont, I believe,' he said, nodding towards Angela.

'You poor thing!' exclaimed Mrs. Sheridan to Angela. 'It must have been the most awful shock for you.'

'Don't mind me,' said Angela. 'I'm quite all right. It's you I am more concerned about.'

'Did—anybody see him before he died?' said Mrs. Sheridan.

'I saw him the night before he was found,' said Lomax.

'Oh!' said Mrs. Sheridan, and looked at him as though wanting to know more.

'He was rather down,' said Lomax.

'I see,' said Mrs. Sheridan, still waiting.

'I'm afraid he mentioned that you'd had a row,' he said in a rush at last. 'He thought you'd gone for good. He was unhappy, but I never really expected him to do what he did. I thought it was just words. People say that sort of thing every day.'

'What sort of thing?' said Mrs. Sheridan.

Lomax shifted uncomfortably.

'He said something about life not being worth living any more,' he said at last. 'Never took him seriously, though. I ought to have stayed. All my fault.'

'Oh, don't say that, Jack!' cried Mrs. Sheridan. 'You couldn't have known.'

Lomax shook his head.

'I'm sorry, Virginia,' he said.

While this exchange was going on, Angela had the oddest feeling that Jack Lomax disliked Virginia Sheridan. She did not have much to go on, but she noticed that Lomax avoided Mrs. Sheridan's eyes when she was looking at him, and that when she turned away he regarded her with a mixture of fascination and fear, as a small animal might stare mesmerized at a large and hungry predator. Virginia now put her hand on his arm and Angela noticed that he looked deeply uncomfortable and shrank away. Lomax stood to take his leave and Mrs. Sheridan said:

'I'll come with you. I must get home now, as there's such a lot to see to.'

He looked as though he would like to object but said nothing and merely waited politely.

'Shall I come up to the house later?' said Mary. 'I can help with your things.'

'Oh, yes please, Mary, that's terribly kind of you,' said Mrs. Sheridan, and she and Jack Lomax left together, followed shortly by Jonathan.

'Doesn't Mr. Lomax like Mrs. Sheridan?' said Angela as soon as they had gone.

'Why, it's funny you should say that, because I've often thought it myself,' said Mary. 'I don't think he does like her much, no.'

'Why not?'

'I'm not sure,' replied Mary. 'You know he doesn't talk a lot, but I get the impression he thinks she was bad for Raymond. She does require a lot of attention, as you may have noticed.'

'I had, rather,' admitted Angela.

'Well, some people are better at dealing with things than others,' said Mary. 'Virginia is one of those types who need a lot of help.'

'And she seems to get it, too,' said Angela.

'She has just lost her husband, of course,' said Mary. 'It's only right that one's friends should rally round in circumstances such as these. I shall go along to the house in a little while and see what I can do. Oh dear—I do hope she's going to be all right.'

Mary had things to do and so shortly afterwards Angela left and walked slowly back to the hotel, thinking about the events of that morning and in particular Jonathan's theory that the Quinns had been responsible for driving Mr. Sheridan to suicide. It was an extraordinary theory, certainly, but Angela knew little about hypnotism and so had no idea whether or not it was feasible. From what she had heard of the art, she seemed to remember that a hypnotized subject might be induced to do things he would not normally be inclined to do in the wakened state —but whether that extended to killing himself she could not tell; it seemed unlikely to her that a subject could be persuaded to act against his own safety. Furthermore, in this particular case, the theory did not satisfactorily explain the matter of Raymond Sheridan's shoe-laces. Why had he left the house without first fastening his shoes and his jacket? Had it been only one shoe-lace then that might be easily explained by its having come undone on the walk down to the summer-house. But for two to come loose in that short distance? From what Angela had observed of Mr. Sheridan, who had struck her as fastidious in all matters of dress, it seemed most unlike him.

She arrived back at the hotel and went in to lunch, idly wondering what was required to institute a post-mortem investigation on a dead body in Italy. Ought she to speak to

Mr. D'Onofrio again? But he already knew as much as she did about the manner of Mr. Sheridan's death, and he had made no mention of such an investigation, and of course it was none of her business anyway: she could not simply start making demands of the local police or instructing them as to how to conduct their inquiries. No—she would leave well alone and allow Mr. D'Onofrio to act as he saw fit, and in the meantime she would carry on with her holiday.

And yet the nagging doubt remained there in her mind.

Chapter Fourteen

Elsa had gone to Lugano for the day and so Angela lunched alone. Afterwards she fell into conversation with Mr. Morandi, who could always be relied upon to be fully apprised of all the latest gossip. As she had expected, he had heard the rumour about the Quinns' supposed inheritance, but to her surprise he explained that he had heard it from the Quinns themselves, who had been most indignant about the stories that had been circulating about them and had gone straight to Mr. Morandi himself, rightly supposing him to be the quickest conduit through which to quash the rumours.

'Mrs. Quinn was very upset when she heard it,' he said. 'She says it is a dreadful calumny and that if Mr. Sheridan did leave her some money then she knows nothing of it.'

'Why is it a calumny?' said Angela. 'Does she mean that people are suggesting there may have been foul play in some sense?'

Mr. Morandi lowered his voice.

'There have been suggestions that all is not—how do you say?—above the board,' he said.

'But what are they meant to have done?'

He shrugged.

'If I told you half the things I have heard about Mrs. and Miss Quinn in the past two days you would be shocked. And then you would look at the Quinns and say to yourself, "No, this is absurd, and the people who spread rumours are very stupid. I shall listen no more." That is what I have done.'

He then went off, and Angela was left with a burning curiosity to know exactly what stories had been going around. If even Mr. Morandi was refusing to pass on the rumours, then they must indeed be preposterous ones.

It was another fine, sunny day and as she had been sitting down all morning she decided to take a walk along the lake-front in the direction away from the town. The sun was sparkling off the surface of the water and the landing-stage was busy with day-trippers, tourists and boatmen getting into and out of the various pleasure-craft which plied their trade on the lake, and Angela stopped to watch for a moment, tempted to join them and spend the afternoon on the water. She decided against it, however, and continued her walk. A little farther along, away from the hotels, the front was quieter, and here Angela found Jack Lomax with his two pupils, who were taking advantage of the favourable light to paint the lake from an unaccustomed angle. Angela was a little surprised that Lomax felt capable of working so soon after the death of his friend —and indeed he had an air of preoccupation about him— but then she reflected that for such a dedicated artist perhaps painting was a means for him to forget his troubles for a little while.

'I hope you're feeling better now,' said Angela to Christopher Tate, after she had duly examined and admired their work. 'I understand you haven't been well.'

'Yes, thanks, I'm perfectly recovered,' he said. 'It was the weather, you know—that sort of heavy humidity has never agreed with me, and it always gives me the most ghastly headache, but it's quite passed now, thank goodness!'

Angela looked at him and wondered whether Christopher could possibly be telling the truth, for to her he still looked very ill. His face was white and drawn, and there were dark circles under his eyes. He fidgeted continually as he talked and at one point nearly knocked over a water jar full of brushes. As he painted he darted frequent glances at Jack Lomax, who was abstracted and did not seem to have noticed. The hero-worship was still in evidence, but it seemed to have grown even more intense in the past few days. Angela watched as Lomax praised some aspect of Francis's painting, and saw that Christopher's face immediately fell and became disconsolate. Lomax seemed to have noticed it too, for soon afterwards he came over to look at Christopher's painting and remarked upon its fine brushwork. Christopher seemed relieved, which struck Angela as an odd reaction. Perhaps he had blotted his copy-book in some way and was attempting to win back Lomax's favour.

She saluted them and walked on, and soon came to the gates of the Villa Pozzi. There she stopped and glanced up the drive. A little way ahead was the summer-house, and she gazed at it thoughtfully, trying to bring to mind anything she might have forgotten about the events of Wednesday afternoon. After a few moments she shook her head impatiently and was preparing to pass on when she heard a voice calling her name and saw Mary Ainsley and Virginia Sheridan walking arm-in-arm down the drive towards her.

'Mary has been helping me to unpack,' explained Mrs. Sheridan, 'but the house is so gloomy and stuffy that I simply couldn't bear to spend another moment there and I had to get outside or I thought I should burst.'

Angela regarded Mrs. Sheridan sympathetically. She looked a little better than she had that morning, with slightly more colour in her cheeks, although she still clung to Mary like a child.

'Virginia was just saying she thinks she might have to sell the place,' said Mary. 'I can't say I blame her, after what's happened.'

'No,' said Mrs. Sheridan. 'It's such an awfully big house for one person, and I can't possibly manage the gardens by myself. Oh, dear, and they were Raymond's pride and joy.'

Two large tears appeared in the corners of her eyes, and she fumbled for a handkerchief.

'No, I promised I wouldn't be like this,' she said after a moment or two. 'I must think about practical things, mustn't I, Mary?'

'That's probably the best idea,' replied Mrs. Ainsley. 'It will help take your mind off what's happened. Oh, by the way, Angela, I do wish we hadn't mentioned anything to Jonathan this morning about the Quinns. I think he is going to be quite impossible on the subject.'

'Really?' said Angela. 'In what way?'

'Why, he's fastened onto this silly hypnotism idea, of course. He was silent all through lunch, and then quite suddenly came out and asked me if I'd ever felt myself feeling sleepy while talking to Mrs. Quinn, and had I ever thought they might be trying to persuade me to do something against my will? Naturally, I gave him my best snort and told him in no uncertain terms that he ought to forget about the Quinns and start concentrating on his worshippers, in case he lost them altogether, but I don't think he was listening. He went out and said he was going to visit Mrs. Rowe.'

'Is Mrs. Rowe the woman who was supposed to be planning to include the Quinns in her will?' said Angela. 'The one whose son wasn't happy about it?'

'Yes, that's the one,' said Mary. 'I dare say Jonathan is haranguing her at this very moment, trying to get her to admit that she was hypnotized into it. Poor woman. And she walks with sticks so she can't even run away.'

'Oh dear,' said Angela, trying not to laugh at Mary's rueful face, since she saw that her friend was genuinely worried.

'Yes,' said Mary. 'I am rather worried that he's going to cause trouble. I've told him that it's unchristian to spread rumours, but he's adamant that it doesn't apply in the case of the Quinns, since they are as good as criminals and he is doing a good turn to society in warning people against them.'

'I don't think he's the only one, though,' said Angela. 'I was speaking to Mr. Morandi earlier and he said he had heard a lot of silly rumours about them. He wouldn't tell me what they were, but I gather there has been a lot of talk in the town over the past couple of days. It looks as though the Quinns are under rather a cloud of suspicion at present.'

'Poor things,' said Mary. 'Even if they aren't quite the thing I don't suppose for a moment they had anything to do with what happened to Raymond, but once a rumour takes hold there is no quashing it.'

Virginia Sheridan had been listening to all this with astonishment.

'Do you mean to say that people think the Quinns had something to do with Raymond's death?' she said. 'How are they meant to have done it?'

Reluctantly, Mary told her about the hypnotism theory and she opened her eyes wide.

'Why, surely that's nonsense!' she said.

'Of course it's nonsense,' said Mary, 'but I'm afraid reports are going about that he left them some money in his will, which supposedly gives them a motive. You don't happen to know whether he *did* leave them anything, do you?'

'He never told me anything about it if he did,' said Mrs. Sheridan. 'But he never made any secret of the fact that he was very grateful to them, so I shouldn't be a bit surprised if he had left them something. I doubt it would be very much, though—and certainly not enough to induce them to—' she tailed off.

'That's exactly what I said to Jonathan,' said Mary, 'but he wouldn't be convinced. I really must persuade him to take a holiday. I think the strains of the job are getting on his nerves, rather.' She suddenly remembered something. 'But Angela,' she said, 'I quite forgot to ask you what happened during your séance. You never told me your impressions of the Quinns.'

'No, I didn't, did I?' said Angela, who had almost forgotten about the thing in view of subsequent events. She recounted what had happened during their sitting, and told Mary what she had thought of the Quinns—that is, that they were harmless charlatans who provided a little excitement for a modest fee.

'I thought you'd say that,' said Mary.

'Perhaps I was the wrong person to look into it,' said Angela. 'I am a naturally sceptical person with no particular susceptibilities and so was unlikely to be terribly badly affected by it. I'm fairly sure they didn't try to hypnotize me, at any rate—not least because the sitting went so badly —but I can't say what influence they might have on someone of a less—let us say robust—disposition than mine.'

'Someone like me, you mean?' said Mrs. Sheridan suddenly. 'What effect do you think they'd have on me?'

'I don't know,' said Mary, 'but I do hope you're not planning to go along and find out.'

'Why not?' said Mrs. Sheridan.

'Why, because you've just lost your husband, darling,' said Mary. 'It would be quite absurd.'

'But surely that's why I am the very person to do it,' said Mrs. Sheridan. 'Raymond *was* my husband, after all, and if anyone has an interest in finding out how he died then I do. If they really have been hypnotizing people in order to bend them to their will, then someone needs to find it out and stop them.'

'But you can't do that by yourself,' said Mary. 'How on earth will you know if you *have* been hypnotized? If they really are guilty then they will surely be cunning and do it without your knowledge. Now, Virginia, I really don't think you ought to be thinking about anything of the sort at present. You simply aren't well enough.'

'There's nothing wrong with me,' said Mrs. Sheridan. 'Really, there isn't. And someone must do it.'

In vain Mary tried to dissuade her but she was quite obstinate. She would sit for the Quinns at all costs and judge for herself whether they had had a hand in the death of her husband. She wanted to do something useful, she said. Mary saw that she was determined and said:

'Very well, then—do it if you must, but I won't let you go alone. Angela, suppose you go with her? Jonathan would never forgive me if I did it.'

Angela had seen this coming as soon as Mrs. Sheridan spoke, and had already resigned herself.

'Very well,' she said. 'I agree that it would be best for

two of us to go, although I don't suppose we'll discover anything conclusive.'

'Perhaps not,' said Mrs. Sheridan with a little sob. 'But I could never live with myself if I knew that Raymond had died in suspicious circumstances and yet did nothing.'

'No-one will ever accuse you of that,' said Mary soothingly.

Virginia Sheridan set her jaw.

'Very well, then,' she said. 'I shall go to the hotel now and tell Mr. Morandi to call the Quinns and arrange a séance. Will tomorrow afternoon be suitable, Mrs. Marchmont?'

Angela said that tomorrow afternoon would be perfect, and they parted, Mary and Virginia to go to the Hotel del Lago and Angela to continue her walk.

Chapter Fifteen

WHEN SHE RETURNED, Angela sought out a quiet, shady spot in the hotel garden and sat down in a deck-chair by a beautiful flowering camellia to read her book. After a few minutes spent staring at the page without taking in anything much, however, she tossed it aside and lost herself in thought. Truth to tell she was feeling rather dissatisfied with herself. Mary had summoned her to Stresa to investigate the Quinns, but what had she done in reality? Very little, it seemed. She had been out on the lake, visited Milan and had a picnic. All very enjoyable, of course (apart from the picnic), but hardly what she was supposed to be doing. As to *that*, she had achieved practically nothing —had merely sat for the Quinns once, immediately taken them at face value and dismissed them as being of no importance. But now a man was dead and she had nothing to show for her visit: no evidence, or hunch, or anything at all that might allow her to step forward and say, 'I suspect the Quinns are guilty,' or even, 'I know the Quinns to be innocent.' True, she had not particularly wanted to come to Stresa, and was still mourning the loss of Venice, but she had made Mary a promise and surely she owed it to her to follow it through to the end.

Very well, then: tomorrow she was going with Virginia Sheridan to sit for Mrs. and Miss Quinn, and this time she would approach things more seriously and make more of an effort to find something out. There were several questions that demanded answers, but the most pressing one now, of course, was: did the Quinns have anything to do with Raymond Sheridan's death? If so, *how* did they do it and *why* did they do it?

As to the *how*, they had already debated it that morning at Mary's house: either he must have been drugged in order to prevent him from struggling, and then strung up afterwards, or he must have been somehow induced to do it himself. If he had been drugged then only a post-mortem examination would confirm it, and she had no idea what Mr. D'Onofrio was planning in that regard. If Sheridan had been induced to do it, though—Angela paused uncertainly here. Leaving aside the matter of whether or not it was *possible* to hypnotize someone into killing himself, there remained the question of whether it was actually *illegal* to do it. Even supposing it could be proved, was there a law against influencing others, by whatever means, to take their own lives? Angela knew of no such law in England, and had even less knowledge of the position in Italy.

She abandoned that line of thought and moved onto the second question of *why*, which immediately gave rise to two further questions: had Mr. Sheridan left the Quinns anything in his will and, more importantly, had they known of it? If they had no knowledge of it then they had no motive that Angela could see, but how could one *prove* that they knew nothing? It seemed an almost impossible task.

She now thought back to the conversation she had

had with the Quinns on the day Raymond Sheridan had been found. She had never told the Ainsleys about Miss Quinn's warning to Mr. Sheridan and now she was glad of it, for it would surely give more grist to Jonathan's mill in his attempts to prove that the Quinns were responsible for what had happened. But what was it Asphodel had said about a letter? Yes, that was it: Mrs. Quinn had upbraided her daughter for writing to Mr. Sheridan to warn him of her vision that he was in danger, and Asphodel had mentioned something about an angry note he had sent in return. Either of those letters might be a useful piece of evidence: the first might show whether or not the Quinns had been trying to influence Mr. Sheridan in any way, while the second might help shed some light on his state of mind in the period leading up to his death.

Yes, thought Angela, she would be very interested to see those letters. But how could she get hold of them, if indeed they still existed and had not been destroyed? The first was easy enough, she supposed. At some point Virginia Sheridan would have to look through her husband's things, and it would inevitably be found. But getting hold of Raymond Sheridan's reply was a more difficult matter, since the Quinns presumably had it and it would not be found without a search of their apartment. But how to do that? Angela vaguely remembered Mrs. Quinn's telling her that they had a special room for sittings and she racked her brains for a while, wondering if she could somehow trick them into allowing her to leave the room while Mrs. Sheridan sat for them. Perhaps she could pretend to be taken ill and ask to lie down, and then search the place quickly while they were otherwise occupied. It was not an ideal solution, of course—especially since she was meant to be there to look after Mrs. Sheridan—but for the moment she could think of no other answer to the problem.

She was still musing fruitlessly on this topic when she heard footsteps approaching behind her, and knew immediately who it was without needing to turn around.

'I hope I didn't disturb your nap,' said Edgar Valencourt as he stood before her.

'I wasn't asleep,' she said with dignity. 'I was thinking. I do indulge in the pursuit occasionally.'

'I'm glad to hear it,' he said. 'What were you thinking about?'

'Oh, lots of things,' she said. 'You're still here, by the way.'

'So I am.'

She regarded him thoughtfully.

'Have you *any* intention of leaving, or am I wasting my breath?' she said.

'Well, I—'

'Oh, never mind,' she said, for an extraordinary idea had that very second darted into her head and she wondered if she dared do it. She glanced at Valencourt sideways.

'Why are you looking at me like that?' he said suspiciously.

'Like what? I'm not looking at you like anything.'

'Yes you are. You're examining me as though I'm some sort of exotic species of insect you're about to dissect for the purposes of science.'

'Don't be ridiculous,' said Angela.

'I'm not being ridiculous. You're up to mischief, I can tell, and I want to know what it is.'

'We-ell,' said Angela, reaching a decision, 'do you remember when you were so horrid to me the other day?'

'I thought we'd agreed to forget that.'

'And so we have,' she assured him. 'Consider it forgotten. However, I *do* seem to recall your promising to make it up to me.' She stopped and eyed him speculatively.

'Ah, now we come to it,' he said, amused. 'I ought to have known you wanted something. Come on then, what is it?'

'How should you feel about a spot of burglary?'

She said it all at once, then paused half-fearfully and glanced at him to gauge the effect of her words. For a moment he looked astonished, then he burst out laughing.

'Just when I thought nobody could ever surprise me again,' he said, 'here you are, cool as a cucumber, proposing breaking and entering and I don't know what else besides.'

'Is that a yes or a no?' she said, somewhat relieved that he had not immediately run in the opposite direction.

'I'd like an explanation first,' he said, and threw himself down on the grass beside her. 'Tell me more.'

It was only fair, of course, and so Angela explained as briefly as possible why she had come to Stresa and what she wanted to find out.

'I see,' he said. 'So instead of going to Venice you ended up here, investigating fake clairvoyants.'

'Yes,' said Angela. 'Or, rather, no. I seem to have done very little investigating up to now, despite my promise to Mary. I feel quite guilty about it, and after all that's happened I think I shall have to stay in Stresa until I've found out some answers. I don't suppose I'll have time to see Venice at all now, which is a great pity.'

She looked a little wistful.

'Yes, it is a shame to miss Venice,' said Valencourt. 'You'd like it, Angela.'

'Well, never mind about that now,' she said. 'At present I am more concerned about finding that letter. Mrs.

Sheridan and I are going to sit for the Quinns tomorrow at their home. All I need is for someone else to get in and search the flat while they are nicely distracted.'

'Oh, so that's all you need,' he said. 'Not much, is it?'

'But will you do it?'

'I'll have to go and take a look at the place first, and find out whether it's possible,' he said, thinking.

'You must have seen the building,' said Angela. 'It's the red one on the corner of that little street just past the English church, and the Quinns live on the first floor. All the apartments have balconies, and they're bound to have their windows open in this weather, so it ought to be easy enough to get in. As a matter of fact, I *believe* there is a rather handy tree nearby that might be useful for climbing. Mrs. Sheridan and I are going along there at about five o'clock, so it's probably best if you wait until a little after that, when we're all settled, and then you can get on with it.'

'You've thought it all out, haven't you?' he said.

'It was hardly difficult,' she said. 'But I can't do it myself, which is why I asked you.'

'Are you *using* me, Angela?' he said suddenly, and there was a wicked glint in his eye.

She turned a wide smile on him.

'Why, yes, Mr. Valencourt, I believe I am,' she said. 'Have you any objection?'

'I can think of several,' he replied, 'but when you smile at me like that I forget them all.'

'Splendid,' she said. 'Then we're agreed.'

He laughed.

'You knew I'd say yes,' he said. 'And by the way, Mrs. Marchmont, I hope you know I am most offended that you seem to consider me to be some kind of cat-burglar, when I'm nothing of the sort.'

'I know you're not,' she replied. 'And I know what you are, too.'

'What am I, then?'

'Why, you're a confidence-man. You talk people into things—or out of things, rather, and I've no doubt you're very good at it.'

'You seem to be pretty good at it yourself,' he said, 'to judge from what you've just persuaded me to do. So I'm a confidence-man, am I? I suppose that sounds better than "common thief," which is what you called me last time we met.'

'Did I?' said Angela vaguely. 'How very rude of me.'

'Well, quite,' he said. 'I'm not in the least bit common. I can trace my family line back to all sorts of important people.'

'I see,' she said, amused. 'And every one of them as honest as the day is long, no doubt.'

'Yes, and as dull as ditch-water to boot,' he agreed.

'Well, now I've given you the chance to have a bit of excitement,' she said. 'It must be awfully dreary for you here, hiding away with nothing to do.'

'Oh, I shouldn't say that,' he said. 'I'm finding the company very pleasant, at any rate. You do know, don't you, that I'm putting myself in some danger by doing what you ask? At the very least you must promise to dance with me again in return the next time they have an orchestra on.'

'I should be delighted,' said Angela, who was certain that either he or she would be gone by that time. 'I shall make a note on my dance card.'

They fell silent and watched as people began to pass to and fro through the garden. Jack Lomax went past in company with Mrs. Sheridan, and Angela waved. Lomax looked rather reluctant, she thought. Two military policemen strolled by in the other direction. Angela was about to remark on them to Valencourt when she noticed to her surprise that he had disappeared, and that her lap was full of pink camellias which had certainly not been there before. She picked one up and twirled it idly for a moment or two, then stuck it in her hat.

'Idiot,' she said to herself, more for the sake of relieving her own feelings than for any good it might do. Then she realized she was smiling and hurriedly straightened her face.

It was getting towards dinner-time, so she collected her things together and stood up, scattering flowers, intending to go and change. As she headed up the path she encountered Christopher Tate, who was walking alone, without his friend. He barely heard her when she greeted him, and seemed most upset about something. Angela glanced after him in concern, and wondered whether she ought not to have a word with Francis, who was meant to be keeping an eye on him.

'Angela!' said a voice, and she looked up and saw Elsa Peters, who had evidently just returned.

'Hallo, Elsa,' said Angela. 'How was Lugano?'

'Oh, absolutely filthy,' said Elsa. 'Full of other people. The heat and the noise were quite ghastly. I was hoping to have the place to myself, but no such luck. Do you suppose it's too late for an *aperitivo*? Purely for the sake of my nerves, you understand. Do let's. We can have dinner later.'

They sat down on the terrace. Mr. Morandi soon joined them, and as Elsa talked to him Angela was left to reflect on what had just passed between her and Edgar Valencourt, and to wonder whether the heat was starting to affect her brain. Had she really asked him to break into the Quinns' apartment for her? And had he really agreed to do it? It was quite extraordinary, and she could only hope that the search would prove fruitful, or who knew what might happen next? She had no desire to get drawn into an ongoing exchange of obligations with Edgar Valencourt—not least because his manner was so engaging that it was all too easy when in company with him to forget just what and who he was. But of course that was exactly how he operated, as she had seen for herself in Cornwall. He had fooled her then, but she was not about to let him fool her a second time. No: she might have charmed Valencourt into helping her today, but flirting with jewel-thieves was a risky business and she was determined that that should be the last of it.

Chapter Sixteen

THE NEXT MORNING, Angela was just emerging from the post-office when to her surprise she found herself accosted by Asphodel Quinn, who looked as though she had been waiting for Angela to come out.

'Good morning, Miss Quinn,' said Angela, but Miss Quinn was not interested in exchanging pleasantries.

'Mrs. Marchmont, I want to speak to you about this sitting,' she said all at once.

'Oh yes?' said Angela.

'Yes,' said Miss Quinn. 'We've agreed to do it but I don't like it. Why does Mrs. Sheridan want to see us now? What good will it do her?'

'Well—' began Angela, nonplussed at the question. Surely a medium ought to know why a potential client might want to hold a séance. That was Miss Quinn's business, after all. 'She is very upset and wants to try and communicate with her husband,' she said eventually.

'Is that what she told you?' said Miss Quinn. 'But why?'

'Perhaps you ought to ask her that,' said Angela, 'but as far as I understand it, she is very worried that she may, through her own actions, have caused Mr. Sheridan to take his own life, and she is seeking reassurance.'

Asphodel considered this for a moment.

'Yes, that might be true, I suppose,' she said. 'But I still don't like it.'

Angela was starting to feel quite uncomfortable.

'Might I ask why?' she said.

'Because no good can come of it,' said Asphodel. 'I've the most awful feeling about it.'

'What sort of feeling?'

'I don't know,' said Miss Quinn. She evidently realized that this was an unsatisfactory answer, for she went on, 'It's difficult to describe without sounding ridiculous, but the best I can do is to say it's a feeling like hardness under softness.'

'Hardness under softness?' repeated Angela, none the wiser.

'Oh, of course it sounds absurd when I put it like that,' said Miss Quinn. 'I only wish I were better at explaining things, but unless you see things as I do then it's hard to make myself understood.'

'Does the feeling refer to a person or a thing?' said Angela.

'A person, I think.'

'Mr. Sheridan, perhaps?'

'Perhaps,' said Miss Quinn. 'All I know is that someone is going to get into the most terrible trouble if we do the sitting.'

'Who is going to get into trouble?' said Angela, thinking unaccountably of pink camellias.

'I can't tell you. But it's someone who doesn't deserve it.'

'Oh,' said Angela, slightly relieved. She was about to

say something reassuring, when Miss Quinn grasped her by the arm and looked directly into her eyes.

'I'm frightened, Mrs. Marchmont,' she whispered. 'I'm frightened that something awful will happen, and that I shall be held responsible for it all.'

Angela was quite disturbed by the intensity of her gaze.

'But why should you be held responsible for anything?' she said.

Miss Quinn gave a short laugh but did not quite meet her eyes.

'Oh, come now,' she said. 'You must have heard what people are saying about us. Why, it's all over Stresa. Everyone thinks we had something to do with Mr. Sheridan's death. They're saying we drove him to kill himself because he'd left us some money.'

'*Had* he left you any money?' Angela could not resist asking.

Miss Quinn shrugged.

'I don't know,' she said. 'I doubt it, although I can't deny it would come in useful if he did. I know what people say about us, but we've never asked anyone for anything that wasn't owed to us, and we had nothing to do with whatever happened to Mr. Sheridan, d'you hear? Mr. Sheridan was a nice man. I liked him and I'm very sorry he's dead. We're not in the business of bringing people unhappiness, you know—although I seem to have done a lot of that without meaning to lately.'

'Do you believe there was something suspicious about Mr. Sheridan's death?' Angela said. 'After all, you said you knew he was dead before anyone had found him. What else do you know, Miss Quinn?'

Asphodel Quinn looked away.

'Why are you asking me?' she said. 'I might have seen something but you don't believe all that nonsense about visions and stuff, do you? Why, you'd have to be mad, like me. I know people say I'm mad. Mrs. Sheridan told me so to my face when she sat for us last time.'

'Did she?' said Angela, surprised.

'Oh, yes,' said Asphodel. 'She got very upset and told me that I was quite—I think "unhinged" was the word she used.'

Angela tried and failed to picture the delicate Mrs. Sheridan being so rude.

'What did you tell her to make her say that?' she asked.

But Asphodel shook her head.

'I foretold trouble for her and she didn't like it,' was all she would say.

'You were right, though,' said Angela. She saw that Miss Quinn had set her jaw obstinately and went on, 'Look, I'm not especially keen on the whole thing either. Mrs. Sheridan has only just lost her husband and I'm quite certain that a séance so soon after the event can cause her nothing but pain. However, she was quite determined, and so I agreed to come along with her to provide moral support.'

Naturally she did not mention the real reason for their visit, but she was by now feeling quite uncomfortable about the whole thing, and was convinced that Miss Quinn had seen through their little ruse and was intending to warn them off. She was about to excuse herself and walk away when they were joined by Mrs. Quinn, who until then had been engaged in a nearby shop.

'Hallo, Mrs. Marchmont,' she said. 'I expect Saph has been asking you to try and persuade Mrs. Sheridan not to go ahead with our little sitting this afternoon.'

'She says Mrs. Sheridan won't hear of cancelling,' said Asphodel gloomily.

'I don't mind asking her again if you like,' said Angela,

who by this time would have been only too glad to forget the whole thing.

'Oh, no need,' said Mrs. Quinn. 'I know Saph is worried about what might happen, but as I often tell her, you can't go into this business and expect everyone to be pleased all the time. This Gift is a great responsibility, you know. We're blessed enough to be able to bring happiness to many people through our work, but sometimes the opposite happens and—well, things don't turn out the way the client expects. Then we're usually the ones who suffer for it. It's all too easy to blame the messenger in these cases.'

'Does that happen often?' said Angela.

'Once in a while,' said Mrs. Quinn cheerfully. 'When it does we know it's time to move on.'

'We always get driven out eventually,' said Miss Quinn.

'Now, Saph, I shouldn't put it like that. Let's say that we discover we've reached the limits of our ability to help people.'

'People always stop trusting us in the end,' said Asphodel.

The contrast between Miss Quinn's decided gloom and her mother's ebullient determination to look on the bright side of things might have been comical in any other circumstances, but Angela could not laugh. Instead, to her surprise, she found herself feeling some sympathy for the Quinns and their plight. But remembering her investigation, she quashed the feeling firmly. After all, a man had died in doubtful circumstances and the Quinns might well be connected to the mystery. If so, it was her duty to try and find it out, if at all possible.

Angela bade goodbye to the Quinns and continued on her way. She was becoming increasingly nervous about the evening ahead, since she had already begun to regret having asked Edgar Valencourt to search the Quinns' apartment, and now it seemed here was another thing to worry about: the possibility that Miss Quinn knew exactly what Mrs. Sheridan and Angela were up to. Angela had the horrible feeling that she was about to find herself in a very tricky situation of her own making. However, since there was nothing she could do to avoid it now, she determined to put it out of her head for a while.

It was an easy enough resolution to make, but not so easy to keep, for shortly afterwards, on her way back to the hotel, she saw the Quinns again on the lake-front. They were a little distance away, standing in conversation with someone Angela immediately recognized as La Duchessa. She was as expensively and showily dressed as ever, and appeared to be holding forth at some length to Mrs. and Miss Quinn, who listened to her politely. Eventually Mrs. Quinn said something in reply, and La Duchessa took a step back as though she had been slapped. Her face darkened and she began to upbraid the Quinns loudly, although the little group was still too far away for Angela to hear what she was saying. Having given her opinion, La Duchessa turned on her heel and stalked off grandly, a furious expression on her face, while the Quinns exchanged glances. Angela passed on, wondering very much what it was all about.

Chapter Seventeen

AT A FEW MINUTES before five o'clock that afternoon, Angela Marchmont and Virginia Sheridan walked together through the streets of the town, heading for the Quinns' apartment. The weather was growing hot and sultry again, and Mrs. Sheridan was still feeling a little ill and tired, and so they walked slowly to allow her to catch her breath. Angela glanced in concern at the other woman's pale face. Despite her frailty and Angela's attempts to dissuade her, Virginia Sheridan had declared herself quite determined to go through with the séance, come what may—and doubly so now, since at Angela's request she had searched through her husband's things but had found no trace of any letter from Asphodel Quinn. Naturally, Angela had said nothing about the angry note Mr. Sheridan was supposed to have sent Miss Quinn in return—or about the fact that she had enlisted a tame thief to try and find it while they were sitting—but the idea that Miss Quinn might have warned Mr. Sheridan of the danger he faced before he died was quite enough to make Mrs. Sheridan firm in her purpose.

Angela, meanwhile, was still feeling rather nervous, and was trying to compose herself enough to keep her wits about her during the sitting. Her first duty, she told herself, was to remain on her guard at all times, and to try and ascertain whether or not the Quinns really were using hypnotic powers to influence their clients. Even as she thought it, however, she shook her head. The more she considered it the more ridiculous the idea sounded to her, and try as she might she could not shake off a lingering sympathy for the Quinns. But why was she finding it so difficult to be objective? Were the Quinns really as inno-cent as they seemed? Or was there something about Italy that made her more susceptible than usual to the artfulness of charming people?

They were now approaching their destination. The Quinns lived on the first floor of a faded red building which stood on the corner of a narrow street some way out of the centre of town. The street led to a dead end and thus was not troubled with large numbers of passers-by. Angela glanced about her involuntarily as they paused at the outer door of the building, but saw no-one. She could not tell whether this was a good or a bad sign, but it was too late to worry about it now. They rang the bell and were admitted by Asphodel Quinn, who greeted them politely and made no mention of their earlier encounter, for which Angela was thankful. She and Mrs. Sheridan followed Miss Quinn upstairs and through a door, which opened into a long hall stretching to the left and right. As they entered, Angela saw that at the end of the passage to her right was a little sitting-room, furnished comfortably with easy chairs and low tables. A blue-enamelled stove stood in the corner, and she could just catch a glimpse of what looked like a writing-desk. The next room along seemed to be a bedroom. Angela judged that the balcony outside ran along between the two rooms, giving easy access to the place—provided a window was open. But was it? How could she find out? Just then, Mrs. Quinn herself emerged from the sitting-room, leaving the door open wide, and Angela saw to her relief that the French windows to the balcony were a little ajar. It ought to be easy enough for Valencourt to get in, then, if indeed he was intending to turn up.

'I can't tell you how sorry I am about your husband,' said Mrs. Quinn immediately to Virginia Sheridan. 'He was a good man—one of the best.'

'Thank you,' said Mrs. Sheridan, who was pale but quite composed. 'It's been the most awful shock, of course. As a matter of fact, I still can't quite believe it.'

'Well, I promise you that if it's at all possible we'll speak to him this evening,' said Mrs. Quinn, 'and I hope it will bring you comfort. That's the most we can wish for at times like this. Now, then,' she went on briskly, leading them down to a door at the other end of the hall. 'This way if you please. This room here is where we do our sittings. It's not very big, but as you can see it's quite separate and private, and we find it comfortable enough.'

Angela looked round as they entered. As Mrs. Quinn said, the room was a small one and had presumably been intended as a bedroom originally, but the Quinns had fitted it out for their own purposes. It was almost dark, since the small window was covered with a heavy curtain of dark-red velvet, which to judge from its crushed appearance had been folded up and transported many times, and the only light came from a single candle that burned on a little table set against the wall. In the centre of the room stood another table—a round, mahogany one, which was set about with several low easy chairs that looked as though they had seen better days. There were cushions scattered about everywhere, and every horizontal surface appeared to have been clothed in a variety of crocheted mats of all sizes. The room was extremely hot and stuffy.

Mrs. Quinn clicked her tongue and set about lighting some more candles, chatting merrily as she did so.

'Sit down, sit down,' she said. 'Mrs. Sheridan, you look tired, if you don't mind my saying so. Sit here—it's the most comfortable chair. Now what do you say to a cup of tea before we start? Saph boiled some water just before you came and it ought to be just right by now.'

Angela was just about to accept when she suddenly remembered something she had once read about a fake medium whose method for convincing her victims of the reality of what they had seen was to put a drug in their drink that caused them to experience hallucinations. She threw Virginia Sheridan a warning glance, and they both refused the tea.

'I'm sorry we're not quite prepared,' said Mrs. Quinn as she bustled about, 'but we've only now got back from a visit to another client, and we were late visiting *her* because we met someone we knew while we were in town today—it was not long after we spoke to you, Mrs. Marchmont, as a matter of fact—and she kept us talking for longer than we liked.'

Here Miss Quinn gave a short laugh but made no comment.

'Oh, yes, I think I saw you,' said Angela, pricking up her ears. 'It was a lady from the hotel, wasn't it? I believe she is a duchess of some sort.'

'That's right,' said Mrs. Quinn blandly.

'She might be a duchess, but she hasn't got the manners to match,' said the less diplomatic Asphodel.

'Hush, now,' said her mother. 'That's no way to talk.'

'I did notice she looked rather cross,' admitted Angela.

'Is she another of your clients? I thought you offered your services only to the English people here.'

'Oh, no,' said Mrs. Quinn. 'We'll do anyone who asks as long as we all speak the same language. There are plenty of Italians who come to us, for instance. They're great believers in communicating with the after-life, the Italians are.'

'La Duchessa is not Italian, though,' said Angela. 'At least, that is what Mr. Morandi told me. Do you know where she is from?'

'I've no idea,' said Mrs. Quinn.

'Wherever it is, she can go back there as far as I'm concerned,' said Miss Quinn.

'Now, Saph,' began Mrs. Quinn, but Asphodel shook her head defiantly.

'She'd no call to talk to me like that this afternoon,' she said. 'I do my best for people and if they don't like it— well, I can't help it, that's all. I answered her questions, and just because they weren't the answers she wanted she thought it gave her the right to be rude. Well, I shan't speak to her again.'

'Oh dear,' said Angela. 'I hope she didn't upset you too much.' She was dying to ask exactly what had been said but did not know how to do it without seeming impertinently inquisitive.

'Do you remember what I told you this afternoon, Mrs. Marchmont, about people who don't take kindly to being given the message, and who like to blame the messenger for it?' said Mrs. Quinn, nodding significantly. 'Well, this lady is one of those people.'

'I'll say,' said Asphodel. 'She'd been asking and asking, and in the end we had to tell her that she wasn't going to get what she wanted. Some people just want that, you know—they want us to agree that whatever idea they've got into their heads is the right one. But we can't always do that.'

'No,' agreed Mrs. Quinn. 'She was furious, wasn't she? I'd say someone was in for it.'

During this exchange, Virginia Sheridan had said nothing. Angela glanced at her and noticed that her eyes were closed and she was taking deep breaths as though bracing herself for something, while Miss Quinn watched her with narrowed eyes. Asphodel saw Angela watching her and immediately turned her head away.

'Are you quite all right?' said Angela to Mrs. Sheridan, fearful for a second that the Quinns had somehow managed to hypnotize Virginia while her attention had been distracted. But Virginia opened her eyes immediately, and replied in her normal voice:

'Oh, yes, thank you, Angela. I just felt a little hot for a second. I'm much better now. Shall we begin?'

'Why not?' said Mrs. Quinn. 'I think we're all ready. Now, I shall sit in this chair here, a little apart, and see what I can't get for you.'

'Are you going to summon Thutmose again?' said Angela.

'No,' said Mrs. Quinn. 'He's not been back since that day he was so rude to you and Mrs. Peters, but my Roundhead has been about lately. He's much more respectful, I'm very pleased to say. Let's see if we can summon him. I thought we might try and get the departed to speak through me today—it can work better that way if they're so inclined. If not, then we'll try the talking board again. Now, are we ready?' Everyone nodded, and she said, 'Very well, then. I should like everyone to sit quite quietly and try to empty your minds of all thoughts. Mrs. Sheridan, I should like you in particular to bring the image of your husband into your mind.'

Mrs. Sheridan gave a little sob but nodded. Mrs. Quinn smiled reassuringly, then closed her eyes and began to sway in her chair, humming under her breath, just as she had done during the séance at the hotel.

Angela, meanwhile, was trying her hardest to suppress a yawn, which was no easy task in that dark, stuffy room. The heat was stifling and she was beginning to feel sleepy, and after a minute or two she sat up straight and pinched herself hard on the arm.

'Wake up, you idiot,' she said to herself, and wondered whether the heat was a tactic used deliberately by the Quinns to confound the senses of their sitters. She glanced across at Virginia Sheridan, who gave her a wan smile. Angela smiled back reassuringly and resolved to stay alert. She was fairly sure that neither of them had been hypnotized so far, but she was determined not to miss any attempt of that sort.

Mrs. Quinn now appeared to be in a deep trance, and Miss Quinn was watching her mother attentively. There was silence for several minutes, and Angela was beginning to wonder whether anything would happen at all when she heard a quiet *thump*, followed by a rap. For a second she thought it must be Valencourt making a noise next door, and her heart beat rapidly in fear, for she was certain that he must be discovered, but then the sound was repeated, and she realized it was coming from somewhere in the room, for it was now accompanied by a hissing sound and a tinkling of tiny bells, which began almost inaudibly but gradually grew louder and louder until it filled her ears. The sound was quite chilling and set Angela's nerves on edge, and she looked about her, wondering how the Quinns had managed it.

Suddenly Mrs. Quinn's eyes snapped open and she began to talk.

'Now is the time,' she said loudly, and Angela jumped, for the voice was a deep one that was quite unlike her own.

Asphodel Quinn now spoke up.

'What is it?' she said. 'Who speaks? Are you friend or foe?'

'I am neither friend nor foe,' said Mrs. Quinn. 'I am. I am. I am.'

'What are you? Will you help us?'

'I am all,' said Mrs. Quinn. 'Now is the time.'

'The time for what?'

'I cannot help. Cannot help. I am. I am,' said Mrs. Quinn.

'Then we do not wish to speak to you,' said Miss Quinn firmly. 'You may go.'

There was a pause, then Mrs. Quinn opened her eyes. Angela noticed that the hissing and the sound of bells had stopped.

'Any good?' she said in her own voice.

Miss Quinn shook her head.

'I don't know who that was,' she said, 'and he didn't seem too certain either. He couldn't help, though.'

'That's a pity,' said Mrs. Quinn. 'Shall we do it again, or shall we try the talking board instead?'

'May we try the talking board, please?' said Virginia, who was looking faintly horrified at what had just passed.

'All right,' said Mrs. Quinn, and Asphodel stood up and fetched it from a drawer in the corner. 'Now, you've both used this before, so you know how it works. Two fingers on the planchette, everybody, if you please.'

Everybody did as they were told, and Mrs. Quinn closed her eyes again. This time the response was almost immediate, for the planchette began to slide rapidly backwards and forwards, then seemed inclined to attempt a revolution.

'Stop that,' Mrs. Quinn said. 'Whoever you are, you are under our command today. Is that Benedict?'

The planchette paused, then shot towards the letter Y. Mrs. Quinn gave a sniff of satisfaction.

'And how are you today, Benedict? Are you going to help us?'

The planchette jiggled over the Y.

'Thank you. Then can you tell me whether anyone is there with you?'

There was a pause, then the planchette moved slowly away from the Y. It was hovering uncertainly by the N when it suddenly seemed to change its mind, and shot back towards the Y again.

'There is,' said Mrs. Quinn, pleased. 'Can you tell me his or her name?'

This time there was no hesitation, and the letters 'R-A-Y' were spelt out. Virginia gave a little shriek. Angela was wide awake now and watching carefully.

'Please ask him if he would like to speak to us,' said Mrs. Quinn.

The board indicated that the second spirit was indeed prepared to speak.

'Now you must ask the questions,' whispered Mrs. Quinn to Mrs. Sheridan.

'What shall I say?' said Virginia in a quavering voice.

'Just speak to him as though he were here in the room with you,' said Mrs. Quinn.

'Very well, I'll try,' said Mrs. Sheridan, although she looked by no means happy at the idea. She took a deep breath. 'Raymond, it's me, Virginia. Is it really you?'

'D-A-R-L-I-N-G,' said the board.

'How shall I know if it really is him?' said Mrs. Sheridan suddenly.

'Ask him a question that only he will know the answer to,' said Mrs. Quinn.

'Oh,' said Mrs. Sheridan. 'Very well, then. Raymond, if it's really you, tell me—tell me—' She stopped to think for a second. 'Oh, I know! Tell me the Christian name of my father's eldest sister.'

There was a pause, then 'A-D-E-L-A-I-D-E' was spelt out. Virginia gave another little shriek and a sob.

'That's right!' she said. 'Then it really must be him! Oh, Raymond, can it really be you? I'm so sorry about what has happened. But why? Why did you do it? Surely you didn't really believe I wasn't going to come back? Why didn't you send me a letter or a telegram—anything, to tell me how miserable you were? Of course I'd have come straight back if I'd known.'

'S-O-R-R-Y,' said the board. 'I-D-I-O-T T-E-R-R-I-B-L-Y U-N-H-A-P-P-Y.'

'You weren't an idiot at all,' said Mrs. Sheridan. 'I was the stupid one, leaving you alone like that. Please, darling, say you'll forgive me. I shall have to live with the guilt forever but I simply couldn't bear it if I thought you blamed me too.'

They waited, but all was still. Angela glanced up and saw that everyone's eyes were fixed on the board.

'Raymond?' said Mrs. Sheridan, almost in a whisper. 'Are you still there?'

Nothing happened for an agonizing minute, then the planchette began to move slowly.

'M-Y F-A-U-L-T,' it said. 'S-O S-O-R-R-Y D-A-R-L-I-N-G.'

Then it stopped and would move no more. They waited for several minutes, but the spirit or whatever it was showed no desire to return.

'Well,' said Mrs. Quinn at last. 'That was very interesting, I must say. Are you all right, my dear?'

'Quite all right, thank you,' said Mrs. Sheridan quietly. 'If you don't mind, I think I should like to leave now. I want to go home and think about things by myself for a little while.'

'You do that,' said Mrs. Quinn, nodding in approval. 'If you think of any more questions let me know, and we'll see if we can't get him to speak to us again.'

'I shall, thank you,' said Mrs. Sheridan. She seemed slightly dazed. 'Shall we go, Angela?'

They took their leave of the Quinns with thanks and emerged into the street. It was still very warm but at least there was air here, and Angela felt the fug begin to dissipate from her brain.

'Wasn't it hot in there?' said Mrs. Sheridan, breathing in deeply. 'I thought I should die of suffocation.'

'It was, rather,' said Angela. 'It's nice to be back in the fresh air again. Where are you going now?'

'I suppose I had better go back home and get on with looking through Raymond's things,' said Virginia. 'There's such a lot to do.'

Angela looked at her companion in concern, noticing how pale and drawn she was, and wondered whether Virginia had eaten at all since she had found out about her husband's death.

'I hope you are looking after yourself,' she said. 'Suppose you come and have dinner with me at the hotel this evening. I don't wish to be rude, but you look as though you could do with a good square meal.'

Virginia laughed ruefully.

'You're right, I haven't eaten much lately,' she said, 'but I simply don't feel as though I can face food at the moment.'

'The heat doesn't help, I suppose,' said Angela. 'I don't tend to feel very hungry myself in this sort of weather, but I'd hate to think you weren't eating at all.'

'It's kind of you,' said Virginia, 'but you don't need to worry about me. I shall be quite all right.'

Angela saw that her mind was made up and said no more, but she insisted on walking with Mrs. Sheridan back to the Villa Pozzi, ostensibly in order to discuss what had happened at the Quinns' but also partly out of concern that Virginia might faint on the way. It appeared that both women remembered the same things about the séance, which was something of a relief to Angela, since it seemed to indicate that neither of them had been hypnotized—either that, or both of them had, which seemed highly unlikely. That was one concern out of the way, at least. However, both women were hesitant when it came to the actual events of the séance.

'What did you think?' said Angela at last.

'I don't know,' said Mrs. Sheridan. 'It *seemed* very convincing, but it couldn't have been, could it? They must have been doing it themselves.'

'I suppose so,' said Angela. 'The voice of the spirit was rather strange, but I imagine it's not beyond the capabilities of a good actress. I'd like to know how the automatic writing was done, though.'

'That's easy enough, isn't it? You just push the planchette but pretend not to.'

'Well, yes, of course, but how did they know the name of your aunt?'

'I can only assume Raymond must have told them,' said Virginia.

'But why should he do that?'

'I don't know. It does seem a bit odd,' said Virginia, 'but people do pass on odd bits of information sometimes.'

'But don't you think it's rather a coincidence that you should decide to ask a question to which they just happened to know the answer?'

'I don't know,' replied Virginia, then stopped and turned a troubled face to Angela. 'Are you saying you believe that really was Raymond in there?'

'No—no, of course not,' said Angela. 'That would be quite absurd.'

'Yes,' said Virginia. She looked at the ground. 'All the same,' she went on quietly, 'it would be nice to think I really *had* spoken to him, wouldn't it? Just one last time.'

She glanced up, but Angela had no words of comfort to give.

Chapter Eighteen

THE TWO WOMEN parted at the villa, having promised to meet the next day and apprise Mary Ainsley of developments, and Angela returned to the hotel along the lakefront, deep in thought. She was no nearer to knowing whether or not the Quinns had had a hand in Mr. Sheridan's death, and truth to tell, the séance had disturbed her more than she liked. It was not hard to see why people were so easily taken in by spiritualism: if she, a rational, intelligent woman (or so she liked to think of herself) could be swayed by a few candles and a little facile mumbo-jumbo, then it was no wonder that some of the more credulous members of the populace were only too keen to believe. Angela now began to see the truth of at least part of what Jonathan Ainsley had said only a few days ago: there was evidently something about being abroad that tended to cause people to shake off the constraints of home and lose their heads. Angela was certain that she would not have given the Quinns even the slightest benefit of the doubt in a damp, chilly London, but here in the warm sunshine, surrounded by lush greenery and rolling mountains, it was a different matter.

Very well, then: if she could not rely on her own observations to find out answers, then she should have to rely on solid evidence—if indeed any had come to light. Angela had seen no sign of Edgar Valencourt near the Quinns' apartment that afternoon, although she had been looking out for him, and she began to think that he must have decided not to do it after all. She was walking towards the hotel through the garden and wondering whether to be relieved or disappointed when he emerged suddenly from another path and made her jump.

'Well?' she said. 'Did you do it?'

'What do you think?' he said.

'From the look on your face I should say almost certainly yes,' she said, 'but otherwise I have no idea. I didn't hear or see a thing.'

'Of course you didn't,' he said. 'What do you take me for—an amateur?'

'You're not a burglar, though; you told me so yourself.'

'No, but I was a champion tree-climber in my youth. No-one could touch me,' he said. 'And today I discovered that I appear to have lost none of my talent despite my rapidly advancing age.'

'I was rather good at climbing trees myself as a girl,' said Angela regretfully.

'I promise I'll let you do the next break-in, then,' he said.

'Thank you, but that won't be necessary. Now, are you going to tell me about it or not?'

'Let's go somewhere we won't be overheard,' he said. 'The hotel is a bit too crowded for this sort of thing.'

They eventually found a seat on a stretch of the lake-front that was not too busy and sat down.

'How was the séance?' he said. 'Did Sheridan turn up?'

'Didn't you hear it?'

'I heard a few strange noises coming from the room, but I was in rather a hurry and didn't have time to stop and listen,' he said. 'What happened?'

She told him what had occurred, and he listened attentively.

'Just the usual nonsense, then,' he said. 'No special hypnotic powers needed, by the sound of it—just a lot of distraction and portentous mumbling.'

'More or less,' she agreed, 'although it was quite impressive, and I can't help wondering how they knew about Mrs. Sheridan's aunt. Why on earth would Mr. Sheridan have mentioned her name to the Quinns?'

'People often talk about family,' he said.

'Their own families, yes,' said Angela, 'but not about their wives' aunts, surely? Oh, I don't know—perhaps I am thinking about it too much, but I do like to have things tied up neatly in my head, and the matter of Aunt Adelaide is rather a loose end.'

'I dare say you'll find there's a simple enough explanation for it,' he said.

'I dare say you're right,' she agreed. 'Now, then, tell me about your search.'

'There's not much to tell,' he said. 'I got in easily enough, as you said, and had a good look around. They don't seem to have much in the way of possessions—not surprising for people who move around a lot, I suppose, but I did find a few papers in their writing-desk and had a look through them.'

'Oh?' said Angela hopefully, but he shook his head.

'Nothing useful, I'm afraid,' he said. 'The Quinns appear to be exactly what they claim to be. They run their business on honest lines—if we leave aside the nature of the business itself—and I found no evidence that they have ever been in trouble for anything: no convenient clippings of newspaper stories about their latest appearance in the dock, or summonses, or letters from irate clients threatening to sue, or anything of that sort. As a matter of fact, most of their correspondence appeared to consist of letters from delighted old ladies, thanking them for their help. Oh —and there was one rather pompous letter from Jonathan Ainsley, of which you can probably imagine the content.'

'So that was all you found in the writing-desk?' said Angela. 'Did you have a look in the other rooms?'

'Yes, but there was nothing,' he said.

'That's a pity,' said Angela. 'I was rather hoping you might find some trace of this mysterious angry letter that Mr. Sheridan was supposed to have sent.'

'Oh, but I did,' he said. She looked up at him quickly, and he went on, 'It was a lucky chance, though. I was just about to leave when it occurred to me that the sitting-room was awfully hot considering they'd left the French windows open. Then I saw the stove in the corner and realized they'd had it lit, as it was still warm. Of course it's no sort of weather to be keeping the stove alight if one can avoid it, so I took a look inside and found these.'

He put his hand into his pocket and brought out several scraps of burnt paper, which he held out to Angela. She glanced at him in surprise, then smiled and took them gingerly.

'You'd better be careful,' he said. 'They're pretty fragile.'

'Don't worry,' she said.

They put their heads together and examined the charred fragments, which were evidently the remains of a letter, although the signature was lost so it was impossible to tell who had sent it. After a moment's thought, Angela started to lay them out on her lap with the idea of trying to put them in some kind of order.

'You've already ruined one frock this week,' said Valencourt. 'Here, take this.'

He produced an impeccably-folded handkerchief and draped it over her knees, and they bent over the scraps again.

'What have we got, then?' said Angela. 'I assume this "*Thank you—*" goes first, then "*—matters that do not concern —.*" Now, what's next?'

'This one, I think,' said Valencourt.

'"*—outrageous to suggest—*,"' read Angela, 'then "*—lady in question—*," whoever she might be.'

'Then this bit must be last,' said Valencourt.

'"*—assure you I have no intention of putting myself in—*,"' read Angela.

They sat back and regarded the results.

'It still doesn't make a *great* deal of sense,' said Angela. 'It's a pity so much of it is missing. Still, I suppose we were lucky to get anything at all. I don't suppose you can tell me whether it's Mr. Sheridan's handwriting, can you?'

'Not offhand,' he replied, 'but it ought to be easy enough to find out. Someone is bound to have something with his writing on it—as a matter of fact I might have a note or two of his myself at home. I shall have a look later and see if I can't find them for you.'

Angela was looking at the burnt pieces of paper again.

'I wonder what it all means,' she said.

'Well, it looks as though the Quinns have been making outrageous suggestions about a lady,' he said. 'Dear me.'

'Disgraceful,' said Angela solemnly.

'Quite. And the writer is evidently not very happy

about it. Still, whoever he is, he's quite emphatic that he has no intention of putting himself in—what? Danger? Purgatory?'

'The lake?' suggested Angela.

'Who knows? Although he can't have written it too recently in that case, or he'd have been dying to take a dip to cool down.'

'That's true enough,' said Angela. She looked back at the letter, and a thought struck her. 'Can this really be the letter we're looking for?' she said. 'If it is, then why does Mr. Sheridan use the phrase "the lady in question," do you suppose? It seems an awfully formal way of referring to Mrs. Sheridan. Why didn't he just say "my wife?"'

'Yes, I see what you mean,' said Valencourt. 'Perhaps he wasn't talking about his wife at all, then. Perhaps he was referring to someone else altogether.'

Angela raised her eyebrows.

'But who? And why? You don't think Miss Quinn suspected untoward goings-on between Mr. Sheridan and this mysterious woman, do you? Why, I shouldn't have thought he was the type.'

'I shouldn't have thought he was either,' he said. 'But you never know—people do the most surprising things when you least expect it of them.'

Angela paused, considering this new idea.

'Then who is she?' she said.

'I don't know,' he said. 'Probably not an English-woman, though, since there aren't many of those who are younger than about seventy here in Stresa. More likely an Italian.'

'I wonder whether the Quinns were blackmailing him,' said Angela, 'and that's why he killed himself. Perhaps they'd threatened to tell his wife about the other woman and he hanged himself in despair.'

He rubbed his chin.

'It's possible, I suppose,' he said doubtfully.

'Or perhaps they weren't blackmailing him at all,' she went on, warming to her theme. 'Perhaps Miss Quinn was genuinely trying to be helpful in warning him that she knew about the affair, but he took it the wrong way and killed himself because he was terrified of being exposed.'

'In that case, her attempts to help appear to have backfired rather spectacularly, don't you think?'

'Oh dear, yes,' said Angela, trying not to laugh. 'Let's hope that's not what happened, then.'

'If there *was* another woman, I should think it's far more likely that Mrs. Sheridan knew about it,' said Valencourt. 'She admitted they'd had a row and that's partly why she went back to England. Perhaps she was threatening to divorce him and that's why he committed suicide.'

'Well, she's keeping very quiet about it if that's the case,' said Angela. She sighed impatiently. 'I don't know,' she said. 'I'm starting to think that perhaps this isn't the letter I was looking for after all.'

'Oh, I think there's a good chance it is,' he said. 'Otherwise, why decide to burn it *now*? Why light the stove in hot weather just to get rid of a letter if it wasn't something that needed to be destroyed immediately?'

'I see what you mean,' said Angela. 'It seems rather too much of a coincidence that they decide to destroy it just at the time when all this is going on.' She collected the scraps of paper together carefully and put them in her pocket, then gave him back his handkerchief and rose from the seat. 'Thank you,' she said. 'You've been very helpful.'

'You're most welcome,' he said, standing up likewise. 'If you're looking for a man for hire again I shall be more than happy to oblige—although perhaps not in the matter of burglary. I'm getting a bit too old for that sort of thing and prefer a quieter life.'

'Nonsense,' said Angela. 'You look so pleased with yourself that it's perfectly obvious you enjoyed it. There is certainly something of the hedonist about you.'

'And what's wrong with that?' he said. 'We only have one life, so why not enjoy it?'

'Because so often your pleasure comes at somebody else's expense,' said Angela.

'There is that,' he said. 'I thank you for the lecture, and I'll remember it next time you ask me to break into someone's house.'

He sounded a little testy and Angela was about to reply when she heard a voice calling her name. She turned and saw Francis Butler approaching them.

'Hallo,' he said. 'I don't suppose you've seen Chris anywhere, have you? I seem to have lost him.' They both replied in the negative and Francis went on, 'As a matter of fact, I haven't seen him since lunch-time and I'm starting to get a bit worried.'

'Perhaps he's gone off somewhere to paint by himself,' suggested Angela.

'Oh, he probably has,' agreed Francis. 'It's just that he hasn't been himself for the past couple of days and I promised his parents I'd keep a close eye on him, so I don't like not knowing where he is.'

'Is he still unwell?' said Angela. 'I thought he looked a little under the weather yesterday.'

'I think he's been having another one of his nervous attacks,' said Francis. 'He's been fidgeting and talking wildly. He does that when he's not well.'

'Poor Chris,' said Angela. 'Well, I shall keep an eye out for him and let you know if I see him.'

'Oh, I dare say he'll be back soon enough with five or

ten new paintings to add to the clutter,' said Francis. He said it cheerfully but he looked worried.

He departed with a wave, and Angela looked at her watch. It was getting late and there was little time to change before she was supposed to be meeting Elsa.

'You'd better go,' said Valencourt. 'I'll see you later.'

He went off before she could say anything and she was left standing there, alone and not a little disconcerted. It was unlike him not to walk her back to the hotel. Perhaps she really had offended him. True, it was hardly fair of her to have drawn attention to his shortcomings when he had just done her a good turn—however illegal—but she had done it without thinking and had certainly not intended to lecture. She set off back towards the hotel in a state of mixed emotions. On the one hand she felt guilty at having annoyed him, but on the other she was cross that he had *made* her feel guilty by taking amiss a passing remark that happened to be perfectly true. She thought about it all the way back and by the time she arrived at the hotel had worked herself up into a fine state of grumpiness, so much so that she was forced to pause and collect herself before going inside.

'Why, I don't know what's the matter with me,' she said to herself. 'It must be the heat.'

Once back in her room, she changed quickly and was preparing to go back downstairs when she remembered that she had left the scraps of charred paper in the pocket of her other dress. Better put them in a drawer for safe-keeping, perhaps. She took them out and glanced at them before putting them away, then stopped and looked at them more carefully. What was it that had just struck her? When she had picked them up it was as though a light had flashed briefly at the back of her consciousness. What was it? She gazed at the pieces, but it was no good: whatever it was had faded rapidly back into dimness and she knew that it would not come back while she tried to grasp it. It was probably best to let it return of its own accord, she thought. She put the scraps of paper in the drawer and ran downstairs to meet Elsa.

Chapter Nineteen

THE AIR WAS close and sticky and no-one wanted to dine inside, so the hotel terrace was unusually busy that evening. Waiters bustled to and fro—even young Vittorio Morandi could be seen clearing away plates and glasses as though his life depended upon it—and the place was gay with chatter and laughter. Elsa seemed in particularly good humour, and kept Angela entertained with her amusing observations on the guests and the staff. Angela was glad of it, for she was still feeling somewhat out of sorts. She was thinking about Edgar Valencourt and his failure to leave Stresa despite his promise to go—a fact which had, in the space of the last hour or two, become inordinately annoying to her. A day or two's delay she might have accepted—had tacitly accepted, in fact—but it had now been almost a week and he was still here, strolling coolly about the place as though he owned it, and as though the police of several countries were not at present doing their utmost to find him. Furthermore, in Angela's mind his offence in remaining in the area was, somewhat irrationally, compounded by the fact that he had just done her a favour, which made it difficult for her now to report him to the police without looking ungracious to say the least.

Why had he stayed? That was an easy enough question to answer, anyhow. It was perfectly obvious that he believed her to have such a weakness for him that she would never turn him in—hence his complacency in coming here day after day and acting as though no-one could touch him. It was an uncomfortable truth but Angela forced herself to face it, and at that moment she disliked herself intensely for her want of resolution in not having reported him immediately. How must it have looked to him? Naturally he had hastened to take advantage of it, as anyone with half a brain would. It evidently suited him to lie low here, and why should he go when the only woman in the place who knew his real identity was so easily persuaded to keep quiet? He must have been laughing to himself all the while at her stupidity in falling for his nonsense. For a second she wondered what would happen if she *did* speak to Mr. D'Onofrio. The two men might have an unspoken agreement, but she was fairly certain that it held only so long as there were no complaints. She did not think D'Onofrio would arrest Valencourt, but perhaps he might have a quiet word with him, enough to frighten him off. Yes, that might work: that way she could get rid of him without looking too ungrateful for his help that afternoon at the Quinns'. Perhaps she might even persuade D'Onofrio not to bring her into it at all, so Valencourt would never know it had been her doing.

'Are you quite all right, Angela?' said Elsa at last. 'You seem a little subdued this evening—not your usual sunny self at all.'

'Do I?' replied Angela, rousing herself to smile. 'I don't mean to.'

'Are you still brooding about the séance?' said Elsa.

'No,' said Angela truthfully.

'I'd like to have seen Mrs. Quinn in her trance,' said Elsa. 'It sounds like all kinds of fun. We never got anything of the sort out of her, did we? I half-wish now that I'd asked her to read my cards. Perhaps I'll go back to her before I leave and get her to tell me my fortune—although, of course, it's all so vague that the message might mean anything. I couldn't help noticing the other day that each card seemed to have any meaning that Mrs. Quinn cared to put on it. It must be nice to be able to bend things like that to one's own purpose. And I suppose they do the same with the talking board. Just a little push and the planchette goes in whichever direction you want it to.'

'Yes, it does, doesn't it?' said Angela thoughtfully.

The dinner rush had gradually died down, and they were now joined by Mr. D'Onofrio, who had come, he said, to warn the esteemed guests of the Hotel del Lago to watch out for a pickpocket who had been causing no little inconvenience to him over the past two days or so. They need not worry, he said, for he, D'Onofrio, knew exactly who the man was and would soon catch him, but in the meantime, since the malefactor had proved stubbornly elusive so far, he advised them to keep a close eye on their handbags.

He tossed back his grappa and subsided into a complacent silence.

'I don't suppose we need worry at all, with you sitting at our table,' said Elsa, catching Angela's eye. 'Nobody would dare try and steal anything from us.'

'You are right,' said Mr. D'Onofrio, looking even more pleased with himself if that were possible.

He summoned the waiter and ordered another grappa for himself and cocktails for the ladies, and they all sat together sociably for a while. Then Elsa spotted Mr.

Morandi, who was at his best on a busy night, complimenting the ladies, saluting the gentlemen affably and ruling his underlings with a rod of iron, and ran off to persuade him to come and join them. Now was the perfect moment for Angela to speak to Mr. D'Onofrio about Edgar Valencourt if she wished, but while she hesitated, wondering whether to do it and, if so, how to begin, he forestalled her by introducing a quite different subject.

'So, then,' he said, 'you have nothing more to tell me about the death of Mr. Sheridan?'

'Not much,' she said. 'I don't know if you've heard, but there have been rumours that he left a sum of money to Mrs. and Miss Quinn.'

He bowed his head.

'I had heard something of the kind,' he said. 'Is it true?'

'I don't know,' said Angela. 'I don't think anyone's seen his will yet. That hasn't stopped people talking, though. They're saying that the money—if there is any—gives the Quinns a motive for murder.'

'If there is any,' he repeated.

'Well, that's the thing, isn't it?' she said. 'Nobody knows whether there is or not.'

'That is easily discovered,' he said, 'but in the meantime the Quinns could escape. Do you want me to arrest them?'

'Goodness me, no!' said Angela in alarm.

'Ah. Then you yourself do not believe them to be guilty. I see.' He nodded with satisfaction.

Angela thought for a second. By offering to arrest them he had surprised her real view out of her—a view she had not been aware she held until that moment.

'No,' she said. 'I don't think they're guilty—not of

murder, at any rate. They might be guilty of charlatanism, I suppose, but that's nothing like as serious.'

'No,' he agreed. 'And as I believe I told you before, provided they cause no trouble then I have nothing to say to them. It is only if I receive a complaint that I must act.'

'And what about Mr. Sheridan?' said Angela.

He glanced about him and leaned closer.

'Everyone is happy to believe it was suicide,' he said. 'The doctor is happy, Mr. Sheridan's wife is happy, his friends are happy—most of them, at least. No-one wants to know anything different. And why should I argue, if everyone is so very happy?'

'Then that's it, is it?' said Angela. 'We must forget any suspicious circumstances and pretend everything is all right?'

'There were not *many* suspicious circumstances,' said D'Onofrio. 'Only—what? A shoe and a jacket. That is not the kind of evidence that will put a man in prison.'

'No,' said Angela uncomfortably. 'Then I suppose you want me to forget the whole thing?'

He clicked his tongue and shook his head.

'But no,' he said. 'On the contrary, Mrs. Marchmont. I did not say *I* was happy. But I can do very little. You have seen the men in uniforms, I have no doubt. They have been sent here to force happiness upon us all. They make a *brutta figura*—how do you say it?—they cut a bad figure if our English visitors all start killing each other, and so they will pretend for as long as they can that nothing of the sort has happened. And I will probably lose my job if I make a fuss,' he added as an afterthought.

'Then what can be done?'

'Perhaps nothing,' he said with a shrug. 'But if a lady from England should perhaps want to ask some questions, then there is nothing I can do to stop her. And if she should find some answers, then all the better. The men in uniform will ignore an ugly policeman, or perhaps burn down his house, but they will not deny a pretty woman.'

'Good gracious,' said Angela in dismay. 'I don't want to be responsible for your having your house burned down.'

'Perhaps I exaggerate a little,' said Mr. D'Onofrio. 'Besides, I have a long ladder.'

Angela was by no means reassured by this, and was about to say so when she noticed that there seemed to be some sort of commotion going on inside. Mr. D'Onofrio had seen it too, and stood up to see what was happening. The noise seemed to be coming from the entrance-hall, and D'Onofrio strode off to do his duty. After a second, Angela followed him, for she had seen that Mr. Morandi and Elsa appeared to be at the centre of the disturbance. When she arrived she saw Francis Butler looking distraught and wild-eyed and talking loudly and rapidly, which was most unlike him, while Mr. Morandi and Elsa tried to calm him or at least persuade him to sit down.

'Never mind that,' he was saying. 'I won't sit down. You must fetch a doctor immediately.'

'Do not worry,' said Mr. Morandi soothingly. 'You see Mino is telephoning the doctor now. He will come as soon as he can, but now I insist you sit down. Vittorio!' he snapped to his son, who was passing and had paused to watch the fun, '*Un brandy per il signore. Su, veloce!*'

The young man ran off to fetch the brandy and Francis was at length persuaded to take a seat, where he slumped looking utterly miserable while Mr. Morandi fussed about him.

'What is it?' said Angela to Elsa.

'Chris has been taken ill,' said Elsa. 'They're calling the doctor now.'

'Oh dear,' said Angela in concern. 'I hope it's nothing too serious.'

Francis looked up, and the expression on his face was one of utter despair.

'He's not ill,' he said. 'He's dead.'

There was a horrified silence, then Angela spoke.

'Are you sure?' she said. 'Where is he?'

'At the *pensione*,' said Francis. 'I found him in his room. I'd been looking for him all afternoon but he must have been there all the time.'

'But are you quite certain he's dead?' said Elsa. 'Perhaps he's just been taken ill. Perhaps the doctor can do something for him.'

But Francis shook his head.

'No, there's no doubt,' he said. 'I know a dead man when I see one.' A sob escaped him. 'How am I going to tell his parents?' he said. 'I was supposed to be looking after him. I wasn't supposed to leave him alone. I knew he wasn't well, and now he's dead and it's my fault. I ought to have watched him more closely. But please, we must get back and see to him. I can't leave him alone any longer.'

'The doctor will be here very soon,' said Mr. Morandi as young Vittorio returned with the brandy. 'Here, drink this and we will go as soon as he arrives. But you cannot go anywhere like this. Now, tell us what happened. What was it? Some sort of fit, perhaps?'

'No,' said Francis. 'At least, I don't think so.'

Little by little, as the brandy calmed him down, they drew the story out of him. After he had spent the afternoon hunting high and low for his friend without success, it had eventually occurred to him that Christopher might have returned to their little hotel to rest himself. As soon as he had entered the room he had known something was wrong, for Christopher was lying on the bed, quite still and unresponsive. Francis had done all he could to try and revive him, but to no avail, and it was only then that he had noticed the glass by the bedside, the bottle of grappa, which they had bought only the day before, and the little bottle bearing the label 'Chloral Hydrate.'

'Was it an accident, do you think?' said Elsa. 'Does he take sleeping draughts?'

'Not as far as I know,' said Francis. 'I didn't even know he had any of the stuff with him. I can only assume he brought it with him without telling me. Perhaps he meant to—to—' he broke off.

Angela exchanged glances with Elsa. Her mind was working furiously. Two suicides in one week? It seemed rather unlikely.

'Why didn't he tell me?' said Francis. 'He hadn't been himself for a few days—he was very nervy and upset about something, but I never thought he was planning to do anything desperate.'

'Did he say what was upsetting him?' said Angela.

'No,' said Francis. 'That is—perhaps. When he's having one of his spells he gets worked up about all kinds of things, and even the tiniest little difficulty can set him off. I'm used to it, and normally I don't listen much as it's mostly nonsense, and the best thing to do generally is just wait for him to calm down. I do remember that last night he was talking about someone or other and saying that he'd been betrayed, but I just thought it was the usual wild stuff and didn't really pay much attention.'

'Betrayed?' said Angela, and again glanced at Elsa. 'Who betrayed him? Who was he talking about?'

Francis paused for a second in thought.

'I don't know,' he said. 'I think he was talking about a woman at one point, but I've no idea if she was the person who was meant to have betrayed him.'

'Did he have a girl?' said Elsa. 'Perhaps he had had a row with her.'

'No,' said Francis. 'There was no girl. He's never been especially interested in that sort of thing as far as I know.'

'Then who was he talking about?' said Angela.

'I've no idea,' said Francis. He looked about him. 'Is the doctor here yet? I want to get back to Chris. I shall have to send a telegram to his parents, but what on earth am I to say?' He stood up. 'I must go back; there is so much to do.'

'Don't worry about all that now,' said Elsa kindly, taking his arm. 'Gabriele will take care of everything for you. Why don't you move here for the next few days? You won't want to stay in the *pensione* after what's happened, and I'm sure he can find you a room.'

It took Angela a second to realize that by 'Gabriele' Elsa meant Mr. Morandi, and she had barely any time to digest this new information and raise her eyebrows before the doctor arrived. Mr. Morandi explained the situation briefly and he, the doctor and Francis Butler, who insisted on going, went off to examine the body and begin the formalities, leaving the others to remain and wonder at this latest dreadful event.

Chapter Twenty

Elsa was now talking with great animation to Mr. D'Onofrio, who had observed the whole scene with his usual expression of non-committal wariness, and so Angela found herself drifting to the front entrance and gazing after the departing figures of Francis Butler, Mr. Morandi and the doctor, who were now walking briskly out of the front gate. A hundred ideas were revolving through her mind, and she was trying to put them in some kind of order, although they seemed determined to resist.

Of all the questions that had sprung into her head at once, however, one in particular shouted for attention more loudly than the others, namely: was there any connection between Christopher Tate's death and that of Raymond Sheridan only a few days earlier? And if so, what was it? Was it too much of a coincidence to suppose it possible that *two* men had both, within days of each other, decided to commit suicide? It certainly seemed very odd indeed. Taken by itself, of course, Christopher's death was unlikely to arouse suspicion, for he was known to have suffered nervous problems for years, and while his suicide was a shock, it might not be entirely a surprise to those who knew him well. But coming so hard on the heels of a suicide that *had* been unexpected—well, that seemed to throw rather a different light on things.

Angela wandered around the side of the building and into the garden. The ideas continued to whirl through her head and as they did so she thought she began to see a pattern, a possible link between the two events, which would go some way to explaining Christopher's behaviour over the past few days, although several questions still remained unanswered—and she was still not entirely sure where the Quinns fitted into it all. Dusk had fallen, although it was still very warm, and she stopped to gaze for a few minutes at the brightly-lit terrace, which still rang with chatter and laughter and the clatter of plates. It seemed strange to listen to the sound of people enjoying themselves after what had just happened, although of course they did not know about Christopher—and nor could they be reasonably expected to care about the death of a young man of whom they knew nothing. She turned away, and was absently regarding a statue of a woman, indifferently executed in the Roman style, when she was joined by Edgar Valencourt, who had just arrived.

'You were standing so still I could hardly tell which one of you was the statue,' he said by way of a greeting, but she did not smile.

'Christopher Tate is dead,' she said.

'Good God,' he said, startled. 'I'm sorry. What happened?'

'It looks like an overdose of chloral hydrate in his drink. Francis found him at his *pensione.*'

'Was it an accident?'

'Nobody knows yet. The doctor and Mr. Morandi are there now.'

'Ah, yes,' he said. 'Trust Morandi to be in the middle of things as usual, making himself look important.'

'I don't think that's quite fair,' said Angela. 'He couldn't have been kinder to Francis, who is quite distraught.'

'Is that so?' said Valencourt with a shrug. His insouciance did nothing to improve Angela's mood, and in fact only added irritation to the upset she was already feeling at Christopher's death and her vague sense that she ought to have prevented it somehow. She had no desire to be goaded into a display of temper, however, and so decided to do what she believed she ought to have done from the first, which was to remain politely cool and distant. He evidently wanted to walk with her, and so she clasped her hands together behind her back to discourage him from offering his arm. If he noticed it, he did not mention it.

'Have you had another look at those scraps of paper?' he said. 'I'm afraid I don't seem to have anything in Sheridan's writing. I was almost certain I'd kept a note or two from him, but I suppose I must have thrown them away, as I couldn't find them anywhere.'

'Thank you,' she said, 'but I dare say it doesn't matter much any more, since the police are certain to get involved now—and besides, Virginia Sheridan is bound to have something if it turns out to be necessary for the purposes of comparison.'

'Why are the police certain to get involved?' he said.

'Because I shall see to it that they do,' she replied.

'Oh, shall you, indeed?' he said, raising his eyebrows at her tone. 'And why is that?'

'Why, because the whole thing looks distinctly suspicious now that there's been another death, of course.'

'Do you think so?'

'Don't you?'

'Suppose you explain,' he said. If he had not noticed the change in her manner before, it was evident enough now, and he glanced at her curiously.

'I'm talking about murder, of course,' she said. 'I'd been wondering how it was done, since there were obvious difficulties.'

'Really?' he said. 'Couldn't whoever it was just have put the stuff in the fellow's drink when he wasn't looking?'

'I wasn't talking about Chris,' said Angela. 'I meant Mr. Sheridan. Don't you see that Chris's death makes it much more likely that it was murder?'

'I'm not sure I understand,' he said. 'Did Chris kill himself or not? Or are you saying that was murder too?'

'I don't know,' said Angela. 'Given his personality it might have been either.'

'You're talking in riddles,' said Valencourt.

'Am I?' said Angela carelessly. 'I didn't mean to.'

He looked at her curiously again.

'Is something the matter, Angela?' he said.

'What do you mean?' she said, although she knew perfectly well what he meant.

'You seem a little out of sorts,' he said.

'Well, I'm not,' she said. 'At least, no more than one would expect after what has happened this evening.'

They had now come to a little clearing in among the bushes, at the centre of which an ornamental fountain played merrily, its waters glinting in the light borrowed from a well-illuminated path somewhere nearby. The noise from the terrace was muffled here but still audible, and every so often the sound of passing voices could be heard conversing in many languages.

Angela paused here as though in thought, and Valencourt tried again.

'Very well, then,' he said. 'Sheridan was murdered, you say. Do you know who did it?'

Angela glanced at him sideways, and was suddenly seized by an inexplicable and overwhelming urge to provoke him.

'I do have an idea,' she replied, 'but I'm not certain I ought to tell you.'

'Why not?'

'Because I might be wrong, and I don't want it getting about if I am,' she said. 'This is a small place and I don't want to cause any more trouble than I can help. Rumours of that sort can be very damaging.'

'You don't think I'd tell anyone, do you?' he said, then looked at her more closely. 'You don't trust me, is that it?'

The little devil that lurked in Angela's breast at that moment prodded her onwards.

'Of course I don't trust you,' she said coolly. 'Whatever made you think I did?'

'Ah,' he said in sudden realization. 'So now we have it. This is what you really think of me.'

'I thought I'd made it quite clear some time ago what I really think of you,' she said, and had the perverse satisfaction of seeing his expression change from surprise to momentary anger. He was not the sort, however, to indulge in outbursts of rage, and he merely smiled ironically.

'Oh, of course,' he said. 'I forgot. I'm no good—that's what you're saying, isn't it? I'm a wanted criminal who has no right even to show his face in the same town as you. And yet, oddly enough, you're quite prepared to use me whenever it suits you, and whenever you need any dirty work doing. You're far too delicate and well-bred to soil your hands yourself, but you're happy enough to let someone you despise do it for you. Well, at least I'm not a hypocrite. And it all comes out the same in the end, you know. If I'd been caught at the Quinns' you'd have been just as much to blame as I, as far as the police were concerned. Don't think you have any right to feel superior.'

Angela was stung but refused to rise.

'I had a very good reason for asking you to do it, as you know perfectly well,' she said.

'No you didn't,' he retorted. 'You just took it upon yourself to interfere. You set yourself above everyone, but nobody asked *you* to be judge and jury, did they? Has it occurred to you that by sticking your nose into the whole business you might have made things worse?'

'What do you mean?' she said, taken aback.

'Why, that you've created mistrust and suspicion where none existed before,' he said. 'A suffering man decides quietly to take his own life—it happens every day and no doubt it's a tragedy for all his family and friends, but then you come along and start stirring things up with your inquisitiveness, and your questions, and your "are we sure it was suicides?" and your conceited assumptions that you know better than the police. But you're not as clever as you think you are. You'd never have looked twice at the Quinns had you not been listening to that stupid Ainsley fellow with his ridiculous obsessions. Now the whole town is pointing the finger at them and saying that they're somehow responsible for Sheridan's death. Don't you think you might have had something to do with that? And what about this boy? How do we know that people hadn't run away with the idea of murder and started accusing him too? Perhaps that's why he killed himself. Had that occurred to you at all? Can you honestly say that you might not have been partly to blame?'

Angela heard all this without remark, then raised her head and stared at him haughtily down her nose.

'Thank you, Mr. Valencourt, and goodnight,' she said

with apparent calmness, although she was inwardly furious. She turned to walk away, but Valencourt seized her by the arm and pulled her back around to face him. Now he was angry.

'Oh, no you don't,' he said. 'I'm not letting you run away like a coward. You'll stay here and fight it out like a man.'

'Fight *what* out, exactly?' she said. 'I am not fighting, whatever you may care to do. However, since we appear to be exchanging uncomfortable truths, I might tell you one or two in return. You seem to be under the impression that there is something praiseworthy about the way you conduct yourself—that there is some sort of honour in your dishonesty. You think that just because you admit to it, you are somehow absolved from responsibility for your actions. You're not a hypocrite, you say—as though hypocrisy were the worst of crimes, while theft is merely a scrape you occasionally get into without quite meaning to —amusing and waggish and quite forgivable. Well, that's nonsense, and you know it, so please don't throw accusations at me when your own conduct bears so little examination. At least *I* can hold my head up and claim to be a good person, such as I am, but you will always be—what you are.'

Her tone was deliberately superior and intended to irritate, and although her tongue faltered on the last word she could see that the shot had hit home.

'Damn you, Angela,' he said furiously. 'For two straws I'd give you a good shake this minute.'

He gripped her arm more firmly and seemed inclined to put his words into action, and for a split second she felt a little thrill of fear. She was not yet lost, however. She lifted her chin.

'And how exactly would that make you a better man?' she said with superb disdain.

He drew in his breath sharply, then released her arm and stood back.

'You infuriating woman!' he exclaimed as she turned to leave. 'You're as cold as ice. Does nothing ever rattle that maddening self-possession of yours?'

Perhaps it was something in his tone that spoke directly to her own frustration—she could not tell, but at that moment the last vestiges of all her pretence at calmness disappeared, and before she could stop herself she turned back around to face him.

'*You* do!' she cried. He looked startled but was silent, and she went on in desperation, since there was no sense in stopping now, '*Why* can't you leave me alone, as you promised? You said you'd go away. Why are you still here?'

Now there was nothing to do. She had given herself away completely and he had won. And yet there was no sign of triumph in his eye.

'Isn't it obvious?' he said angrily. 'I know I ought to have left days ago—in fact if I'd had any sense at all I'd have decamped the second I set eyes on you, but for some reason all my good sense seems to vanish where you're concerned, and I don't mind telling you I don't like it. I need to keep a clear head, but somehow you've got under my skin and I can't seem to think about anything else or tear myself away, however hard I try. If you must know, I've been waiting all week for you to lose patience and turn me in, but you haven't. Why not?'

While he spoke he had moved close to her almost unthinkingly and was gazing into her face, demanding an answer.

'Why not?' he repeated when she did not reply.

'I don't know,' she whispered at last, unable to turn her

eyes away from his. Her heart was pounding so violently that she was sure he must be able to hear it.

'I think you know very well,' he said.

They stared at each other in silence, then with great deliberation he drew her to him, and she did not resist but gave herself up entirely to the moment.

'Look here, this won't do,' she said breathlessly after a short interval.

'Then why does it feel so awfully nice?' he murmured into her hair.

Angela felt vaguely as though she ought to disentangle herself, but for some reason her arms were refusing to do as her brain instructed.

'You've spoilt a perfectly good row,' she said instead. 'I'd just thought of a brilliantly devastating retort.'

'We can start it again from the beginning, if you like,' he said. 'Who knows how it might end this time?'

'Well, it *ought* to end with my storming off in a tremendous huff—which, incidentally, is what I still intend to do once you've let go of me.'

'What makes you think I'm going to let go of you?' he said, and gripped her even more tightly to him.

Another minute passed, after which Angela decided that she really ought to make an effort. One did not trade mortal insults with an enemy only to throw oneself immediately afterwards into his embrace. It made one look embarrassingly weak of purpose, to say the very least. She extricated herself with some difficulty, although he would not let go of her hand and kept it firmly imprisoned in his.

'It really *won't* do, you know,' she said.

'I dare say you're right,' he said, 'but it's such a dreadful pity. We do seem to go rather well together, don't you think?'

Angela had no intention of answering that question.

She had now fully returned to her senses, and although her attempts at maintaining a cool distance had admittedly proved a resounding, nay, spectacular failure, she was determined to end it now, if necessary by leaving Stresa herself that very night. She was about to say something suitably brisk and off-putting, despite the fact that he was at that moment distracting her by twirling a lock of her hair gently around his finger and smiling into her eyes, when she suddenly heard the sound of someone approaching along the path. He heard it too and they instantly sprang apart.

Whoever it was paused for a second before coming into view, and Angela was just about to take the opportunity to escape when to her surprise La Duchessa entered the clearing. She was dressed in a magnificent evening-gown that shimmered in the dim light, and as always she looked much too exotic for the simple, pretty surroundings of Stresa. Instead of saluting them politely and moving on, La Duchessa glanced briefly at Angela and then turned her attention to Valencourt, who suddenly looked not a little apprehensive. She snapped something at him in a language Angela did not recognize, and he replied to her politely in the same tongue. His answer seemed to displease La Duchessa, for she shook her head rapidly several times and tapped her watch sharply. He replied with a shake of the head, and she drew herself up with a little 'Ha!' of indignation and began to fumble in her evening-bag.

'I am sorry,' she said in English to Angela, as she finally found what she was looking for. At first Angela had no idea what she was talking about, but then to her astonishment she saw that La Duchessa was holding a pistol and pointing it directly at Valencourt, who had set his jaw.

'Get out of the way,' he said grimly to Angela, and she had barely a second to register his command before two shots rang out loudly and he fell to the ground. La Duchessa calmly replaced the gun in her bag and, without even stopping to look behind her, strode away and out of sight, leaving Angela standing there, stunned, with Valencourt lying at her feet.

Chapter Twenty-One

Instantly Angela was on her knees and bending over the prostrate body of Edgar Valencourt. His eyes were closed and he was quite immobile. She patted his face gently and felt for a pulse, but her fingers were trembling and she could find none.

'Oh, goodness me,' she said in the greatest dismay. 'Edgar! Edgar! Are you all right? Speak to me! Oh, what shall I do?' She sat up and looked about her. 'A doctor,' she said. 'Where can I find a doctor?'

'Are you quite mad?' he said, opening his eyes, and she gave a little gasp of shock.

'I thought she'd killed you,' she said.

'I'm not certain she hasn't,' he said weakly.

'Don't move,' she said. 'Let me have a look. Where did she hit you?'

'In my side,' he said. 'She only hit me once, I think.'

She pulled open his jacket and examined him as best she could in the dim light.

'It's difficult to tell,' she said. 'It might be just a graze, but I can't see well enough to be sure. We must get you to a doctor—and we must call the police and tell them to arrest La Duchessa immediately.'

'We can't call the police, you idiot,' he said.

'Oh, but—' she said, and paused, aghast. Of course the police must not be called. La Duchessa was safe. 'But surely you can see a doctor?'

'How can I explain what happened? If I turn up with a bullet wound he's bound to ask questions, don't you think?'

'But then what shall I do?' said Angela. 'I can't leave you here, bleeding all over the place. You'll frighten the guests.'

'You must get me to my car,' he said. 'I shall go home and see what I can do for myself.'

'Don't be ridiculous,' she said. 'You can't possibly drive in that state. I'll take you. Do you think you can stand up?'

He tried to protest but she cut him short, and indeed he was not entirely reluctant for he was in some pain. With difficulty she raised him to a sitting position, where he remained for a minute or two to fetch his breath, and then helped him get to his feet.

'Can you walk?' she said.

'Of course I can,' he said. He took a few steps but then his legs buckled under him and she only just managed to prevent him from falling.

'You're most likely in shock,' she said. 'We'd better get you home and into bed. Where's your car?'

'On the road outside,' he said. 'It's quite near.'

'Good,' she said. 'Now, put your arm around my shoulders. If we meet anyone we'll say you're dead drunk.'

'Splendid,' he said dryly, but did as she said, and they walked slowly in the direction of the road.

They reached the car without incident, and although they met one or two people on the way nobody gave them more than a glance of curiosity. Angela helped him in carefully and got in herself.

'Don't fall asleep,' she said, for he was beginning to look a little groggy. 'I have no idea where you live.'

'Of course,' he said. 'It's up in the hills, just outside Stresa. Just follow this road and I'll tell you when to turn.'

Outside the town it was pitch dark and Angela had to take great care not to drive off the road.

'Can't you go a little slower?' said Valencourt, grimacing as she hurtled around a bend at breakneck speed.

'Sorry,' she said, glancing at him in concern. 'How far is it now?'

'Just here,' he said, indicating a side-road that led up through the trees. It was bumpy, and Angela drove as slowly as she could to avoid causing him further pain, but still he looked rather pale when they finally drew up outside the little villa in which he lived.

'Is this your house?' she said.

'It belongs to my family,' he said. 'We used it as a holiday home many years ago.'

'Do they know you're here?' she said curiously.

'I doubt it,' he said. 'They have more houses than they can possibly use, and they've probably forgotten about this one.'

He looked as though he were about to say more, but then changed his mind.

'Let's get you inside,' she said.

Here in the hills and among the trees the air was cooler, which was something of a relief after the closeness of Stresa. She helped him into the house, then found a lamp and turned it on. They were in a little sitting-room which was sparsely furnished—so much so that it looked almost as though no-one lived there at all. He sat down in sudden exhaustion on the nearest chair.

'Better have a look at you, I suppose,' said Angela, and helped him remove his jacket. His shirt was torn to shreds at the left side and soaked with blood, and she grimaced. He saw it and attempted a smile.

'How long do you suppose I have left?' he said.

'I'll be able to tell better when we've got that shirt and tie off you,' she said. She saw his look, and said tartly, 'Let's imagine for the purposes of this examination that I'm your mother.'

'What a horrible thought,' he said, but sat obediently as she briskly removed the articles in question. She knelt down and peered dispassionately at the wound.

'Hmm,' she said a minute or two later, frowning. She sat back on her heels. 'Well, it doesn't look as though you're in any immediate danger, at least. I think it's probably just a graze, as there's no bullet in you as far as I can see, although you've bled rather a lot and I shouldn't be at all surprised if it splintered a bit of rib as it passed. Have you any water? The wound ought to be cleaned immediately.'

'In the kitchen,' he said.

'I'll need some bandages too,' she said. 'Or sheets will do just as well, if you don't happen to have any. And I think you could probably do with a drink,' she added.

She found some whisky and poured him a stiff measure, then busied herself about in the kitchen. When she returned carrying water and bandages she found that the whisky had revived him slightly, for some of the colour had returned to his face. She put down her burden and poured him some more.

'Drink that,' she said as she knelt down again. 'This is probably going to hurt a bit.'

'Try not to enjoy it too much,' said Valencourt, and she glanced up at him.

'I think the patient will do very well,' was all she said, and set to work. He bore it stoically, with only the occasional wince, and it was all done sooner than might have been expected. Angela examined her handiwork and then straightened up.

'There,' she said. 'That's the best I can do in the circumstances, I'm afraid.'

'I'd like to say it feels better,' he said, 'but it doesn't, much. Still, I'm sure you've done a fine job. Thank you, nurse.'

'I'm sorry about the sheets,' she said, looking at the damp and bloodied rags that lay about the floor. 'I think they were rather good ones, unfortunately, but I couldn't find anything else. They do make excellent bandages, though.'

'No matter,' he said. 'Sheets can be replaced. I say, you're rather efficient at this sort of thing, aren't you?'

'"Efficient" is the word, yes,' she said. 'I can patch up a wound but I'm not very good at the sympathy bit. And think yourself lucky I didn't have to give you any stitches. My competence with a needle is limited, to say the least. Now, it's getting late and what you need is some sleep. You must be exhausted.'

'I am, rather,' he said, stifling a yawn.

He stood up and she helped him into his bedroom, which was furnished just as sparsely as the sitting-room. Angela glanced around. Since he spent so much of his time on the run presumably he had no opportunity to make the place comfortable.

'Well, this has been a most interesting evening,' he said as he lowered himself gingerly onto the bed.

'You were very lucky she didn't kill you,' said Angela.

'Should you have come to my funeral if she had?' he said.

'Oh, I don't think so,' she said. 'I look dreadful in black.'

'I'm quite sure you look delightful in any colour,' he said, and winced. 'Damn the woman! Why on earth did she have to shoot me?'

'I'm sorry you got hurt, but I think she may have done me a good turn,' said Angela.

'That's hardly kind, when we were getting along so well,' he said.

'A little *too* well, I think,' she said. 'Why *did* she shoot you, by the way? What did you do to upset her so much?'

'That's right,' he said. 'Assume immediately it was my fault, why don't you?'

'I'm sorry,' she said, trying not to laugh, 'but it's an easy assumption to make. I have found myself at the wrong end of a gun once or twice in my life too, and each time it's because I have offended in some way, however unwittingly.'

'I'll tell you all about it tomorrow,' he said. His eyes were growing heavy but suddenly they snapped open. 'You're not going, are you? Please say you're not.'

'No,' she said. 'I'll sleep in one of the other rooms.'

He fumbled for her hand and raised it to his lips.

'Thank you,' was all he said.

'Try and get some sleep,' she said, and went out.

Chapter Twenty-Two

When Angela went in the next morning, carrying a tray with a bowl of water and a pot of coffee, she found Edgar Valencourt, looking tired and drawn but slightly more like his usual self, sitting on the edge of the bed and flexing his left arm experimentally.

'You ought to be lying down,' she said.

'I'm just testing to see how much my side hurts when I do this,' he said. 'The answer is quite a lot.'

'Yes, it's probably going to be pretty sore for a good while yet,' she said, 'and waving your arm about won't help. Now, get back into bed. I've brought you some coffee, for which I apologize in advance.'

'Why, what have you put in it?' he said, sitting back reluctantly against the pillows. 'Arsenic?'

'For all I know it tastes like it,' she said, regarding it doubtfully. 'I haven't made coffee for such a long time, you see. Normally I have Marthe to do it for me, and I'm afraid I've been quite spoilt. I'm sure I used to be very capable, but one forgets such a lot when one is constantly looked after.'

'Ah, yes,' he said. 'I know all about you society women with your rich husbands and hordes of servants. Your hands grow soft and weak. A nice long spell of scrubbing dishes or picking blackberries would do you no end of good.'

'I have precisely *two* servants, and I've never taken so much as a penny off my husband,' she said haughtily. 'Even supposing he had a penny, which I very much doubt.'

'Don't tell me you live on the proceeds of a life of crime,' he said. 'If that's the case then we are clearly meant for one another.'

'Of course not,' she said, laughing. 'My money is my own, and was honestly come by. If you must know, I am a business-woman, and a rather successful one at that.'

'Good Lord,' he said, entertained. 'How very modern. What is it? A shop of some sort?'

'Not exactly,' she said. 'More in the way of an office. Now, if you've finished that coffee and you're quite sure I haven't poisoned you, I'll take a look at your wound and change the bandage, and you can tell me about La Duchessa. I confess I don't like to think of her out there on the loose, since she's evidently very dangerous.'

'I don't think there's much to be done,' he said. 'She'll be miles away by now. I'd like very much to know how she managed to follow me all the way here, though.'

'Where did she follow you from?'

'Antwerp,' he said. 'That's where I know her from, at any rate.'

'Were you—' she began, and hesitated, embarrassed.

'Goodness me, no,' he said in surprise. 'It's nothing of that sort. No,' he went on, 'I'm afraid she holds me responsible for her husband's presently being in gaol.'

'Oh dear,' she said. 'Who is her husband? And *were* you responsible?'

'Of course not,' he said indignantly. 'He made a promise he couldn't keep and he paid for it.'

'This is all very mysterious,' she said. 'Perhaps I oughtn't to have asked.'

'No, I suppose it's only fair to tell you,' he said, 'since you're indirectly involved yourself.'

'I?' she said, glancing up from her work in astonishment.

'Yes,' he said. 'I dare say you remember a little holiday you took in Cornwall last July?'

'Of course I do,' she said.

'And no doubt you also remember that I happened to be there at the same time, and that we were both searching for a certain item.'

'A diamond necklace, yes,' she said. 'And we found it and I handed it in to the police like the good girl I am, and everybody was happy except you—at least, I seem to recall that's how it went.'

'An admirably concise summary,' he said. 'The only thing was, I'd rather promised it to this fellow, er—'

'Mr. La Duchessa,' put in Angela helpfully.

'—who lives in Antwerp and makes his money by helping people such as myself who need to get rid of things in a hurry.'

'A fence, you mean,' said Angela.

'Exactly,' he said. 'Now, as it happens, Mr.—er—La Duchessa had in turn quite rashly promised the necklace to someone else, an immensely wealthy private collector of important paintings and works of art and jewellery, who is very well known in the less reputable circles as a buyer of dishonestly-obtained goods. I have no idea who he is—I don't think anyone does, as a matter of fact—but I do know that he is prepared to pay quite enormous sums of money to get his hands on these things. To those who deliver the goods he is incredibly generous, but he can also be rather vengeful if his expectations are not met.'

'I see,' said Angela. 'And Mr. La Duchessa couldn't deliver the goods because he didn't have them.'

'Exactly.'

'You might have had the necklace, you know,' she said. 'I couldn't have stopped you from taking it from me if you'd wanted to.'

'I know,' he said, 'but I won't use violence against a woman. And besides, you rather shamed me into letting you have it.'

'I'm glad to hear it,' she said.

'At any rate, this fence had to explain that the necklace would not be forthcoming. The news was not well received, threats were made and the next I heard the fellow had been clapped in irons.'

'Dear me,' said Angela. 'Do you think this collector was responsible for giving him away to the police?'

'I've no doubt of it,' said Valencourt. 'He's done it before. He doesn't take kindly to being crossed, you see.'

'And now presumably La Duchessa blames you for it.'

'Yes,' he said. 'She turned up the other day, and said now that her husband was in prison she wanted money.'

'Couldn't you have given her some?' said Angela. 'Presumably even criminals' wives have to eat.'

'It's hardly my job to support another man's wife,' he said. 'And besides, it wasn't money to feed herself she wanted—it was reparation. She wanted me to pay her the value her husband would have got for the necklace had he sold it on. I was hardly going to do that, since firstly I didn't have that sort of sum and secondly it wasn't my fault he'd made a rash promise to someone else, was it? At any rate, she gave me until last night to come up with the money, on pain of unspecified action on her part.'

'Well, now you know what she meant, anyhow,' said Angela.

'Yes,' he said with a grimace. 'Next time I shall take her more seriously.'

'There, we're all done,' said Angela, and straightened up. 'Well, it's a pretty story, I suppose.' She was in two minds as to whether or not to believe a word of it, since he had told her similar stories in the past which had turned out to be misleading, to say the least. She did not like him very much when he talked so carelessly of these things, and at that moment was glad that they had been interrupted in the garden, even though she would not herself have chosen that particular sort of interruption.

'You've gone all cool again,' he observed. 'I'm sorry it offends you, Angela.'

'I'm afraid it does,' she said. 'I can't help it.'

'I suppose you think I ought to retire,' he said.

'It's nothing to do with me.'

'Oh, but it has everything to do with you.'

'I told you before,' she said. 'Your conscience is your own affair. I won't be held responsible for it.'

'Then you're very unusual,' he said. 'Most women would jump at the chance to reform a sinner.'

'Not I,' said Angela emphatically. 'I know to my own cost that it's a waste of time even to try.'

She saw him regarding her curiously and looked away.

'Did your husband make you *very* unhappy?' he said at last.

'He did, rather,' she replied, busying herself with the discarded bandages so he would not see her face. 'Still, I suppose it was partly my own fault: I married the man after all—no-one forced me to do it. I can't even claim I wasn't in my right mind at the time, as I knew perfectly well what I was doing.'

'I'm sorry,' he said. 'You don't deserve to be treated badly.'

She waved his words away and turned to put the bandages on a nearby table, on which one or two letters and bits of paper lay.

'Oh!' she said in surprise, as she saw what was on top of the pile. It was the little sketch of her done by Jack Lomax.

'Ah, yes,' he said. 'I got that off him and I was going to get it framed for you, but I haven't had the opportunity yet.'

She picked up the drawing and looked at it thought-fully for some time without speaking.

'What is it?' he said.

'It's very nice,' she said after a pause, 'but I should say it flatters me.'

'Do you think so?' he said.

'Yes,' she said. 'He's given me much too pretty a nose. It ought to be longer—all the better for sticking into other people's business.'

She glanced at him slyly.

'Did I say that?' he said. 'I do apologize. I was very angry with you, wasn't I?'

'Yes, well,' she said. 'I was angry enough myself. Perhaps it's better for all concerned that we forget what happened last night.'

'I'll forget the row with pleasure,' he said, 'but I won't forget the rest. Please say you won't either.'

She met his gaze.

'No,' she said. 'Of course I won't.'

There was a short pause.

'Can't we try again, Angela?' he said. 'You could leave the hotel and hide with me up here until you go back to England. No-one would ever know. It would be our little secret.'

She could not help laughing.

'I must say, I have to admire the sheer impudence of a man who can attempt seduction from his sick-bed shortly after taking a bullet in the side,' she said. 'And in return for that I won't put on a display of outraged modesty at the suggestion.'

'Thank heavens for that,' he said. 'But I take it the answer is no.'

'It is,' she said. 'I am going back to Stresa shortly, and this time I should like you to keep your promise to stay away until I leave. It ought to be easy enough, since you're not exactly in the fittest state at present.'

He looked down at the bedclothes.

'Very well,' he said after a moment. 'You have my word. I won't bother you any more. I'll keep away from you and you'll go back to England and we'll never see each other again.'

Angela's heart gave a treacherous thump at this, but she ignored it.

'Thank you,' she said. 'It's for the best.'

'I expect it is,' he said. He glanced at her. 'You know,' he said, 'I've always been in the habit of seeing what I want and taking it, but I can't do that with you, can I?'

'No,' she said. 'Some things are not for the taking.'

'And yet I've never wanted anything more,' he said softly.

Angela stared determinedly at the floor. She would not look into his eyes, for she was afraid of the effect they might have on her.

'Very well, then,' he went on at last, in much more like

his usual manner. 'I shall leave you to return home and no doubt be claimed by a better and a duller man.'

'No fear of that,' she said. 'No, I shall be perfectly happy on my own. As you have no doubt deduced, I seem to be afflicted with a constitutional weakness for men who are very bad for me, and so I've rather sworn off all that kind of thing. Last night you caught me off guard, but I won't be taken like that again.'

'You talk as though it were a deliberate move on my part,' he said. 'It wasn't, I assure you. You took me by surprise just as much as I did you.'

'Well, no matter,' she said, for she wanted to bring an end to the subject. 'Now,' she went on briskly, 'I shall have to take your car, I'm afraid. You can have the people at the hotel return it to you later. You won't be needing it for a few days anyway.'

'You're going to cut quite a dash, strolling into the place wearing a bloodstained evening-dress first thing on a Sunday morning,' he remarked.

She looked down at herself in dismay.

'Oh dear,' she said. 'You're right—look at the state of me. I shall probably attract all kinds of unpleasant attention. But it's still early, so with any luck things will be quiet when I get there. Otherwise I expect I shall have to climb in through a window or hide until nightfall.'

'I'd lend you something, but I don't tend to keep a supply of women's clothes here,' he said. 'I shall know better in future, naturally.'

'No need for that,' she said. 'Unless you're planning to get shot again, of course.'

'I'll try most things once,' he said, 'but I think once was quite enough in this case.'

She cleared the old bandages away and returned to find him looking tired again.

'You'd better get some more sleep,' she said. 'In fact, I should advise you to stay in bed for a few days at least. You were lucky enough this time, but bullet wounds are not to be taken lightly—even minor ones.'

'So you really are leaving me,' he said.

'Yes,' she said, 'I am.'

'Then shake hands before you go,' he said.

They did so, formally.

'Goodbye, Angela,' he said.

He seemed inclined to keep hold of her hand. She withdrew it gently.

'Goodbye, Edgar,' she said. 'Be good.'

'I'm not sure I can remember how,' he said.

He looked so rueful and forlorn that Angela was forced to bolt out of the room before he began to work on her sympathy. The car was standing where they had left it the night before. She got in, turned it with some difficulty and set off back to Stresa.

Chapter Twenty-Three

THE DAY WAS dull and overcast, but Angela hardly noticed the weather as she drove the short distance back to Stresa, lost in her own thoughts. Being a sensible woman not generally prone to excessive sentimentality, she congratulated herself on her success in having escaped from an extremely awkward situation with at least some—although certainly not all—of her dignity intact. Clearly, it was quite impossible for her to continue to have any sort of association with Edgar Valencourt, and she was pleased with herself for her strength of purpose in having acknowledged the fact and acted upon it promptly—or at least she knew she *ought* to be pleased with herself, but something that she recognized to her annoyance as a sharp twinge of regret *would* keep on nagging at her and puncturing her complacency. From there it was an easy step to feeling cross with him again, and within a very short interval her thoughts had revolved in so many directions that by the time she turned back onto the lake-front she could not have said whether she was happy, sad, angry or merely rather puzzled.

As she approached the hotel she forced her thoughts away from Valencourt and turned her attention to other matters. The important thing now was to resolve her current predicament, which was how to get to her room without attracting attention, for she really did look quite dreadfully disreputable. It was just after eight, and she hoped that most people would be either at breakfast or still in bed. Rather than walk in through the front door, she decided to try and creep in through the quieter side entrance, and accordingly stopped the car as near to it as she could. She looked down at her pale-green evening-dress, which was bloodstained in several places, and wished fervently she had worn something darker last night. Still, it was too late now: she would just have to make a run for it and hope for the best.

She waited until the coast was clear, then alighted from the car and hurried up the path, but immediately saw someone coming out through the side door and had to duck behind a bush, feeling rather foolish. She waited until the man had passed, then emerged and ran as fast as she could through the door. As she entered she heard the clink of plates and cups and the sound of voices coming from the restaurant, and paused to reflect for a second. The lift would not do at all, of course, and neither would the grand staircase. No: she would have to go up the back stairs by the kitchen. It was a pity her room was on the fourth floor, she thought—although before today she had never considered the fact as an inconvenience.

There were a few people in the hall and she was just slipping discreetly past them while trying not to draw attention to herself, when she heard a voice she recognized as Mr. Morandi's call out her name. She pretended not to have heard and, throwing all caution to the winds, put her head down and made a dash down the corridor that led to the kitchen, and through the door to the back stairs. She ran up all eight flights, meeting only one startled house-maid on the way, and to her relief made it to her room, panting for breath, without encountering any of the guests. After the extraordinary events of the past twelve hours or so she was almost astonished to find that the room looked exactly as it had when she had left it. The bed looked very tempting, and she suddenly realized that she was feeling extremely tired, not having slept much the night before. A lie-down—just for half an hour or so—would be just the thing to refresh her, she thought. She took off her soiled dress and lay down.

When she awoke she found to her surprise that she had in fact slept for almost four hours, and that it was gone noon. She lay for a while in a pleasant state of abstraction until an uncomfortable emptiness in her stomach reminded her that it would soon be lunch-time, and that she really ought to get up. She rose and debated the possibility of a bath. There was unlikely to be any hot water at this time of the day, but the weather was warm enough for it not to matter much, and so she decided to take the risk. After-wards, scrubbed clean and looking entirely respectable in a light summer dress, she felt much refreshed and ready to face the world—or at least that portion of it that was to be found entertaining itself in the public rooms of the Hotel del Lago. She went down—in the lift, this time—and looked about for Elsa, whom she soon spotted coming in from the garden.

'Goodness, Angela, I've been looking for you every-where,' said that lady. 'Where on *earth* have you been? You disappeared last night without so much as a word, and then I missed you at breakfast this morning. I was starting to think you must have gone back to England without telling anyone.'

Angela said—for to tell the truth was obviously impossible—that last night she had been afflicted with a terrible headache and had had to go to her room and lie down. She had spent the morning in bed but was feeling much better now.

'You poor darling,' said Elsa. 'Well, if you really are better you must be feeling awfully hungry by now. Let's go and have lunch.'

'How is Francis?' said Angela as they went in and found their table. 'Have they taken Chris away?'

'Oh, of course, you went off in the middle of all the uproar, didn't you?' said Elsa. 'Poor Francis—and poor Chris! Yes, they went along to the *pensione* last night and I'm afraid it's all true. It looks very much as though he killed himself, although nobody is quite sure why. There have been vague mutterings about nervous trouble, but I shouldn't have thought that would be enough reason to kill oneself, should you? I mean, even people who suffer from their nerves generally have to have a *reason* for that sort of thing, even if it's just the fact that they were served some tough beef at dinner. Something must have upset him enough to make him do it, surely.'

'Yes, I suppose so,' said Angela. 'What does Francis say? Does he believe it was suicide? Or might it have been an accident, do you think?'

'Why, I don't know,' said Elsa, 'and I don't suppose he does either. He seemed just as shocked and confused as the rest of us last night. Quite distraught, in fact, the poor boy.'

'That's understandable,' said Angela.

'I've rather taken Francis under my wing,' said Elsa. 'He reminds me so much of my youngest son, you see. We brought him back to the hotel last night and he's staying here now, since the owner of the *pensione* had rather a fit at what happened and wanted nothing more to do with him.'

'Dear me.'

'Well, quite,' said Elsa. 'Look, there he is now.' She waved at Francis, who was just then entering the dining-room, and he saw her and came over to their table. He looked tired and even more subdued than usual.

'I've just been talking to that police chap, D'Onofrio,' he said. 'He was asking me all sorts of odd questions about Chris.'

Angela pricked up her ears.

'What kind of questions?' she said.

'It's too bad of him to disturb you like that when you've just had such a shock,' said Elsa in concern. 'He might have waited a day or two.'

'No, no, he was very kind,' said Francis, 'but he wanted to get the facts straight, he said, just to make sure that everything was done correctly—for Chris's sake, you see. He wanted to know where Chris got the chloral hydrate. I said he must have bought it here in Italy, as I'm certain he never had anything of the sort in his luggage. I've been thinking about it all night and I'm sure of it. You see, I was going back to the *pensione* to fetch something one day and he asked me to look out something of his. As you can imagine, he's not—he wasn't—the tidiest of fellows, and I spent about twenty minutes searching through his things and never saw anything of the kind. If I had I'd have said something at the time, because it would have worried me.'

'Did you happen to get a look at the bottle when you found him last night?' said Angela. 'Was the label in English or Italian?'

Francis thought for a moment.

'Why, English, now you come to mention it,' he said. 'I'm pretty sure I saw the words "Chloral Hydrate" on the label. If it was in Italian then I shouldn't have understood it, should I? I suppose that must mean he *did* bring it with him, then, although he must have kept it pretty well hidden. How odd. I wonder why I never found it.'

He excused himself a moment as he had spotted Mr. Morandi and wanted to speak to him about something. Elsa watched him go in sympathy, and sighed.

'Goodness me,' she said. '*What* a week it's been! Why, there's been nothing but trouble, it seems.'

Angela glanced up at her quickly and seemed about to say something, but changed her mind.

'What is it?' said Elsa.

'Trouble,' said Angela after a moment. 'That's a word I keep hearing lately.'

'Well, what else would you call it?' said Elsa.

'Oh, it's a perfectly good word to use in the circum-stances,' said Angela, 'but—I don't know. There's some-thing odd about it.'

In fact, she had just remembered something that Asphodel Quinn had said—something about having fore-seen trouble for the Sheridans. Angela wondered very much whether Miss Quinn had seen something similar for Christopher Tate, and had half a mind to ask her. Illogical as it was, Angela could not shake off the feeling that Miss Quinn knew more than she was prepared to tell—but whether because of her supposed clairvoyant abilities or for some more prosaic reason she could not say. She made up her mind to speak to the girl if she got the chance, and see if she could persuade her to speak.

After lunch Angela set off to walk into Stresa, for she had agreed to meet Virginia Sheridan and Mary Ainsley to discuss the séance—an event that now seemed part of an earlier age after all that had happened since, although in reality it had taken place only yesterday. As she walked along the lake-front she saw Mr. D'Onofrio coming towards her. He nodded politely, and seemed to be wondering whether or not to approach her. She made up her mind and went across to him.

'So then,' he said. 'Another man is dead, it seems.'

'Yes,' said Angela, 'and I wish it hadn't happened.'

'There is no stopping a man who wants to end his life,' said D'Onofrio.

'Then you don't think it was an accident? Or perhaps —something else?'

He shrugged.

'Again, I have no evidence to the contrary,' he said. 'This boy is a nervous type who carries a medicine with him to help him sleep, and one day, when life seems just a little too hard for him to struggle on with it, he makes a decision to stop struggling. He takes the bottle of medicine, puts a few too many drops of it in his drink and then drinks it all up, and so it ends.'

'I don't believe it,' said Angela.

'Why not?'

'Because Francis Butler was almost certain that the drops were not Chris's,' she said. 'And it's just too suspicious coming after the death of Raymond Sheridan.'

'Go on,' he said.

Angela hesitated. She did not wish to tell him how to do his job, but she felt this was important.

'I don't know how things work here,' she said at last, 'but if you can, I think you ought to try and arrange for a post-mortem examination to be carried out on Raymond Sheridan.'

'I see,' he said. 'And if I do that, what do you think they will find?'

'I shouldn't be a bit surprised if you were to discover

that he died of an overdose of chloral hydrate, just like Chris,' she replied.

He nodded.

'I think it is possible,' he said. 'But of course, if we do discover that, people will begin to say that Mr. Tate murdered Mr. Sheridan and then killed himself out of remorse.'

'Yes, they probably will,' said Angela, 'and it's all nonsense—although no more so than the idea of the Quinns' being responsible for Mr. Sheridan's death, I suppose.'

'But still they will say it,' he said.

'Then we must prove he had nothing to do with it,' she said. 'Will you try and arrange for the examination?'

'Very well,' he said. 'I will do what I can.'

'If you're worried about having your house burned down, tell them a determined English woman is loudly demanding an investigation. I'm quite happy to take the blame for the trouble. They can't burn *my* house down— although I suppose they can throw me out of the country if they like.'

He snuffed in dry amusement.

'I do not think that will be necessary, *signora*,' he said. 'But I will keep it in mind just in case,' he added.

She regarded him closely.

'I believe you know—or at least suspect—what happened,' she said.

He met her eye briefly then glanced away, out towards the lake.

'People talk,' he said eventually, 'but I cannot always listen to everything.'

'You really ought to in this case, you know,' she said gently.

'I am beginning to think you are right,' he said, still looking out at the lake.

They both watched as a pleasure-cruiser arrived at the jetty and began to disgorge its cargo of chattering tourists, then he turned back towards her as though he had reached a decision.

'I believe you also have an idea of what happened, Mrs. Marchmont,' he said. 'Will you help me?'

'I'll try,' she replied. 'What do you want me to do?'

'Talk to people,' he said. 'You are not in any way official, and perhaps people will speak to you more easily than they would speak to me.'

'Yes,' said Angela, thinking. 'I can do that. I don't know exactly what happened—or at least, I'm not entirely sure why—but I think there's one person in particular who might be able to tell me. Very well, then, I will do what I can. I only hope that some conclusive evidence can be found, though. If there's no proof, then this whole thing will remain forever unresolved and the rumours will never be quashed.'

Mr. D'Onofrio sighed.

'It is a great pity that these things must happen,' he said. It was the nearest thing to a moral pronouncement Angela had ever heard him make. He gave her a little bow and departed, and she went on her way.

Chapter Twenty-Four

WHEN ANGELA ARRIVED AT THE AINSLEYS' apartment she found that Virginia Sheridan had already arrived and was sitting with Mary in their little sitting-room, looking even more unwell than before, if possible. Angela once again wondered whether Mrs. Sheridan was eating properly and could not help inquiring after her health.

'Yes, I confess I am a little under the weather,' she replied, 'but I assure you it's nothing serious. I shall be quite all right.'

'Oh, but you must look after yourself *now*,' said Mary who, it appeared, had also been upbraiding Virginia before Angela's arrival. 'Think of what Raymond would say if he knew, and what he would tell you to do.'

'Of course I'm thinking of Raymond,' said Virginia sharply. She caught herself and lowered her head. 'I'm sorry,' she said. 'I didn't mean to snap. I promise I shall do my best.'

'I know you will, dear,' said Mary, and busied herself with serving tea, an activity which occupied the conversation for the next few minutes.

Naturally, the first topic to be introduced once they had all been served was the death of Christopher Tate. Mary and Virginia were full of wonder and consternation at this latest tragedy and wanted to know everything Angela could tell them, since she had been there when Francis had come to the hotel to report it. Angela told them what she could and said that it looked as though Christopher had killed himself. At this, Virginia Sheridan gave a little exclamation of distress.

'I hope he didn't get the idea from Raymond,' she said. 'I should hate to think it influenced him in any way.'

'I doubt it,' said Mary. 'Why, it's not as though they died the same way, is it? I shouldn't give it a second's thought if I were you. You have enough to worry about as it is without getting worked up by that sort of idea.'

Angela, who was by now fairly certain that Mr. Sheridan's death had led almost directly to Christopher's, said nothing, but sipped her tea.

'Poor Francis,' said Mary, after a pause. 'I suppose he will have to go home now. What will happen to Chris's paintings, do you think?'

'I dare say his parents will take them,' said Angela.

'And once Francis goes home Jack Lomax will have lost both his pupils at once,' said Mary. She sighed. 'It's quite astonishing how many people are affected by one person's death, isn't it?'

'I wonder what drove him to it,' said Virginia.

'I gather he hadn't been well,' said Mary. 'He had a nervous complaint, I understand—but as to what was bothering him in particular I have no idea. Do you know, Angela? You've spoken to Francis, haven't you?'

'Francis says he doesn't know either,' said Angela.

'I wonder,' said Mrs. Sheridan, considering. 'Perhaps

Jack will know. Didn't Chris rather hero-worship him? I'm sure someone told me he did.'

'He did, rather, from what I saw,' said Angela.

'Then I do hope it wasn't something Jack said,' said Virginia. 'He can be a little brusque at times, and if this boy really was the nervous type then it might only take the slightest remark to upset him enough to—' she faltered, unwilling to voice the thought.

Angela glanced up but said nothing.

'Well, no doubt it will all come out sooner or later,' said Mary. She poured out more tea. 'Now, then, Angela,' she said, 'we have been waiting to hear your opinion of this séance. Virginia was just telling me what happened when you arrived. It's all most mysterious, don't you think? But can you be quite sure they didn't hypnotize either of you in any way?'

'Quite sure,' said Angela, who had now completely abandoned the idea of the Quinns' being guilty of murder and was almost inclined to think that if anyone had hypnotized her it was Jonathan, for she could think of no other reason—apart from possibly her own natural gullibility—why she should have believed such a ridiculous theory in the first place.

'It was rather impressive, though, wasn't it?' said Virginia hesitantly.

'I suppose it was,' said Angela, 'but I dare say a real expert in these matters could explain immediately how they did it. I couldn't tell you myself, but I expect there's a simple enough explanation.'

'Oh dear,' said Mary. 'Then I shall have to find a way to tell Jonathan. I don't suppose he'll be pleased.'

'I imagine not,' said Angela, 'but I'm afraid he will just have to accept the fact that there is nothing he can do about the Quinns, however much they annoy him.'

Mary was about to answer when Virginia Sheridan interrupted gently and asked if she might have a glass of water.

'Of course, dear,' said Mary. She got up and fetched the drink, then fluttered about Virginia in concern. It appeared that the Ainsleys had offered to help Mrs. Sheridan make a list of the effects at the Villa Pozzi with a view to holding a sale.

'I'm afraid I don't know where to begin,' said Virginia. 'There is such a lot of stuff, you see, and some of it is rather valuable.'

'Well, Jonathan and I can help you clear out any unwanted things that won't fetch anything,' said Mary. 'You won't want to be bothered with all that, will you?'

'Are you selling the house?' said Angela.

Virginia nodded.

'Yes, I think so,' she said. 'It's far too much for me to manage alone. Mary and Jonathan are very kindly going to help me arrange everything.'

As Virginia and Mary began to discuss what was to be done, Angela was once again struck by the apparent ease with which Mrs. Sheridan induced other people to do things for her, just as Edgar Valencourt had said. At the thought of Valencourt, she felt a little stab as she remembered that only last night he had accused her of doing almost exactly the same thing when she had persuaded him to search the Quinns' apartment for her. She would not soil her own hands, he had said, and she was stung anew at the memory. True, he had been angry, and she had returned fire with interest, but was he right? After a moment's reflection, however, she concluded that the accusation had been unjust, since she would have been perfectly willing to do it herself had she been able to. She wished she had had the presence of mind to make the point at the time, and for half a second was resolved to tell him of it the next time she saw him. Then she remembered that it would not be possible, that he had promised to keep away from her, and that they were not to see each other again. Still, there was some satisfaction in the thought that he had been wrong, and that she was nothing like Virginia Sheridan, since she was entirely able to do things for herself.

Her thoughts running along these lines, Angela watched absently as Mary flapped about Virginia. Then she sat up straight and almost laughed at her own obtuseness as a thought darted into her head and she suddenly understood something that she had completely missed before. How could she have been so blind when it was so perfectly obvious? Why, even a child might have noticed it. Angela shook her head in wonder at her own lack of perspicacity, and could only assume that her mind had been so occupied with other things that she had not been paying full attention to the matter at hand.

It was all very well seeing the thing, however, but the real question was: what did it mean? Was it a coincidence, or was there something more to it than that? Did it, in fact, hold the key to the mystery? For a few moments Angela debated with herself as to whether to speak directly to Virginia Sheridan about it, but after a moment concluded that it might be unwise, and so decided to say nothing for the present. At that moment she wanted nothing more than to go somewhere quiet and think about things by herself, and so after a few minutes she took her leave and set off through the town, intending to find a seat overlooking the lake and attempt to put the pieces of the puzzle together. But when she reached the lake-front she changed her mind, for there, sitting on a bench and gazing out across the water was the familiar figure of Asphodel Quinn, who for once seemed to be without her mother.

Angela hesitated for a second and then made up her mind. She went across to the bench and stood before Miss Quinn.

'May I sit down?' she said.

The girl glanced up. From the state of her eyes it looked as though she had been crying. She indicated that she had no objection and Angela sat down next to her.

'I wondered if I might ask you something,' she said.

'Yes?' said Miss Quinn.

'I seem to remember your mentioning a letter you sent to someone once, warning him that he was in danger.'

'Yes, and what of it?' said Miss Quinn rudely. 'You might also remember that it didn't work, so why remind me of it?'

'You know very well why,' said Angela. 'Two people are dead in mysterious circumstances and there's a very real possibility that it was foul play.'

Miss Quinn looked up, surprised.

'Do you mean this boy?' she said. 'Why, what are people saying about him?'

'Nothing, yet,' said Angela, 'but I should imagine they will start sooner or later, and quite frankly I can't understand why you're not more interested yourself in solving the mystery, since you and your mother are the ones who are suffering the most from all the rumours that have been flying around about Mr. Sheridan.'

Miss Quinn shrugged.

'Oh, well,' she said. 'It's nothing we're not used to. We've survived this kind of thing before and we can do it again. People don't like our sort, you know. They're only too happy to speak our praises as long as we're telling them what they want to hear, but as soon as the skeletons start to come out of the closet we get the blame. No matter, though—it's easy enough for us to move on.'

'But aren't you interested in justice?' said Angela.

'How can justice be served in this case?' said Miss Quinn. 'There's no proof of anything, only rumours and stories.'

'I think evidence may be found shortly,' said Angela. 'I believe the police are planning to conduct a post-mortem examination on Raymond Sheridan.'

Asphodel Quinn glanced up sharply.

'Is that true?' she said. She seemed to consider this idea, then shook her head. 'But in any case, don't you see?' she said. 'Even if they do find proof that he was killed, then the wrong person is going to suffer for it.'

'What do you mean?' said Angela. 'Who is going to suffer?'

Miss Quinn bit her lip. She seemed to regret her remark.

'I didn't mean anything,' she said. 'Please forget I said it.'

Angela decided the time had come to confront her. She turned and looked directly at Asphodel Quinn.

'Are you talking about Jack Lomax?' she said.

Chapter Twenty-Five

ASPHODEL QUINN GAVE a little gasp and stared at Angela, who went on:

'It was to him you sent the letter, wasn't it? I misunderstood you at first and thought you'd sent it to Raymond Sheridan. You *did* tell Mr. Sheridan you believed his life was in danger, but you told him in person, not in writing. But you wanted to warn Jack Lomax too, and so you wrote to him since he wasn't a client of yours.'

Miss Quinn hesitated a second, then nodded slowly.

'But the warning to Jack Lomax was of quite a different sort,' said Angela. 'You were worried he was about to do something dreadful—something he would regret.'

'He didn't believe me,' said Miss Quinn, almost in a whisper. 'He wrote back and said it was all nonsense. But it wasn't. Of course, he couldn't have known what would happen, and how things were going to change.'

'How did you know?' said Angela. 'It wasn't just one of your visions, I suppose. I believe you witnessed something.'

Miss Quinn turned her head away and looked out at the lake.

'Yes, I did,' she said at length. 'It wasn't much—just a look—but it was clear enough what was going on.' She paused. 'Have you ever seen a mouse hypnotized by a snake, Mrs. Marchmont?' she said. 'The snake fixes its gaze on the mouse and the mouse crouches there, frozen, half in fear and half in fascination. It's almost as though it sees its fate and welcomes it. Well, that's what I saw—or something very like it.'

'I think I understand,' said Angela.

'Do you?' said Miss Quinn, turning back to her almost eagerly. 'Perhaps you do. Then you'll see why I simply knew something dreadful was going to happen. It was as though a black cloud had come down over him—over both of them, in fact. I couldn't see clearly, but I knew they were about to do something terrible. Then I just had to write and warn him. Mother said I oughtn't to have, and now I realize she was right. I oughtn't to have said anything at all. But what else was I to do? I couldn't just let it happen. And yet it did.' She looked down at her feet. 'Sometimes I wonder whether I mightn't have put the idea into his head myself,' she said.

'I doubt that very much,' said Angela.

'Oh, but what if I did?' said Miss Quinn. 'Then I've got him into dreadful trouble—and after all, he's not the one who is really guilty.'

Angela shook her head.

'I'm afraid that won't wash,' she said. 'You do know another person has died, don't you? Once might be understandable, but to kill twice—well, one can't just go on making excuses for him. He's a grown man and is responsible for his own actions.'

'Perhaps the second death had nothing to do with it,' said Asphodel feebly.

'It had everything to do with it,' said Angela.

'Then I'm very sorry,' said Miss Quinn after a pause. 'Of course you're right. I oughtn't really to defend him, although I'm afraid I burnt his reply to me so it couldn't be used as evidence. I just felt as though somehow it wasn't his fault.'

'If he did it then he is very much to blame,' said Angela.

'How did you know?' said Miss Quinn suddenly. 'I mean, about Mr. Lomax?'

Of course, Angela could not explain that she had seen the burnt letter, or that she had recognized the same hand-writing in the signature on Lomax's portrait of herself, so she merely said:

'He was the last person known to have seen Mr. Sheridan alive, and so was bound to come under suspicion if it *was* murder. But he couldn't possibly have disposed of the body alone, since Mr. Sheridan was far too heavy to lift, and so he must have had someone to help him. Now that Christopher Tate is dead it's rather obvious who that someone was.'

'Then you believe Mr. Lomax killed him to keep him quiet?' said Miss Quinn, aghast.

Angela nodded.

'I'm afraid so,' she said.

'What do you propose to do now?' said Miss Quinn.

'I don't know,' said Angela. 'There's not a lot can be done until the results of the post-mortem examination come back, and even then there may be no evidence to connect Mr. Lomax with the deaths.'

'I almost hope there isn't,' said Asphodel.

'But then the rumours will continue to circulate and

you will probably have to leave,' said Angela. She looked at Miss Quinn's stricken face. 'None of this was your fault, you know,' she said gently. 'You mustn't blame yourself.'

'I only wish I could see things as you do,' said Miss Quinn sadly.

Angela had no further reassurance to give. She took her leave and wandered slowly along the lake-front. What a mess the whole thing was turning out to be, she thought, and wondered whether the situation would ever be resolved. She was very much afraid that Miss Quinn was right in thinking that only half the story—at most—would ever come out.

The sky was still overcast but it did not look like rain, and since Angela did not feel like mingling with the crowds but rather preferred to wander alone, she passed the Hotel del Lago and continued along as far as the Villa Pozzi. Without thinking much she drifted through the gates and wandered up the drive as far as the summer-house, where she stopped. The door was unlocked and she opened it, although she did not go inside but merely stood in the doorway and glanced around the dim room. Everything had been put back in order and the place was perfectly tidy. There was no sign of the dreadful events that had taken place only a few days ago: no overturned chair, no rope hanging from a beam—nothing to say that anything out of the ordinary had occurred.

Angela gazed about her, trying to picture what must have happened on Wednesday morning before the picnickers had arrived. Or had it perhaps all taken place on Tuesday night? No, it must have been Wednesday morning—yes, of course it was, thought Angela, suddenly recalling something Francis Butler had said on the evening after Mr. Sheridan had been discovered. According to Francis, Chris had gone out on Wednesday morning and come back upset about something, and then shortly after that had been struck down with one of his nervous attacks. That must be when it had all happened, then. On Wednesday morning Jack Lomax and Christopher Tate had carried the body of Raymond Sheridan down to the summer-house, lifted him up and suspended him by the neck from the ceiling. Even with two of them it must have been immensely hard work, but she supposed that urgency must have given them strength. But how had Lomax persuaded Chris to help him? Or was Chris himself somehow mixed up in Mr. Sheridan's death? There was no connection between the two and it did not seem likely. But Chris was dead now, and could not answer the question, and the only person who *could* answer it was unlikely to speak.

After some minutes spent in meditation, Angela roused herself and found that it was later than she had thought. Then she remembered that Jonathan and Mary would be expecting her at church for the evening service, since she had missed the morning one, and if she did not hurry she would be late. After the events of the past few days perhaps a little spiritual edification would do her some good, she reflected, as she shut the door of the summer-house and set off briskly back down the drive.

Chapter Twenty-Six

DESPITE HER BEST EFFORTS, Angela arrived late for church. She slipped through the door during the first hymn, found a spot at the end of a pew and glanced about her. The place was fuller than she had expected, and for a second she wondered why Jonathan had been making such a fuss, since it seemed a perfectly respectable turnout to her; then it occurred to her that perhaps people had heard about the deaths of Raymond Sheridan and Christopher Tate, and had come to church in the hope of getting some thrilling gossip. Jonathan Ainsley was in his element, and looked particularly pleased at the size of his congregation. Angela watched as he exchanged smiles with his wife, who was sitting near the front.

The hymn ended and the service began, and if those present were hoping for some interesting news they were disappointed, for apart from a single brief mention of the two tragic losses suffered in Stresa that week, followed by a short prayer to help the dead men on their way, Jonathan made no mention of Mr. Sheridan or Christopher Tate, but instead launched into his rewritten sermon, of which the original had been ruined during Wednesday's storm. In spite of her reservations about Jonathan, Angela could not help but be impressed with his abilities, for he spoke well and sincerely and with a strong sense of purpose, and for perhaps the first time she felt she was seeing him at his best.

The service came to an end and the congregation filed out. Angela stood out of the way to let people past, since she intended to wait for Mary, who had just gone into the little vestry. As she did so, she noticed to her surprise a lone figure still sitting on the end of a pew at the back of the church, his head in his hands. It was Jack Lomax. Without stopping to think, she approached him. He glanced up as he heard her coming, and she was shocked at the change in him, for his once-handsome face was sunken and drawn and his eyes were hollow. He looked as though he had not slept in days.

Angela stopped in front of him, and they regarded each other for a moment. He looked as though he were waiting for something.

'Why did you do it?' said Angela.

He showed no surprise at her question, but turned his eyes away and looked straight ahead.

'Which one?' he said. 'Raymond, you mean? It was an accident. Never meant to kill him.'

'Did you drug him with something?' said Angela.

'He said he was having trouble sleeping since she'd left him,' he said. 'I told him I'd the very thing. Put some drops in his whisky. Must have given him too many by mistake. Went back the next morning and he was dead.'

'Then why didn't you confess it at the time?'

'I should have done, but then Chris saw me and I panicked,' he said.

'Chris saw you?' said Angela.

'Yes. He must have followed me. Saw him looking through the window. He was horrified. I let him in and explained what had happened, then I realized how unconvincing it sounded and thought people might think it was deliberate. Rather lost my head and begged him to help me disguise it as suicide. We got rid of the empty glass, put Raymond's jacket and shoes back on him, then carried him down to the summer-house and strung him up.'

His face contorted at the stark horror of his own words.

'I wish I hadn't done it,' he said. 'Too late now, of course.'

Just then Angela glanced up and saw Jonathan. He had come in from saying goodbye to his congregation, and to judge by the expression on his face had heard everything Lomax had said. Angela shook her head in warning, but it was too late, for Lomax had already seen him.

'Hallo,' he said in resignation. 'You might as well stay and hear the confession. You're the right fellow for it after all.'

'Hallo, Jack,' said Jonathan. 'I'll listen to anything you want to say, never fear.'

'What about Chris?' said Angela. 'Was that an accident too?'

'Don't know,' said Lomax. 'I missed the drops and thought I must have left them somewhere. Was rather worried about it, to be perfectly frank. If anyone found them I might be in trouble. But he must have taken them. Perhaps it was an accident, perhaps it was deliberate. We'll never know. My fault, though. I oughtn't to have dragged him into it. Ought to have known he was delicate. Nervous. Must have disturbed him. Not much fun trying to hang a dead man, you see.'

'No,' said Angela.

'Raymond was my friend,' he said, 'and I killed him. I don't know what to do now. I suppose you'll have to call the police.'

'I'm afraid we will, Jack,' said Jonathan. 'But if, as you say, it was an accident, then I don't imagine you'll have anything to fear—although they may not be too happy about your attempts to disguise what happened.'

'Probably not,' agreed Lomax.

'Wait here,' said Jonathan. 'I shall go and fetch Mary. Someone will have to tell Virginia.'

'Please,' said Lomax. 'I don't think I can bear to face her myself. Cowardly, I know.'

Jonathan laid a sympathetic hand on Jack Lomax's shoulder and then went into the vestry to fetch his wife. Angela remained behind and regarded Lomax thoughtfully.

'Are you quite sure you've told us everything, Mr. Lomax?' she said.

He turned pink.

'What do you mean?' he said.

'I think you know what I mean,' she said.

He was silent for a second, then said:

'I don't suppose you can imagine what it's like to make a mistake and be trapped by it forever, can you? Well, that's what I've done. I made one false step. One false step that led to another, and then another, and now my oldest friend is dead because of me, and whether I go to prison or not my life will forever be a living hell. Raymond was worth ten of me and I killed him, and now I have to live with the fact until the day I die.'

He was so patently distraught that there was no doubt he regretted what he had done. No, no doubt at all, and had Raymond Sheridan's death been the start and end of it Angela might have let it lie there—might have believed the accident story and inquired no further. But other people had suffered too. What of Christopher Tate? Tall, energetic Christopher Tate, with his infectious love of art, and his enthusiasms, and his hero-worship of his art tutor. And his loyal friend Francis Butler, who now had to deal with the death of his childhood companion and confess to Chris's parents that he had been unable to look after him as he had promised. What of them? How were they meant to get justice? For justice was what was missing here, Angela was certain of it. Lomax's story was convincing enough; it wrapped everything up neatly with no loose ends and would certainly be enough to satisfy the people of Stresa, at any rate, but Angela was not satisfied, and only wished she knew what she ought to do.

Jonathan and Mary came hurrying out just then and all was confusion and dismay. They took charge of Jack Lomax and led him away, and Angela was left alone in the church to struggle with a tumult of conflicting emotions.

Chapter Twenty-Seven

THE NEWS of what had happened soon leaked out, and by Monday morning the tragic events were the talk of the place. As Angela had predicted, everybody seemed perfectly satisfied with the story that was put about. There was much sympathy for Jack Lomax and his plight, and the question on everyone's lips was: how would Virginia Sheridan take the news that Lomax had been accidentally responsible for her husband's death? By Monday evening the story was circulating (courtesy of Mr. Morandi) that the two had met, and that through her tears she had assured him that she bore him no ill-will and forgave him from the bottom of her heart. At this news there was an almost palpable sigh of relief from all the guests of the Hotel del Lago—all except Mrs. Marchmont, who was still dissatisfied with the whole thing. She kept her thoughts to herself, however—at least until Tuesday morning, when she happened to spy Mr. D'Onofrio as he took his coffee at his usual table on the terrace.

'Good morning, Mrs. Marchmont,' he said, with his

usual expressionless look. 'So you see, everybody is happy again.'

'I'm not,' she replied.

'No,' he said. 'I did not think you would be.'

'I don't like having the wool pulled over my eyes,' she said.

'*Come?* I beg your pardon?'

'I mean I don't like being deceived.'

'You think someone is deceiving us, then?'

'I'm almost certain of it,' she said.

'But it is such a beautiful and tragic story,' he said.

'Yes, it is, isn't it?' she said dryly. 'But it's far too neat for my liking. Two inconvenient people are put out of the way and nobody gets into trouble? Yes—*far* too neat.'

'Then what do you propose?' said D'Onofrio.

'I don't know. I only wish there were more evidence,' said Angela.

'I think some might be found,' he said. 'Perhaps you think the police do nothing here in Italy—and it is true that we are very different from your Scotland Yard—but even here we know all about finger-prints on a bottle, and what it means when some prints are missing which ought to be there.'

Here he paused significantly, and Angela raised her eyebrows.

'I see,' she said.

'And who knows?' he went on. 'We may find something else that will come in useful—especially if we can find a motive.'

'Oh, that's easy enough,' said Angela. 'Motive without evidence won't make a case, though.'

'You are right,' he said, 'but it will help us in our investigation. But tell me, Mrs. Marchmont: are you quite sure you want to spoil such a beautiful story for an ugly reality? Sometimes it can be better to leave things alone for the peace of all.'

Angela was looking at Francis Butler, who was sitting alone at a nearby table, looking glum. She turned back to Mr. D'Onofrio.

'I'm quite sure,' she said firmly.

'Very well,' he said, and rose to leave. 'I will see what I can do. In the meantime, I rely on you to ask more questions of your friends.'

He gave a little bow and went off, leaving Angela wondering what to do next. Tomorrow she was returning to England, but the case was still unresolved—to her mind, at least—and she did not wish to go home without receiving some confirmation at least of what she believed to be the real truth. But Italian justice appeared to move extremely slowly from what she had seen so far, and it seemed as though she might wait for months before hearing anything. This was unsatisfactory, and she debated whether or not she ought to take action herself.

She wandered out through the front door of the hotel and onto the lake-front. The weather was fine once again, and everybody was going about their usual business. Angela watched the scene for a few minutes, then made up her mind and decided to pay a call. She set off briskly and was very soon walking up the long drive of the Villa Pozzi. When she reached the house she rang and was taken through a number of grand salons and into a smaller drawing-room which was elegantly and comfortably furnished in the Italian style. There she found Virginia Sheridan, who was standing by the window, staring out thoughtfully across the garden.

'Hallo, Angela,' said Mrs. Sheridan. She still looked

very pale. 'Do sit down. I suppose you've heard all about what happened.'

'I have,' said Angela. 'I think the whole town has heard about it.'

'Everyone has been tremendously kind,' said Virginia. 'I'm very lucky to have such good friends. Oh, but poor Jack! Think of what he must have been going through. It must have been hell for him, coming back here the next morning and realizing what he had done. I can hardly blame him for wanting to pretend it had never happened. I've told him so, but I'm afraid he will never be able to forgive himself. Still, I'm determined that nothing shall change between us. It wasn't his fault and I won't let him think I blame him.'

With her wide, sad eyes and gentle manner she was the very picture of womanly forgiveness, and for a moment Angela almost forgot her purpose in visiting, but then she remembered Francis Butler's face that morning and set her jaw.

'Are you still intending to leave the Villa Pozzi?' she said.

'Yes, I think so,' said Virginia. 'It costs such a lot to run, you know, but I have been told it will fetch quite a large sum if I sell it, and—well, it rather looks as though I'm going to need the money soon.'

'Ah, yes,' said Angela. 'As a matter of fact that's why I'm here. I wanted to congratulate you. I ought to have noticed before but I'm afraid I must have had other things on my mind. It was only yesterday that I realized why you've been feeling so ill. It is that, isn't it?'

Virginia blushed delicately.

'Yes, it is,' she said. 'And thank you. I'm just so terribly sorry that Raymond died before I could tell him. Now he will never know his child.'

Angela took a deep breath.

'Perhaps that's a good thing, don't you think?' she said.

'What do you mean?' said Virginia.

'Why, because the child is not his, of course.'

Angela had been wondering whether she was about to make the most awful fool of herself, but when she saw Mrs. Sheridan's instantaneous reaction to her words she knew immediately that she had been right. Instead of looking shocked and puzzled, Virginia narrowed her eyes for a split second, and a calculating look came across her face.

'That's rather ill-mannered of you, Angela, to suggest such a thing,' she said.

'But it's true, isn't it?' said Angela. 'You were having an affair with Jack Lomax and the child is his.'

Virginia eyed Angela. She still showed no shock at the suggestion, but instead seemed to be considering.

'The child is Raymond's,' she said eventually. 'But even if it weren't, it would be stupid of me to admit it, don't you think?'

'Oh, I didn't expect you to admit it,' said Angela. 'I just wanted you to know that you haven't got away with it. The police suspect it wasn't an accident and they're collecting evidence, but at the moment they don't have a motive. This is a big enough motive, though, isn't it?'

'Nonsense,' said Virginia. 'Are you suggesting that Jack killed Raymond on purpose?'

'I'm almost sure of it,' said Angela, 'and the post-mortem examination ought to confirm it.'

'How?' said Virginia, looking interested despite herself.

'Well, if I were going to murder a man by drugging him with a sleeping draught, I should take good care to put enough of the stuff in his glass to make absolutely sure of killing him—far more than could be explained by an accidental overdose,' said Angela. 'I'll bet that's what Jack did. I shouldn't be surprised if they find enough of the stuff in your husband's system to have killed him several times over.'

'That still doesn't prove anything, though,' said Virginia.

'No, but it's highly suggestive,' said Angela. 'And then there's Chris. I don't believe for a moment that he stole the bottle of drops and used them to kill himself.'

'No?' said Virginia politely. 'What do you think happened, then?'

'As a matter of fact, I'm fairly sure he saw the two of you together and came to the conclusion that he'd been duped into helping to disguise a murder as suicide. I saw him myself the other day in the hotel garden, looking terribly upset, shortly after I'd seen you and Jack walking together. I imagine Chris confronted Jack—or perhaps even both of you, and accused him of betrayal. But of course then he became a danger to you, and so he had to be put out of the way.'

'Nonsense,' said Virginia. 'The bottle was found by his bedside. Of course Chris did it himself.'

'Then why weren't his finger-prints on the bottle?' said Angela.

Virginia opened her mouth, but said nothing, and Angela went on:

'I was speaking to Mr. D'Onofrio this morning. He is highly suspicious of the whole thing. He doesn't believe the accident story either, and he's searching for evidence to prove it was murder.'

Virginia Sheridan was looking a little rattled.

'I can't believe it of Jack,' she said. 'And in any case, even if what you say is true, I still don't see why you are telling me. If by some remote chance Jack *was* in love with me and decided to put Raymond out of the way, then surely I am the victim. I'm certainly not guilty of murder. Why, I wasn't even here at the time.'

'No, but you're rather clever like that, aren't you?' said Angela. Virginia was silent, and she continued, 'Let me tell you what I think happened. I think that a few months ago you began an affair with Jack Lomax, perhaps because you were bored, or perhaps because you really did love him—I don't know. At any rate, you found out that you were expecting a child and were thrown into a panic. You were terrified that Raymond would divorce you when he found out, and so rather than suffer the humiliation of a court case you determined to put him out of the way. I'm not sure why you didn't simply plan to pass off the child as your husband's—after all, it's been done enough times before—but I can only imagine that in some way you were certain that he would know it wasn't his and would be very angry.

'The trouble is that when someone dies unexpectedly, the finger tends to point at the dead person's wife or husband. Naturally you didn't want that, and since you were certain that nobody knew about your affair with Jack you began to work on him. It has been pointed out to me by several people—and in fact I have observed it myself—that you are very good at getting people to do what you want. I don't suppose for a second that Jack would have killed his oldest friend unless he had been persuaded or charmed or badgered into it in some way, but I imagine you worked on his sympathy, pretended to be terrified of your husband's rage, and altogether made Jack feel as though he were doing it to protect you. Whatever the case, eventually he agreed to do it. The plan was that you would go to England so that no suspicion could possibly fall on you, and while you were away he would do the deed. Of course, since nobody knew about the two of you no-one would ever suspect him either, since he had no apparent motive.

'You agreed that you would manufacture a row with Raymond and then leave. That way, once he was dead, you could put about the story that he believed you had gone forever and was depressed about it, then everyone would think he had killed himself. So that's what you did: you deliberately fell out with Raymond then went away and left Jack to do as he had promised. At first, all went according to plan: on Tuesday evening Jack visited Raymond, slipped the chloral into his drink and left. The next morning he went back, intending to make sure that Raymond was dead and that nothing had been forgotten. Unfortunately for him, he was spotted by Chris, who followed him to the house and peered through the window. It was this room he died in, wasn't it?' said Angela, looking about her suddenly. 'On that sofa there.'

Virginia said nothing but regarded Angela unblinkingly. Angela was reminded of what Asphodel Quinn had said about a snake hypnotizing its prey, and resolved to maintain a wary distance from the other woman. She went on:

'I don't know what Chris saw, exactly, but he evidently realized that something was very wrong, and that Jack was the cause of it. Jack must have got a tremendous shock when he saw Chris at the window. He knew immediately that he had to come up with a convincing story then and there or he would be in trouble. Luckily for him, Chris was only too willing not to have his illusions shattered, and so he fell for Jack's lie about having accidentally given Raymond an overdose, and agreed to help Jack disguise the death as a suicide by hanging. I suppose Jack thought that Chris was less likely to talk if he was involved in the thing himself—and of course, he must have known about Chris's hero-worship of him, so I imagine he thought he was safe.

'That evening Jack came to the hotel and told every-body—with apparent reluctance—that Raymond had mentioned ending his own life. Then on Friday you returned and hinted delicately at the same thing. You both played your parts very well, by the way. You took care not to hammer the point home *too* hard, presumably for fear of arousing suspicion if you did. I think the séance was a mistake on your part, though.'

'What do you mean?' said Virginia.

'Why, because of Aunt Adelaide, of course,' said Angela. 'Assuming that Raymond wasn't really in the room with us, who else would have known the answer to that question except you? It wasn't the Quinns who were manipulating the talking board at all—it was you, wasn't it? I don't know exactly what you were trying to do. Presumably you wanted to direct suspicion towards the Quinns—either that or you thought I was credulous enough to fall for whatever nonsense might come out during the séance. Either way, the whole thing was just a little too much and you ought to have let well alone.'

'I rather think it is *you* who ought to have let well alone,' said Virginia. 'As I said before, there's no proof of anything.'

'Not of your involvement, no,' agreed Angela. 'You can count yourself lucky at present, because Jack is sticking firmly to the accident story and has refused to give you away—naturally, since if he were to admit to your affair then that would immediately present a motive for murder, and then the whole thing would start to look deeply suspi-cious and he might be arrested. But I shouldn't congratulate myself just yet if I were you. You see, if evidence *does* emerge that Raymond and Chris were deliberately killed, then Jack will have no further reason to keep quiet about you—rather the opposite, in fact, since he will be looking for someone to blame for having persuaded him to kill his friend.'

For the first time, a look of fear crossed Virginia Sheridan's face. It was gone almost immediately, however, and her expression once more became impassive. There was a pause, and Angela held her breath. She was still not certain that she had done the right thing in confronting Virginia, but since there was some doubt as to whether a prosecution would ever be brought, she wanted Mrs. Sheridan to know that someone, at least, knew what had really happened. If she and Jack Lomax *were* to get off scot-free, Angela was determined not to allow them to do it in peace. They would have to live in the knowledge that the truth was known to others, including the police. It was poor punishment, but it would have to do for the present.

Virginia Sheridan opened her mouth to speak, and for a second Angela was convinced she was about to admit everything, but then she seemingly changed her mind. Instead, she stepped forward.

'It was so kind of you to come, Angela,' she said. 'I'm sorry you have to hurry off, but thank you so much for the congratulations. Raymond would have been *so* happy.'

She held out a hand. Angela hesitated, then shook it uncertainly. There seemed nothing else to do.

'Goodbye,' said Mrs. Sheridan.

'Goodbye,' said Mrs. Marchmont.

They regarded each other for a moment, then Angela turned and left the Villa Pozzi for the last time, wondering whether she had perhaps dreamed the last half an hour. She set off down the drive, forcing herself to walk at a gentle pace, since she was sure that Mrs. Sheridan was watching her from the window. It was not until she was certain she was quite out of sight that she began to hurry, and by the time she reached the gates she was almost running.

Chapter Twenty-Eight

THAT EVENING the Hotel del Lago was in festive and hilarious mood, for Mr. Morandi and Mrs. Peters had decided to announce their engagement and Mr. Morandi had ordered that all his guests be treated to free champagne. There was much merry-making and many speeches —mostly from Mr. Morandi himself, who could not praise his lady highly enough and would have held forth about her merits the whole evening had Elsa not called him an idiot and told him to shut up, at which everybody laughed.

Angela was more pleased for her friend than she could say, and took the first opportunity of congratulating her heartily. Elsa was not the sort to blush, but she beamed.

'Thank you,' she said. 'You will come to the wedding, won't you?'

'I should love to, if I can,' said Angela.

I'm rather surprised at myself, to be perfectly honest,' said Elsa. 'Until Gabriele asked me I should have said I was far too old for this sort of thing, but now I feel as fluttered and silly as an eighteen-year-old—quite ridiculously happy, in fact.'

'How delightful,' said Angela, smiling, for Elsa's happiness was infectious. 'Then I suppose you will be staying in Stresa now.'

'Oh, no, I have to go home and tell the children,' said Elsa.

'How will they take the news, do you think?'

'I should think they'll be all right,' said Elsa. 'They're all grown up now, and have their own concerns. I dare say they'll be pleased that there's no danger any more of my coming to live with them when I get old and grumpy.'

'I can't imagine your ever being grumpy, Elsa,' said Angela. 'Why, you simply don't have it in you.'

'I'm sure I could if I tried,' said Elsa. 'Perhaps when I've had to deal with one too many rude guests I shall discover reserves of bad temper I never knew I had.'

'So you are going to help run the hotel?'

'Yes,' said Elsa. 'I'm rather looking forward to it, as a matter of fact. I love having lots of people around me, and now I shall.'

'I do believe you and Gabriele are very well suited,' said Angela.

'We are indeed,' said Elsa, 'and another advantage of marrying a hotelier is that there's no danger of his crashing a plane into a field.'

They laughed, and then paused as young Vittorio Morandi approached their table. He had ostensibly come to clear away their glasses, but instead he stopped, glanced about to make sure his father was not looking, then kissed Elsa quickly on the cheek. Elsa laughed again as he ran off with an air of repressed mischief.

'I see you have won him over already,' said Angela.

'I hope so,' Elsa replied. 'I think there are the makings of a fine boy in him, but he needs a mother to put him right.'

Angela was reminded of Francis Butler, and she looked about for him.

'Where is Francis?' she said.

'He's gone home, the poor darling,' said Elsa. 'I made him go, as I didn't think this place was doing him any good. He needs to be back in England with his family. Gabriele can deal with all the formalities for him here. And what about you, Angela? You are off to England tomorrow too. You never did get to see Venice after all, did you?'

'No,' said Angela. 'It will have to wait until another time, as I have promised to visit my brother and his family shortly.'

'You don't look particularly happy about it,' observed Elsa.

'I'm not, especially,' said Angela. 'I'm afraid he and his wife disapprove of me. He's quite painfully respectable, and I understand he finds my occasional appearance in the newspapers embarrassing. Investigating murders is an unwomanly pursuit, you see. And to make things worse, there is the fact that I can't produce a convenient husband when required, despite being a Mrs. and not a widow.'

'Well, you must admit it is dreadfully modern and scandalous of you, darling,' said Elsa. 'However, I should have thought anyone in their right mind would be terribly excited to have a detective in the family. I know I should.'

'As a matter of fact, I am rather thinking of abandoning all pretensions to detective ability,' said Angela glumly. 'I seem to be far too easily swayed by what people tell me. I ought never to have let myself be persuaded into investigating the Quinns—and I especially ought not to have believed that they had anything to do with Mr. Sheridan's death.'

'Don't blame yourself for that,' said Elsa. 'Rumour is a very powerful thing, and if you truly believed there was something suspicious about his suicide then it was your duty to do something about it. And as we now know, there *was* something suspicious about it. At least the truth has finally come out.'

Angela was silent, for of course the truth had not come out at all. She glanced about her and saw no sign of Jack Lomax or Virginia Sheridan, although that was hardly surprising in the circumstances. Angela wondered whether Virginia had been in communication with Jack to tell him that they were both under suspicion. Or would she continue to pretend that nothing had happened, as she had that morning? Angela felt very dissatisfied with herself about the whole thing, and was half-inclined to think that she might have made the situation worse by interfering.

Mr. Morandi had now come to join them, and Angela excused herself tactfully and wandered out onto the terrace. There she spied the Quinns sitting at a table. They saw Angela, and Mrs. Quinn beckoned to her to join them.

'Well, Mrs. Marchmont,' she said. 'It looks as though someone has been doing something she oughtn't—and Saph seems to think she had a hand in her husband's death, too.'

'Yes, I rather think she did,' said Angela, 'although nobody knows that except ourselves so it's probably better not to put it about for the present.'

'I gather she's in the family way,' said Mrs. Quinn. 'It's all out in the open now, although Saph says she saw it some time ago.'

'I knew she was in trouble,' said Miss Quinn, nodding.

'Ah, of course,' said Angela, who suddenly understood something that had been nagging at her.

'Do you suppose they'll arrest her?' said Mrs. Quinn.

'I can't say,' said Angela. 'It all depends on the results of the post-mortem examination and any other evidence they find. Mr. D'Onofrio is doing his best—at least, I think he is: he's so laconic that it's difficult to tell—and really, it's all up to him now. However, I rather fear that justice may not be done in this case.'

'I hope it will be,' said Asphodel. 'I'm a witness, you know. I saw Mr. Lomax and Mrs. Sheridan together, and I shall speak up if necessary.'

'Then I suggest you talk to Mr. D'Onofrio,' said Angela. 'The more proof he can get the better.'

'Poor Mr. Sheridan,' said Mrs. Quinn. 'Even if it was an accident, it's not right to string a man up and deprive him of his dignity. Still, at least everyone knows now that it had nothing to do with us.' She lowered her voice and went on with a touch of glee, 'In fact, if you'll believe it, Mrs. Marchmont, even Mr. Ainsley came and shook my hand this morning.'

'No!' said Angela in surprise.

'Oh, but he did. He said he was sorry if he had inadvertently been responsible for spreading untrue stories about us. He said he knew it was an unchristian thing to do, but he had believed at the time he was only acting out of concern for his congregation. But now the truth had come out, he realized he'd acted wrongly and hoped we would pardon him.'

'And did you?' said Angela.

'Of course I did,' said Mrs. Quinn. 'And if that makes me soft in the head then so be it. We'll be leaving Stresa soon, you know, and I don't like to part with people on bad terms.'

'Oh?' said Angela. 'Where are you going?'

'I don't know, exactly,' said Mrs. Quinn. 'I've a fancy to see Naples and Sicily, so I imagine we'll head South at first. I suppose you'll be going back to England soon.'

'Tomorrow,' said Angela.

'Well, I hope you have a good journey,' said Mrs. Quinn. 'It's been a pleasure to meet you. I'm only sorry we never managed to speak to your husband. Still, perhaps it's for the best.'

Angela went a little pink at this, but Mrs. Quinn appeared not to notice, as she had just spotted someone she knew coming up the steps to the terrace. She stood up.

'Excuse me a moment, won't you?' she said, and hurried off, leaving Angela with Asphodel Quinn. Miss Quinn turned her dark, intense gaze on Angela and seemed to be making her mind up to something.

'I know I ought to keep my mouth shut after everything that's happened,' she said at last, 'but you've been kind, so I won't. Don't be shocked, but I'm rather afraid I see danger ahead for you too, Mrs. Marchmont.'

Angela was disconcerted in spite of herself.

'Oh?' she said. 'Of what nature?'

'I don't know, exactly,' said Miss Quinn. 'I'm sorry, that's not very helpful, I know. It's not imminent, though. I mean, you're not going to get run over by a train tomorrow, or anything.'

'Well, that's a relief,' said Angela dryly.

Miss Quinn was thinking hard.

'That man,' she said at last. She seemed to be staring at something over Angela's shoulder. Angela glanced involuntarily behind her, but saw no-one.

'Which man?' she said.

'The nice-looking one with the deep blue eyes,' said Asphodel. 'You know, the one who comes to the hotel sometimes.'

She paused again.

'Is the danger to do with him?' said Angela.

'I'm not sure,' replied Miss Quinn. 'I'm not certain what I can see, exactly, but I think perhaps he might save your life. Or is it the other way round? How odd—I can't tell which it is.'

'Perhaps it's both,' said Angela politely.

Miss Quinn was now staring into space and seemed not to have heard; indeed, it looked as though she had entirely forgotten Angela was there. Angela waited a moment, then departed quietly and went back inside. There was certainly something odd about Asphodel Quinn, but whether her prophecies were accurate or not was impossible to say, since they were invariably so vague that they might mean anything or nothing. Angela returned to her table and received an enthusiastic greeting from Elsa and Mr. Morandi, who pressed another glass of champagne into her hand, and within a very few minutes Miss Quinn's words had disappeared completely out of her head.

Chapter Twenty-Nine

ANGELA MARCHMONT TOOK a final look around her hotel room to make sure she had not forgotten anything, and then stepped out onto the balcony one last time to admire the view over the lake. Despite the dreadful events of the past week she was sorry to be leaving Italy. How dull it would be to go back to chilly England after all the recent excitement! Angela had been rendered especially peevish by a letter which had arrived from her brother that morning. It had evidently followed her from Florence, and in it Humphrey spent the best part of a page and a half enjoining various impossible standards of behaviour upon her during her forthcoming visit, which promised to be painfully tedious. Perhaps it was a penance imposed upon her for having enjoyed herself too much lately. For a second she smiled at the thought of what Humphrey would say if she were to tell him that she had very nearly been enticed into embarking upon a love-affair with a wanted criminal, but then caught herself. No: she would not think of that. For the past three days she had forced herself through sheer effort of will not to think of Edgar

Valencourt, and this was no time to begin. She would go home and have no regrets, and soon she should forget him entirely, she was quite certain of it.

Having fortified herself thus, Angela turned and left the room, as she wanted to say goodbye to her friends before she left. She had already taken leave of Mary Ainsley, who had come to breakfast at the hotel that morning to say farewell. Jonathan was feeling a little chastened, Mary told her, for since Jack Lomax's confession he had begun to feel that he had spent too much time worrying about the Quinns, and had neglected his flock.

'He believes he ought to have seen that Jack was unhappy about something,' she said. 'I think he feels guilty that he was unable to provide comfort when it was most required.'

'I don't think there's much he could have done,' said Angela.

'Perhaps not,' said Mary. 'Still, I must say the change is proving to be quite refreshing. He has even taken it upon himself to be polite to Mrs. Quinn.'

'Yes, so I had heard,' said Angela. 'Perhaps he has finally begun to listen to you, Mary.'

'Let us hope so,' said Mary. 'I'm very fond of him, you know, even though he can be rather exasperating, and I do want him to be happy—not least because it makes my life so much easier.'

They both laughed, and Mary rose, for she had to go back.

'I want to thank you for everything you've done, Angela,' she said. 'It was so very kind of you to interrupt your holiday like that—even if it did turn out to be more or less a wild-goose chase.'

'It was my pleasure,' said Angela. They bade each other farewell and Mary went off, promising to write soon.

Now, as she waited for the lift, Angela thought about that earlier conversation with Mary. The Ainsleys more than anyone had gone out of their way to be kind to Virginia Sheridan following her husband's death. What would they say when—or if—they found out the truth? Would they support Jack if he went to prison? And what if Virginia were arrested? Would they support her too? Thinking on these lines, Angela remembered that she had not yet told Mr. D'Onofrio about her conversation with Virginia Sheridan. Now was about his usual time for visiting the hotel, however, so perhaps she would be able to speak to him before she left. As luck would have it, he was just on his way out as Angela emerged from the lift, and she ran after him and caught him up. He greeted her politely and observed that she was dressed for a journey.

'Yes,' said Angela. 'I'm going home today. I'm glad you're here, though, as I wanted to talk to you. I went to see Mrs. Sheridan yesterday.'

'Ah,' he said. 'And did she tell you anything useful?'

'No,' said Angela. 'To be perfectly honest, I should have been surprised if she had, but I'm afraid she denied everything.'

'I see,' he said. 'No matter. I have decided that perhaps it is time to pay her a little visit myself. But first I will visit Mr. Lomax and tell him of the evidence of the bottle. Since his are the only finger-prints on it, then he must have been the one to administer the drug to Christopher Tate. Perhaps we can surprise him into a confession.'

'I hope so,' said Angela, 'since I fear that may be the only solution in the end.'

'You may be right,' he said.

'I shan't be here to find out what happens,' said Angela, 'but I have friends here who will write to me, I'm sure, if any developments occur.'

'Then I hope they will soon have news for you,' he said.

'I'm only sorry I couldn't be more helpful,' said Angela.

'You have done what you could,' he said. 'And in any case, you are not a policeman, and so nothing is expected of you.'

'True,' she said.

His face broke into a rare smile, then he gave a little bow and went off, leaving Angela standing alone in the hall, deep in thought.

An hour later, having finally taken her departure from the Hotel del Lago with many salutations and kisses and promises to write, Angela arrived at the station in Stresa. For the whole of the short journey, the taxi driver had kept up a bewildering stream of conversation in broken English, and it had taken all her concentration to follow what he was saying. Once they arrived, however, all his friendliness disappeared, and he took down her small bag containing her things for the journey (the rest of her luggage having been sent on earlier), dropped it at her feet, and abandoned her abruptly at the entrance. Angela looked around for a porter, but there seemed to be nobody about, so she picked up her bag with a sigh and set off for her platform. She was a little later than she had planned, and the train had already come in and was puffing gently in preparation for its departure for Milan, where she was to change. She walked along the platform until she found a likely-looking carriage, then glanced at her watch. There were still five minutes before the train was due to leave, and she wanted to buy a newspaper, for she had nothing to read. She put down her little case and began rummaging about in her handbag for her purse. Then she glanced up and started violently as she saw Edgar Valencourt standing before her.

'Hallo, Angela,' he said.

Angela tried and failed entirely to look cross.

'Tell me, Mr. Valencourt,' she said when she had found her voice, 'does your word mean *anything* at all? Or is it just something that comes out of your mouth quite accidentally while you're thinking of other things?'

He tried and failed entirely to look ashamed of himself.

'It's not fair to extort a promise from a man when he's sick and not in his right mind,' he said. 'I couldn't possibly be expected to keep it.'

There were a number of suitable replies to that, but instead Angela said:

'Oughtn't you to be resting? You certainly can't be in any fit state to drive.'

'I'm all right,' he said. 'And anyway, I wanted to see you.'

'Well, now you have,' she said, somewhat ungraciously.

'Yes,' he said. 'I have.'

He was gazing at her earnestly, and once again she was reluctant to look into his eyes, for fear of what they might induce her to do. She ought to have known that he would not let her escape so easily. She had congratulated herself on her strength of purpose in not thinking about him and in refusing to admit regret, yet now she was discovering that it was one thing to be firm in his absence, but quite another to manage it when he was standing in front of her, looking pale and drawn and lost. She gripped her handbag tightly for support and glanced about, but nobody came to rescue her from herself. No matter—there was a way out just behind her, for the train was due to leave at any moment. She could bid him goodbye with every appearance of equanimity and then flee to safety inside her iron refuge.

'It's very kind of you to come and see me off,' she said, in an attempt at formality.

'Kindness has nothing to do with it,' he said.

A guard walked past as they stood in uncomfortable silence.

'*Salgano i signori passeggeri*,' he said. '*Signora*, the train is about to leave.'

'Well, then, goodbye,' said Angela.

'Please don't go,' said Valencourt.

'But I must,' she said in surprise. 'I can't stay here. I have things to do at home.'

'Listen, Angela,' he said, and at the appeal in his voice she looked up and could not look away. 'I couldn't let you go without at least trying to see you one last time. Perhaps you think this is all a joke, that I'm not sincere—God knows I've hardly the best reputation for truthfulness—but I swear to you I'm perfectly serious. Can't you stay another day or two?'

'No,' she said. 'I can't, and you really oughtn't to be here, Edgar. What's the use in prolonging this when nothing can ever come of it? You must see it's impossible. Why, the very notion is quite absurd. You've chosen your way of doing things and I've chosen mine, and the two are hardly congenial, to say the least.'

'Yes, and I'm sorry for it,' he said. 'I never knew how much until now.'

It was the first intimation he had ever given that he might be less than perfectly satisfied with the path he had taken in life, and she was briefly surprised. But it was not enough. She would not be swayed.

'I'm sorry, too,' she said, then looked towards the guard, who was gesticulating energetically at the train. 'I must go.' She picked up her little case and turned to get on board.

'Come to Venice with me,' said Valencourt suddenly.

'What?' she said, turning back.

'You wanted to go to Venice,' he said. 'Then let's go together.'

She stared at him, half-doubting.

'Oh, but—' she said.

He pressed on while he had her attention, sensing an opening.

'You're right, of course,' he said. 'I have chosen my way of doing things, and now I have to live with it—in fact I might have died because of it, had it not been for you, and I'm more grateful to you than I can possibly say. I'd forgotten such kindness existed. But Angela, can't you be kind to me one more time?' He smiled ruefully. 'Mine's rather a solitary life, you know, and I should be very glad of the company—*your* company, at least—for a little while. Come with me to Venice. We'll be as proper as you like, I promise. It's not as though I'm well enough to try anything funny even if I wanted to. We'll go and sit in a gondola and wander by the canals and get lost in the alleyways, and you'll be kind to me again and forget everything you hate about me, just for a few days. Please, Angela, say you will. Please don't leave without even a backward glance as though I didn't matter to you at all, when you matter so very much to me.'

While he was speaking she had made the fatal mistake of meeting his eyes, and now she was transfixed. All her common sense told her that she ought to get on the train immediately; that he was deliberately appealing to her sympathy and exercising the same charm he used when talking his unsuspecting victims out of their valuables. She knew her weakness—as did he—and she was quite certain that he was taking advantage of it, and that she ought not to listen to him. For some reason, however, all she could think about was that night in the hotel garden when he had taken her in his arms; she recalled the jolt of feeling when his lips met hers, and the desolation she had known when he had been shot and for a few moments she had thought he was dead.

Would it be so *very* bad if she went with him to Venice? After all, she had been especially keen to see the place, but had given it up to help someone else. Now here was her opportunity to go at last. He was hardly the wisest choice of companion, but he was injured and had promised that she should be safe from him. Of course they could not be lovers—that was quite impossible—but surely she could enjoy his company as a friend. There was no need at all to be drawn into anything further.

The practical problem, of course, was that her brother and his family were expecting her in a day or two. She thought of the disapproving letter she had received that morning. Humphrey would be so cross with her if she put him off—but then he was always cross with her, so did it really matter all that much? Surely the visit could wait a few days. She could say that there had been a mistake with the tickets, or that she had been ill and could not travel. There were plenty of possible excuses. *Could* she go to Venice? Would she regret it forever if she did?

It took only an instant for these thoughts to flash through her mind, but in that instant she was lost. The guard, who could see well enough what was being negotiated between the lady and the gentleman but had no time to wait and find out the result, shook his head and blew his whistle. The train hissed loudly and pulled slowly out of the station. Angela watched as it disappeared into the distance, and as she did so, Jonathan Ainsley's words about people who came to Italy and lost their heads suddenly came back to her. She could not be one of those people, could she?

She turned back to Valencourt. There was a long silence.

'You needn't look so pleased with yourself,' she said at last.

'I can't help it,' he said, and held out a hand to her.

———

New Releases

If you'd like to receive news of further releases by Clara Benson, you can sign up to my mailing list here: clarabenson.com/newsletter.

Books by Clara Benson

THE ANGELA MARCHMONT MYSTERIES

THE FREDDY PILKINGTON-SOAMES ADVENTURES

SHORT STORIES

Angela's Christmas Adventure

The Man on the Train

A Question of Hats

COLLECTIONS

Angela Marchmont Mysteries Books 1-3

Angela Marchmont Mysteries Books 4-6

Freddy Pilkington-Soames Adventures Books 1-3

HISTORICAL FICTION

In Darkness, Look for Stars (published by Bookouture)

The Stolen Letter (published by Bookouture)

OTHER

The Lucases of Lucas Lodge

Printed in Great Britain
by Amazon